PARTHIAN BOOKS

A White Afternoon
& other stories

New Welsh Short Fiction

Selected and translated by
Meic Stephens

PARTHIAN BOOKS

Parthian Books
53, Colum Road
Cardiff
Wales
CF10 3EF
www.parthianbooks.co.uk

First published in 1998.
Reprinted in 2000

ISBN 1 902638 00 X

The publishers would like to thank the Arts Council of
Wales for support in the translation and publication of
this book.

Typeset in Galliard by NW.

Cover art from original painting by R.Elfyn Lewis
Copyright 1998.

A CIP catalogue record for this book is available from
the British Library.

The Stories

∞

A White Afternoon

Sonia Edwards

The first cold of autumn is lying thinly over everything; it's come this year without anyone noticing, lightly and mildly, like milk forming a skin. From my mother's bedroom window I can see the mountains, sleepy and still, like the shadows of old, old cattle. The sky is a bulging patchwork of grey and blue, with tufts of cloud sticking out of it, like the fur of a white cat on a coverlet.

They're getting married at two o'clock. Mam and Emlyn. She's been ever so nice to me, whispering secrets and saying funny things as if she were my big sister.

'Why don't you have something to eat? A drink of milk and a Welsh cake?' Her fingers are cold against my cheek. 'It'll be tea-time by the time we have lunch today, you know, and your stomach will be rattling.'

But although my stomach is empty I haven't any room in it. It feels tight and small inside me as if someone has tied string around it. Outside, under the window, the trees are still, holding their heads together to let the sunshine dapple through their leaves here and there like rust. They haven't any choice, just waiting for it to happen as I was after playing in Luned's house when she had chicken pox. I had it worse than her in the end. I still have a small round scar on my forehead where I picked one of the scabs. It's out of sight under my hair, quite tiny, smaller than a baby's tear. But I know exactly where it is, white and pearly and there for ever.

'You'd like to help me get dressed, wouldn't you, Mari?'

I've helped her dress many times before, lifting the coils of her hair so that I can do up the top button of her frock, smoothing out the creases in the material to feel her body warm and familiar, and knowing that I can't touch anyone else in the whole wide world as I touch her, nor put my cheek against the nape of anyone else's neck and feel the hairs there soft like the fluff under Jinw's belly when she was a kitten.

But today's different from all the other times. Today I feel as if I'm her mother, and we are reaching for her things on the bed together and she's wiping her hands on her dressing-gown before touching anything as if she's afraid the trembling in her fingers will soil the brandnew material. It's she who reaches for the white, flimsy underwear. She turns her back to me for a moment in order to open the oblong box with the name of that expensive lingerie-shop we went to in Chester written on its side in pretty, wavy letters. As she shakes the contents bit by bit out of the folds of the box, the silky paper rustles and goes quiet in turn, making me think of a bird fluttering its way through a thorn hedge. And then, suddenly, complete silence. No rustling, no sound, no thin material whispering through her fingers. Nothing. And I see her shoulders heave slightly, making her seem frail and vulnerable. It's not the noisy crying for attention that Luned and I go in for. It's more a sort of quiet, soft sighing that comes and goes in her eyes like needles of sunlight stitching through wet hoarfrost. She lets me hold on to her tightly and it doesn't matter that she's just powdered her face and put lipstick on. I can press my cheek against hers and let her flowery perfume remind me of lovely things. Of birthday parties and Christmas and all the other best-dress days we have shared together.

'I'm alright now.' She tenderly pulls away from my grasp and puts me to sit neatly on the side of the bed as if I'm a doll. 'Come on, we'd better get a move on or your grandmother will be here with Ifan and Enid and I shan't be half ready.'

There won't be a crowd of us. No fuss. Only close family because Emlyn's a widower and Mam's been married before. And then I'll be going to stay with Nain for three or four days over the half-term holiday while they go off somewhere to ged rid of their shyness, as Mam said. Luned frowned when she heard this.

'People say the daftest things,' she said. 'How can they be shy when Emlyn's been sleeping in your mother's bed?'

That's what she said to me and now I'm beginning to regret telling her. But at the time I had to share the secret in order to stay friends with Luned because the bedroom across the landing had become a strange and distant place. And their low, careful laughter was even more frightening when I head the slow rasp of the key in the keyhole. I don't want to know what they do in that big, hard bed. And hearing Luned say that everyone has to do it some day doesn't help at all. Especially if they want babies, she says, and she wouldn't be surprised at all if Mam had another one after she marries Emlyn. What does Luned know about anything? I could believe what she says better if she were able to write properly and copy things out correctly in her exercise books.

Mam is taking off her dressing-gown as if she's forgotten I'm here and her body looks so white until she starts to put her expensive underwear on; the newness of the lace is whiter even than her skin, bright and starchy like the driven snow.

'There's a car stopped outside. Nip down, will you, and tell them I shan't be long.'

It's Uncle Ifan and Auntie Enid, and Nain like a duchess in the rear of the big grey car. I wait until I hear the car doors slamming before going to open the door to them, trying to decide which cheek to offer for the lipsticky kisses of Auntie Enid and the coarse hairiness under Uncle Ifan's nose. But I'm not worried about kissing Nain. She always holds me tightly without worrying about creasing her clothes and there's a faraway, old-fashioned smell to her scent, like the smell of roses from the bottom of the garden on late summer evenings when it's damp underfoot and the gnats make the sky shimmer.

Enid comes sailing through the door, carrying flowers on the lid of a box.

'Here, Mari, take hold of this, will you? Good gracious, this

9

girl's grown every time I see her! You are getting to be a bonnie lass, aren't you?'

I can't stand it when people call me 'a bonnie lass'. I take the flowers from her so that she can tidy her clothes and arrange the coat of her costume to hide the two buttons which tighten dangerously across her chest every time she lifts her arms.

'What's that smell, Nain?' A strong, sweet smell, as if someone's spilt a bottle of scent.

'Friesias.'

She puts the bouquet under my nose and I look for them amid the other flowers, expecting to see something large and grand-looking. But they're shy, tiny little things, like rows of bells hanging downwards, and she smiles at my surprise, touching the bouquet with her fingertips, which are cold as dew.

'Sit down, Ifan. You make the place look untidy!'

Enid. Interrupting everyone and everything. From nowhere and everywhere. I must escape the noise of her. Her voice fills the kitchen and takes the shine out of Nain's eyes as she nags Uncle Ifan all the time.Going on and on. Following me out to the yard where the afternoon is heavy with the cold that breathes from the earth and the primitive taste of rotting branches. Overhead there are birds migrating in a ribbony line. That's the only thing moving — that black line in the sky that quavers suddenly before splitting into two parts like an old shoelace snapping.

I know everything will be different after today. When I come back from Nain's house. As if we had visitors who are going to stay for ever. And I'll have to make sure that I keep my shoes tidy and pass the dish of potatoes across the dining-table so that he can help himself first. It was I who always used to serve my father, and knew exactly how much to put on his plate. I never put too much or too little, he used to say. After he'd finished, I would fetch his tobacco tin and he'd smile because he didn't have to ask. Mam used to pretend to be upset because she would find small strands of tobacco between the dirty dishes, sticking to the tablecloth like the legs of flies.

'Well, good luck to her, I say!' Auntie Enid's voice carries like a bell because the back-door's wide-open and there's not a sound from anywhere else. 'She deserves a bit of that, Gwyn doing what he did, leaving her for another woman!

That's the first time I've heard one of them saying his name for a very long time. My father's name, falling crisply into the midst of the kitchen, into the shadows where there's a smell of friesias. Not one of them notices me watching it all — the familiar shapes of the furniture, the dishes on the dresser winking at themselves in the reflection of the window, the shadow of Uncle Ifan's wife falling messily over everything. I've been here for a long while, with my nose pressed against the window, then I hear someone calling my name and I'm too scared to budge until I realize it's Mam.

'What are you doing out here? You've gone and left everyone.'

But there's no rebuke in her voice. There's not much anything in it. Her words hover in the air, just like this white afternoon that's been caught between two seasons and is expecting something to waken it.

'You look pretty, Mam.'

Her smile darkens her eyes, turning them the same blue as the suit she's wearing. I follow her back into the house, through the kitchen and the talk and the cold perfume of the flowers on the table. It's dark in the front-parlour because the heavy green curtains are only partly open. A dark, green room that's kept especially for visitors. Where the wedding photograph used to be. My father's face young and thin and Mam pale and dressed all in white. There's something quiet and serious about this room, and I think of the minister who came to see us after we had buried Taid. I don't remember much from that time, except that I'd never seen Nain weeping real tears before. Huge tears like a glass necklace and the minister sitting with his knees together, just like a woman does, drinking tea from a bone-china cup.

'You'd better have this now, Mari.' Her wedding-ring. 'It's much too big for you at the moment, but perhaps you'd like to wear it some day.'

But I don't know whether I'll want to do that. She tugs it off her finger and puts it, a small, warm, yellow ring, in the palm of my hand. There's an empty band on her finger without it.

'I'll be having a new one today, you see.'

'Yes. From Emlyn.'

'Yes.'

'He thinks the world of you, doesn't he?'

'Yes, of course he does. And of you.'

It doesn't matter very much to me. I'm not very sure whether I want him to think the world of me. I'm not terribly sure of anything.

'He'll think you look very, very pretty today, won't he?' I say.

The shop's smells are on her clothes, new, sharp smells mixed with scent, and the pearly buttons of her jacket are pricking against my cheek. I wonder if my father's new girlfriend wears clothes like these? Does she have scent and rings, I wonder, like a grand lady in a story? Or does she wear an everyday flowery apron and has she honey-blonde hair that falls in coils around her face after she's been putting washing out to dry and the wind has brought out the colour in her cheeks?

Pity we can't stay here for ever without anyone interfering. But that can't be. So we both of us go back in together, back to the others. Closing the parlour door with its dark furniture. Closing the door on where the minister dropped the crumbs of his afternoon tea onto the cushions of the sofa when Nain was weeping real tears. And on where the afternoon has begun to slip between the curtains and to cast its ripples of white light along the empty place on the piano where the picture used to be. The old picture of them on their wedding day long ago.

Linda's Story

Aled Islwyn

I'm on my own. On my own is what I'll be from now on, I suppose. He's still living with me, of course. But things can never be the same. Though nothing's changed.

He's still kind enough and was never tight with money. I get more than most women for housekeeping and things like that. And he's quite good at mending this and that about the place when I ask him to. And if I need a hand with Llinos, he's only too willing. She's a real Daddy's girl.

Things can never be the same again, though, can they?

Not that he's mentioned it since that night. Strange, that. Not a word. As if I'd never asked. He still goes to work every day and he came for a walk with me and Llinos after lunch last Sunday, as usual. It's normal things like that make me sure the neighbours don't suspect anything. They all think I'm very lucky. Her next door told me the other day she'd be glad to have a husband like David. Seems she's only stayed with hers for the sake of the kids.

How can she understand? She didn't ask him where he went those evenings he stayed out late. She didn't get the answer I got last Wednesday night.

And don't tell me I'd understand better if I asked more questions. I'm too scared. He'd tell me the truth, straight out. I know that now. That's what scared me so much. That's half the trouble.

I'd never guessed. That's what's strange. Hadn't thought it could be another woman or anything like that. Thought he spent his evenings with his workmates. Thought he went somewhere to meet them. I should have twigged, I suppose. He's a great one for his own company. Never kept in touch with his school chums. Lost touch with his mates in the army. I don't know why. He doesn't say much, that's all. That's why I fancied him in the first place. Quiet and didn't do my head in with his talk. Different to the other boys round town.

A man who keeps himself to himself isn't going to have people talking about him. That's what Gran used to say. And David was like that.

What am I saying? Still is like that.

That's why what he said hurt. And his voice was rough.

We didn't used to quarrel, ever. We don't now. That's what I can't understand. Because I still love him, I suppose. Though I can't feel anything about what's happened, either. That's why I feel empty inside.

I can't talk to him at all. I daren't. Daren't breathe a word to anyone.

Getting up from supper last night he said my hair was pretty. I still do it with henna, like the night he saw me the first time. Years ago he used to say that's why he fancied me in the first place.

I blushed to my auburn roots. He hasn't said anything nice like that for ages. And perhaps he won't leave me if I still please him somehow. But who knows what can happen? Last night I was watching him playing with Llinos in the garden. I was by the kitchen window doing the dishes. I could hear my own voice inside my head praying he won't ever leave. Can't get that prayer out of my head.

Daren't tell anyone.

Mam called this afternoon. Thought I was even quieter than usual, she said. I told her what David had said about my hair. If I'd told her the whole story she'd have sworn it was all my fault.

When we started going out together Mam said David was a

hard worker and I'd be alright with him. 'Stick to him, my girl. You've got a good lad there.'

He was all man, too. On leave from the army and coming up for demob. Married after a year's courting. The sun stayed in but the weather was fine.

He's still all man, of course. That's why I don't understand. Though I ought to get used to it, I suppose. Time's flown! And I rushed upstairs in tears.

'Don't be so silly or you'll wake Llinos,' he said abruptly as he stood there in the doorway watching me blubbing on the bed. Always thinks of Llinos.

And when he comes in from work and finds one of our mothers here, he's nice as pie then, too. Kissing them as if nothing's wrong. Perhaps nothing is wrong. Perhaps it's me thinking too much, like Mam says. He still wants me about twice a week. Three times, sometimes. And I never refuse him. Never. I've never refused him. Not even before we were married. 'You hang on to him,' Mam used to say. And that's what I did. Because I've always wanted him. Warm and heavy.

After making love he rolls off me and turns his face to the wall. I'd like him to hold me in his arms for a bit, but he never does. It's not my fault.

I rang that help-line the other night and made more of a fool of myself than usual.

I'd seen the number at the end of some programme on the telly. A phone-line for women like me. A help-line for any spouse with a gay partner, that's what it said. I'm a spouse and he's gay. Though you'd never tell. The line's only open on a Tuesday night and it was a fluke David was out.

After the phone had been ringing for ages, this woman answered all out of breath. Her voice was kind enough, I suppose. She was a good listener, she said. There was no need to be shy. She understood. But I wasn't so sure. If only she'd seen me five minutes before, staring at that phone before plucking up the courage to lift the receiver.

For a few minutes she tried to coax me to say something. I clammed up and couldn't get a word out. But my eyes had plenty to say. They hadn't frozen up. They gushed like two waterfalls and still I couldn't say anything, only bawling my eyes out.

I must have sounded more stupid than usual, because she asked me if I'd be happier having someone to talk to in Welsh. She'd get someone to ring me back. No, I said at last. She'd do.

Easier to say it in English somehow. Less intimate. And I couldn't give my number, anyway. He'd go spare if he ever got to hear about it.

I started by telling her about how he answered me so roughly that time. About the tears. And then the silence. I told her everything. Said it was almost brazen the way he'd stood there going on about what he calls his needs. So cold and shameless. Just bare facts.

I ought to respect him for his honesty, at least, she said. Men usually deny it, it seems. I'd have been glad if he'd denied it to me, I replied. I didn't want to know. Lost my temper with her a bit. Well! Hard not to.

'Does he use condoms?' she asked me then. 'Not with me,' I said. But that wasn't what she meant. It was important for me to understand the risk. Important I knew what to do. I've been doing it ever since I've known him. She didn't understand.

I could hear her getting worked up at the other end of the line. Though she was professional enough at her job. Trying not to show her feelings. But I saw through her bit by bit. Going on about honesty in one breath and all lies in the next.

I asked what I ought to do. But she wasn't there to solve problems, she said. What she wanted to do was give me a chance to talk things over. Another way of running up a phone-bill, I thought. But there was no point arguing. For her it was only a job for a few hours every Tuesday night. And she was nice enough.

Her name's Lucinda. I was welcome to ring any Tuesday night. And I could call her Lucy if I found Lucinda too much of a mouthful. Her kids call her Lucy, she said. She had two boys. And that's why she'd been late getting to the office, it seems. Had to take the boys to the Scouts and something wrong with the car. She said what make it was, but I don't remember. It's David usually sorts out that kind of thing. I got to know quite a bit about her really. But not the kids' names. Nor the husband's. He's left her, it seems. Living in Chester on his own. Lucinda lives somewhere in Clwyd. Close enough for the boys to keep in touch with their dad, I said. But she didn't say anything.

I'm not likely to ring again. Just happened he was out on a Tuesday evening. A round or two in the Club to say goodbye to one of his mates from work, he said. I believe him, of course. As I said to Lucinda, one of the things about him that hurts most is he always tells the truth.

Wednesday today. His mother will be here in a minute. She doesn't work on a Wednesday afternoon and she'll be here, you'll see. In her blue suit and white blouse. Same old conversation, too.

'You were lucky to get this house so soon after marrying. Our David was never afraid of work.'

Everyone agrees he's not afraid of work.

'Yes. Very lucky,' I'll reply, like a parrot.

'And you've got this place all spick and span.'

'I do my best.'

The rest of the afternoon she'll be cuddling Llinos. Filling the place with her scent and staying for tea.

The same old routine. I don't know why I keep going on about it. Because I've got all evening to think about how pointless the day's been, I expect. Wednesday evening, see. After his mother's gone, he'll get ready to go out, too.

The evenings he's out are the worst. He'll probably go to that pub in town, this being mid-week. That's where they all go. He told me. Everyone round here knows about it, I expect. It isn't as if he was worried about that. Good beer there, he said. He never had much of an ear for tittle-tattle. He's got me to do all that for him. To be his ears. To be his housekeeper. To make a home for him in every way.

I'm certainly not a gossip. Whenever I want to say

something important I can't find the words.

Trouble is I don't know what's on his mind. He's so quiet about the place. Says nothing, never smiles. Except when Llinos is around.

Not that he's unpleasant. That's what's so funny. This silence is different to the one that used to be between us. This is a silence I don't understand.

I've got an idea he goes to Chester or Liverpool on Saturday nights. The mileage on the clock went up a lot over the weekend once. I do notice things sometimes, when I remember to look.

I can't stand hearing him in the bedroom sprucing himself to go out. I sit playing with some of Llinos's toys. That's what I do then. Keep my fingers busy and gawp at the telly.

He comes in all smiles and says he'll see me in the morning and not to stay up too late. And when I hear the door shut I can breathe again. And sit here thinking about what I have to do. I hate ironing more than anything, so Wednesday or Saturday night's a good time to do it. It's easier to think how much I detest ironing than worrying about where he is.

At least then the ironing's out of the way by the following morning.

Listen! She's here! Damn! I was going to tidy up a bit before she arrived. This room's in a bit of a state. Clothes all over the kitchen. But why go on about it? I'll be lucky again today. And the place all spick and span.

Another big mistake this afternoon. Mam called and I decided to tell her. Not everything. Not what he told me months ago. Not the silence. Not the fear. I just mentioned the pub. Said David goes there.

She looked me straight in the eye and said only a fool cuts off her nose to spite her face. I'd got hold of the wrong end of the stick, most likely. And anyway, as long as a man earns an honest living and comes home sober more often than not, what the hell does it matter where he goes boozing? That's what I got from her.

And when she heard about the phoning, she went spare. The whole thing was a con job by middle-class people to put up BT's profits, she said. 'There was no such thing as help-lines in my day, my girl. Only clothes-lines. And we were grateful for one of those.'

Mam reckons she's funny. I didn't bother to argue. Just listened. It would be better to save my money for Christmas than waste it like that, she said. David's money, she said.

I ought to be grateful, I suppose. No, she didn't say anything out of the way to him when he came home from work. The usual peck on his cheek. He was all smiles.

A lot of talk over supper. David telling her how much he was looking forward to Portugal next summer. Mam looking forward to Christmas. Both of them getting Llinos all excited with their chatter. I had to clear up after she was sick.

Before we went to bed tonight, David had to bring the tree down from the attic. A surprise for Llinos tomorrow, though there's still a month to go.

Holding the steps at the top of the landing, while he hoisted himself up, I was in a cold sweat, I was that scared. Fear of losing him. Just seeing his body disappear into that hole in the ceiling was like a kick in the guts.

I could see him in that disco in the old Territorials' hut. Where we first met. His mates egging him on to come over to the little mouse and ask her to dance. I did because I was fed up with sitting at that table listening to the other girls going on about themselves. And anyway, he looked so smart. In a pair of real trousers instead of the jeans the town boys always wore.

He didn't say much. Nor me. And that's how it was when we started going together. Killing time in each other's homes. Going to the pictures sometimes. Going for a drink. With some of his army mates sometimes. What was his great pal called, too?

Leigh! Yes, that's it! I don't know what happened to make them fall out. David wouldn't say.

And his girlfriend, Gaynor. A farmer's daughter from over Dolgellau way. Though you'd never tell. That she was a farmer's daughter, I mean. She had great big earrings and bangles on her wrists that would have gone round a bull's neck. She knew all about wine and fancy food and stuff like that. She had a good job with the Council. And we went out for a meal once, the four of us. To that posh restaurant that used to be near the college. Closed now, of course.

The two men stuck to steak and I had everything Gaynor had. Don't remember exactly what. We never eat out now. An ice-cream for Llinos in the park if the van comes round, that's about it.

They got married, I think. Leigh and Gaynor. Married and moved away. Though I don't know why he couldn't be best man, at the last minute like that. Something wrong somewhere, must have been. David was really cheesed off at the time, I remember. 'It's between me and him, no one else. Got it?' That's all. Doors slammed and I was none the wiser.

He hasn't always been ready to give me a straight answer. Not always wanted to tell the truth. He's changed, see. But I can't for the life of me remember when it was.

Nearly five when he came in this morning. I must have dozed off in the end. But I heard the doors. The car door. The back door. The door of Llinos's room. He always looks in on her before coming up to bed. I was lying with my back to the light, pretending to be asleep.

Started thinking then what might happen if he didn't come home at all one night. He could leave me, like that Lucinda's husband. Or meet someone special. The house is in his name, you see. Everything I have is in his name.

Things have been better for months now. In my own mind, anyway. A smashing Christmas. A meal out on my birthday, too. A month ago, that was. But a great night. Well, we didn't have much to say to each other, of course. But it was a good meal and his mother had given him five pounds for the taxi home. When he's had a few he relaxes a bit.

Things aren't too bad at the moment, to tell the truth. He's still nice. Nicer than he used to be, really. I still do my best. For him. For Llinos. For this house. For everything that's in his name.

I'm awful for dwelling on things. I can see that, but I can't do anything about it. Perhaps I misunderstood what he said that night all those months ago. Got the wrong end of the stick.

'You're not going to leave me, are you?' I whispered this morning, half-asleep, just as he was slipping out of the sheets on his way to the toilet.

'I have to, love. I've got a job to go to,' he replied. He'd misunderstood. Just as well, perhaps. He would only have lost his rag.

Had I been for an HIV test? That was nearly the first thing she asked me. I don't remember whether she said the word 'Congratulations' or not. But the main thing was I ought to know my HIV status before going on with this pregnancy. I had some idea what she meant, but not much.

If I'd got the virus I'd have to do the responsible thing and have an abortion. That was what Lucinda thought. There was nothing else for it, in fairness to the baby.

I was sorry I'd rung. I thought she'd be glad to hear the news. More fool me. She was jealous, I think. She wants more kids of her own but she hasn't got a man to give her them.

I'd got to mention it at the clinic, she said. But I don't want to. After the last chat with her I made a point of going through David's things and found piles of condom packets in the drawer where he keeps important papers — bank statements, the mortgage, stuff like that. He didn't think I'd go looking there.

I didn't say anything to Lucinda. None of her business, is it?

I think he cares about us. David. He was over the moon when he heard about the new baby. Surely he won't do anything to harm us now.

I won't be ringing her again. After all, I'm the one who knows him best, I suppose. I'm his wife.

I was pushing Hannah back from the clinic. I'd have known her anywhere. Great golden earrings and an expensive-looking suit on. I was in my old jeans and sweater, looking a real tramp as usual.

'Still married?' she asked, gob-smacked. Real catty she was. But fair play, she made a big fuss of the baby in her pushchair. You could see she always looks on the black side.

Felt awful afterwards when I heard about Leigh, because I'd been having nasty thoughts about her. We went into the Sweet Tooth café. Opposite Smiths. It's pricey in there. All we wanted were two cups of tea and a slice of cake each. I'd heard what it sets you back in there. Over five pounds! But anyway, Gaynor paid and wouldn't let me chip in. I didn't argue.

He'd had meningitis to start with, she said. But it was double pneumonia that did for him in the end.

Only ill for three weeks. Terribly sudden, as they say in the papers.

She looked really great. A pension from the army and she'd got her old job back with the Council. Nothing down in the mouth about her. No sign of grief in her voice or anything. Well! It's not to be expected, I suppose. Not after two years.

I looked great as well, she said. Confident enough to make the best of my flame-coloured hair at last. Made me look younger than when I was twenty, she said.

Dylan's doing, I replied. Had to explain who Dylan was then. One of David's mates. He's a nurse by calling. I had to be careful to say that right. Because the first time he came to tea I asked him what his job was. I was told soon enough that nursing wasn't a job, it was a calling. Not that he took offence, really. He's an awful one for pulling your leg, that's all. Everyone round the tea-table was in fits. Even little Llinos. She didn't understand, of course. I hardly understand myself.

It did her a power of good to see me again. Gaynor. 'Red of hair and loose of tongue', as she put it. That's what eight years of married life do for a girl, I explained. Then I took out the snaps I'd just picked up from Boots. The last film had been in the camera since that holiday in Portugal. The one when Hannah started. Looking at the snaps, though, you'd hardly notice I was on holiday with him and Llinos. There's only a few of me. 'I'm better at taking them than appearing in them, that's always my excuse,' I said for a laugh.

She was thrilled to hear me talking with such confidence. I can sometimes be quite talkative these days. Even in front of David. It's not as if he notices much. As long as I don't go too far.

Her word for him, as I went through the snaps, was 'hunk'. I flicked through the ones of him on the beach and playing in the swimming-pool with Llinos pretty quick, because I could see she was drooling more over him than over her cream gâteau. She said she was sorry to have lost contact with us and forgotten how good-looking he was.

Well! He's not all that good-looking, really. Even I could see she was having me on.

She's lonely, I think. Asked could she come and see us. She'd moved back and realized that 'the old gang', as she put it, had all settled down or moved away.

Leigh's fault, she said. Him and his hang-ups had come between us all. She didn't say anything else. And I didn't ask.

She's coming to tea after work next Tuesday afternoon. 'She's lonely, see,' David said thoughtful like, as if I hadn't worked it out for myself. Lost her husband, poor dab! No kids. A good job and a drawer full of jingle-jangles don't make up for that, do they?

I'm lucky, really. Told him so just now. I was giving the girls a bath and he was getting ready to go out.

He agreed with me. Smiling at me in the mirror as he put on his tie.

That Dylan's just rung. Asking where David is. Arranged to meet him somewhere, it seems, and he hadn't turned up. Perhaps he's stopped going to that pub in town. I don't know for sure.

I won't ask.

Mothers

Meleri Roberts

'What sort of a night did you have?'

'Oh, quiet, you know.'

'Quiet? In this place? You must be joking.'

'No, it was action stations — as usual. Babies are like rabbits, aren't they? They come out after dark!'

They both laughed at the old joke which was so true; generations of nurses could confirm it.

Rhian Jones leant back in her plastic chair, stretching her legs under the table. 'Oh!' — a long sigh of weariness and contentment that had no need of words. It was easy enough to say which of the two nurses at the small table had just finished her shift.

'How many of the little buggers did you have last night?

'Oh, three ... three little girls.'

'Any trouble?'

'No ... well, not like you mean, anyway. You'll see.'

With that, Rhian drained her cup, got up and made for the door.

'Off already, Nurse Jones?' Carol teased her.

'You bet! It's coming to something when I hang around here when I don't have to, doesn't it? See you in the morning.'

She went into the staff-room to change out of her smart white uniform and discard with it the responsibilities and concern that were second nature to her.

Carol looked at her watch. Time to make a start and have a look at the three new babies in the ward. She walked down the long corridor under the glare of the pitiless strip-lighting. It was so strange, she thought, that she and so many like her played such an essential part in the first hours of thousands of little individuals, and then, once the innocent things had gone out through the hospital doors — that was that. The connection was severerd as completely and as pitilessly as the cord between mother and child. A strange world.

'So there's three new members of the screamers' choir!'

Carol saw that Mair was there already, sitting behind a large desk in the middle of the corridor — a small island of orderliness and good sense in the midst of chaos.

'Here we are, Carol. Rhiannon Edwards — a girl; Carys Hughes — a girl; and Sheila Davies — a girl.'

Mair pointed in the direction of the ward where the beds were hidden by flowery curtains. Each mother like a hen settled on its cosy nest, sheltering within and pretending that she wasn't there at all.

'So we have three more little Welsh girls — very good.'

'Yes, well, we'll see.' Mair was unwilling to look on the bright side of things, as usual.

'Mr Edwards is in with baby number one now.'

'Oh, the proud father!'

'Wants to get the fuss over before he goes to work, if you ask me.'

'Mair! You're a real cynic! Where has all your goodwill gone?'

'Lost under all this bumf. But you'll see if I'm not right!'

'I'd better introduce myself.'

Carol parted the flowery curtain and came face-to-face with Trefor Edwards. She read the signs — short camel-hair coat, smart trousers, loud tie, large expensive watch. He glanced at his watch and then at Carol. The proud father? Perhaps he was in a hurry ...

'Mr and Mrs Edwards? I'm Staff Nurse Carol Williams —

congratulations to you both ... '

'Why's that? Look, Rhiannon, I have to go — you know, important meeting. I'll be back this evening ... probably. Excuse me.'

With another glance at Carol, off he went, a whirlwind in a camel-hair coat.

The two women looked at each other across the little nest, not half so cosy now.

'He's very busy, you see — in business.'

Rhiannon was trying to think of excuses — for whose benefit Carol wasn't sure. But she decided it would be best to go along with her.

'Oh, you don't have to tell me — he's probably whacked after being here all night.'

'Um, no ... he wasn't. He was out at a dinner last night — you know how it is. He did ring, mind you, but the nurse said it was a girl.'

She nodded towards the cot by the bed, but not really looking at it. 'So...' The soft, complaining voice went hoarse. Carol went over to the cot and stroked the perfect apple of the baby's cheek. The child slept, unaware and careless of the nuisance her birth was causing.

'Of course we'll try again — perhaps we'll be luckier next time. It doesn't matter, we're both young enough. It'll be a boy next time, won't it, nurse?' She turned imploringly to Carol, as if the nurse had some say in the matter.

'No! No! Take her away!'

The raucous shouting saved Carol from having to answer the woman's question. She rushed to the next bed where she found a nervous young nurse holding a screaming baby, while a girl cursed her from the bed.

'Right, nurse, take the baby away for a moment, please — I'll deal with this.'

The nurse looked gratefully at Carol as she came over and tried to comfort the fragile bundle.

'It's Carys, isn't it?' Carol moved towards the bed and the

hysterical young woman. 'D'you want to tell me what the problem is?'

The girl turned her head away. She couldn't have been more than seventeen. Carol noticed the bleached hair that was starting to show its dark roots, the peeling varnish on her nails.

'Come on, Carys, won't you tell me what's troubling you?'

'That silly nurse — expecting me to let the baby ... ' The words were too much for her, but the look on her face was enough to...

'You don't want to feed the baby yourself — that's it, isn't it?' Carol asked kindly.

'Feed it? Yeuk — no, you bet I don't. What's Cow and Gate for? Yeuk — it's horrible. I don't want to see the little sod, let alone ... yeuk!'

'Perhaps you'll feel different later on.'

'Uh? What's got into you?'

'Er ... Carys,' began Carol hesitantly. 'Have you thought about adoption? Perhaps it would be ...'

'What? Let someone else have her, you mean? No way! She's all I've got, and anyway, the social worker said she'd try to get me a flat or something — I may as well get something for all I've been through.'

Carol stood up and walked briskly away from Carys and her sickening attitude. How could a mother say such things? How could a young girl have such cynical notions? It wasn't her place to ask questions, Carol reprimanded herself. But in a job like this, with long hours and low pay, the thought that she was doing something worthwhile was what kept her going. But now, having encountered these two mothers ...

Sighing, she parted the curtains to see what the third bed had to offer.

'Hello, nurse.' The quiet voice, full of excitement, came from the deep cosiness of the nest. Carol stood open-mouthed, staring at the miracle of mother and child. A middle-aged woman was sitting up in bed, holding her fragile bundle as proudly as if it were the Crown Jewels. Her face was lit up with love and tenderness and her voice purred over the treasure in her arms.

'Would you like to see her?'

She was still whispering.

'She's just gone to sleep, but if you're quiet I'm sure it'll be alright.'

She handed the baby to Carol, who held out her arms to cradle her carefully.

'I'm going to call her Llinos — do you think it suits her?'

Carol looked down at the pink form, and her heart froze. The features of the face, the almond-shaped eyes — all the characteristics of Down's Syndrome. The nurse felt her throat tightening. She looked at the baby again, a child who would need so much care and love, who would face such difficult challenges and be so dependent ...

'Is she alright, nurse? I'm not doing anything wrong, am I?'

'No.' Carol fought to get the words out in a normal voice. 'No, she's fine — champion.' She smiled wanly.

'Yes, she is, isn't she?' the mother agreed, taking the baby back to her warm bosom. Then, looking down at her, she murmured, 'You're alright, aren't you, my little one ... You're perfect.'

Dear Mr Atlas

Angharad Jones

She hadn't slept all night. Too hot. Stifling. No breeze coming into the small room under the eaves of the house. For once, she was glad the morning had come. Anything was better than that sweaty bed. Even a morning of work.

The front door slammed behind her. She'd hoped the fresh air would cool her. But no. There was no breeze outside either, only bright clouds weighing down on the day, and the sun behind them with no warmth — only heat. Heat, heat — such heat! Even breathing was a strain. There was no relief anywhere.

She felt her eyebrows knit and there was sweat under her arms. She licked her top lip in order to get rid of the band of perspiration that had formed there. God, I must smell, and my spots beginning to show under the foundation ...

She walked on. It wasn't fair to expect people to work in this heat, not fair... But what was the point of complaining— there was nothing she could do about it. Work was calling and it had to be answered ... Oh God, and everyone will be cross, she thought. Going on about the heat, the hot rooms, each other ...

Elen hadn't noticed the sound of drilling on the other side of the street, breaking the silence, cracking the concrete to rubble. She hadn't noticed that there was a block in the road, a change. She hadn't noticed.

'Wheet — whi-iw!'

She looked up and saw three bare-chested men. She felt herself blushing at the wolf-whistle, and cursed at having to pass workmen today of all days. She felt so ugly, so heavy, like an awkward seal flopping down the street. She turned the other way, to avoid looking at them, but it was impossible to escape the shouts, the jokes of the men ... How could they, at this time of morning — in such heat? How could they? She started walking faster. Why were they always the same? Whistling, going through the motion of saying suggestive things? Didn't they get fed up of behaving like that? And as she rebuked them in her head, she stumbled and fell. Not sedately, but messily, sprawling all over the place in full view of her audience.

She felt the blushes burning her cheeks as the laughter rose on the other side of the street. The shame! The situation was so squalid — three men seeing her like this! Pathetic.

'You alright, love?'

Oh no ... one of the men was crossing the street! She got up as quickly as she could. She nodded without looking up. Then she felt a hand on her shoulder.

'Hey ... '

She wanted to get away, but the hand was firm.

'Hey ... '

Calm down. It was that kind of voice. And everywhere was blue eyes and brown shoulders. Everything else faded— the pain, the embarrassment, the heat. Everything except the smallest breeze.

'That's better. What's the hurry? You had a nasty fall there. Let me see ...'

A Glasgow accent. Unfamiliar. And he's kneeling to inspect my knee. It's cut, bleeding, and the blood's flowing through my tights, staining the nylon. The sound of laughter on the other side of the street. But I don't hear.

'Nasty.'

And he's getting back up. And his arm touches my knee, touches the cut. A stab. A thrill.

'Sorry, love. You should wash it straight away ... You're sure you're alright now?'

She nods and manages to thank him. He smiles.

'Ta-ra, then,' and he goes back over to his mates. He doesn't look back.

Elen went on her way, the sweat now dry, the panic over. And it didn't matter about the undignified hole in her tights, the ugly cut on her leg. Blue sky had broken through the clouds, a breeze had touched her for a moment. Who could hope for more than that?

Gronw's house was cold, even in summer. Dark, with low ceilings, the windows small holes struggling to let the light in. A Welsh cottage.

Elen ought to have been happy. Another day in the office over, an evening with her boyfriend ahead. But as she drew near the cottage, she felt its low ceilings and dark windows weighing on her, like the morning's clouds. She felt the morning's sweat returning, soaking her skin, stifling. She hoped that Gronw wasn't in a bad mood ...

'Hello—o!'

No answer. She opened the door.

'Gron?'

Silence. The sound of his grandfather's clock in the hall. Or was it his great-grandfather's? She could never remember, although she'd heard the story many times. The hall was dark. Come to think of it, perhaps it was his great-great-grandfather's ...

'Gronw?'

She went up the stairs, breathing heavier with each step. He was slouched over his desk, writing. He hadn't heard her come into the house. She found herself staring like a stranger at the rounded shoulders and the lank hair. And the arms! So white and feeble, busy at the desk, like a hamster on its treadmill ... Gronw suddenly turned around.

'Elen! You startled me!'

No answer. She went on staring at the hands and arms.

'You're early. Go down and make a cuppa or something. I

want to finish this chapter. I shan't be long'

'You look tired.'

Flat. A lie. He always looked tired, with shadows under his eyes. Not interesting shadows, which made you want to guess how they got there, but the kind caused by thousands and thousands of academic paragraphs. And his eyes! Pink and yellow and grey at the same time, reminding her of the stuff that grows on the top of a pot of old jam. That's what Gronw's eyes were like — there was something stale in them.

A shiver went down her spine and she felt her stomach turn.

'Does that surprise you? I'm so busy ... up till four this morning.'

'But it has to be done.'

'Exactly. It's my responsibility, as a Welshman, as some kind of artist ... '

His mouth went on moving but she no longer heard what he said. In fact, she was finding it hard to breathe in the cramped room. It was so stuffy, and everything seemed to be turning yellow — the wallpaper, the furniture, Gronw ...

'Why don't you open the window, Gron? It's close in here.'

'I'm freezing.'

'Freezing? There were three men this morning without any shirts ... '

'I'm cold, Elen.'

'But fresh air would be ... '

'Listen. If I opened the window, the sound of the bloody sheep would disturb me. And the birds. You know how I need quiet ... '

God, he's so ugly. Frowning like that, one knot of a twisted artist. Frowning out of his little cloud. God, he makes me sick. Even when he touches me, he makes me sick ...

'What are you staring at?'

'Nothing.'

Oh, where are those blue eyes and brown shoulders, the strange accent, to unknot my knitted brows, to lighten this heavy feeling, the worry ...

'I'll go, then, Gronw.'

'What about my cuppa?'

'Oh yes. Sorry. Just feeling quite ... odd for a moment. Can't breathe — you know ... '

And she closed her eyes and smiled.

'Elen! ELEN! Your knee's hurt!'

Smiling. Yes ... But then I feel fingers gripping my arm. A cup of cold water on my skin and I'm in such a long warm bath...

'Elen? What is it?'

I open my eyes.Gronw's in my face. He's like a spot, full of self-centred poison. In need of bursting.

'Nothing, Gronw, nothing.'

What had she seen in him? Just because he was 'a sensitive creature', going to be a Figure of Importance ... But she knew now. Knew. He could write the most beautiful Welsh on the face of the earth but he would never have blue eyes and brown shoulders.

'Are you sure? You've been acting odd.'

'Sorry. It's just that I've had a hard day. You know how I hate that place.'

A sigh. His bones slacken on her arm.

'Not this again.'

'Gron ... '

'It can't be that bad.'

I close my eyes.

'Well, your salary's quite a bit better than mine.'

I open them. Back to Numero Uno, eh, Gron?

'But at least you're doing what you want to do.'

'Want? WANT? Have to do, Elen. I haven't got time for want, I thought you understood that.'

'Oh, yes. I understand. I understand that wanting is a sin, that having to is a virtue, but I want, want, want ... '

Gronw didn't look upset now, just bored. He had very little patience with her tantrums. They occurred every now and then, usually just before her period. And it was the same old tune every time: how awful the office was, how boring, that she wanted more, wanted to get away, wanted to go back to college, wanted everything and nothing. She got on his nerves when she was like this. She needed a direction — a cause, a religion, a crusade, as he had — something to drag her from this self-obsessed stagnation. She gave him a headache with his woolly uncertainty, all these words ...

Oh Gronw, Gronw, all these words. Why all these endless words?

'Shh, don't cry.'

'I'm not crying. I'm just tired, so tired ... '

She got to her feet.

'I'd better go home — it's this weather. It's hot, so hot — makes my head spin ... '

She gave him a peck on the cheek. She couldn't help noticing how yellow the spot on his face was, how really yellow.

'I'll be back tomorrow night, Gronw.'

'Ok.'

'We'll go out or something ... '

She rushed downstairs, hearing Gronw whining.

'Don't expect a piss-up or anything, I have to keep a clear head ... '

But the car's engine had started and she was on her way to her small room under the eaves.

She got up early next morning, taking more care than usual with her dress, hair and make-up. It was hot again, but the heat was not so unnatural as the previous morning. She glanced in the mirror. She looked better today, without that band of sweat on her lip. And there was no need for foundation, either — her skin had cleared remarkably.

Her heart missed a beat as she heard the door slamming behind her. The clouds were low again, but not oppressive.

She walked down the street without sweat under her armpits, or a frown disfiguring her eyebrows. She walked briskly, confidently, enthusiastically. Enthusiasm! She'd almost forgotten what it was like. And inside there was such a picture of the sky in blue eyes, and of the earth in brown shoulders ...

She knew the drills would be starting. She turned the corner as if she were diving into a crystal-clear river after baking in the relentless sun for too long ... She stopped dead. There was no one there. No drills, no rubble, no bare shoulders. And the street was flat, quiet. Repaired, with everything in place, the concrete smooth, not so much as a scar to prove the men had ever been there. And there was no whistling or embarrassment or fall. No reason to fall, to get hurt or to feel.

She walked on. It was only Tuesday morning. A Tuesday morning like any other in old Wales. Nothing had changed. It was just an ordinary street — a bit of excitement for a while, before falling silent, back into its usual ways. Nothing had changed.

But without warning, she felt warmth trickling down her leg. The cut had opened. Blood was flowing. She smiled.

Dean and Debs

Aled Lewis Evans

Not even the video and satellite are company enough in the end, though I'm kidding myself. Neither are the cans of beer, though there's plenty of them too. I was setting out from the house with two cans when an old schoolmate called; he's the only one who does except for Mam, fair play to her. Perhaps she feels she has to after I found out everything. She's good to me. Brings me clothes and says I ought to spruce the place up, and have more than one chair now that Debs has gone. It's Mam who'll do the sprucing. The three-piece suite's gone, and I lost Debs the same time as the job. Not that I blame the buses completely: I'm happy enough as a bus-driver, but there was too much temptation involved. Mainly schoolgirls saying 'Hiya!' and smiling at you all daft, and a few others, like Alison.

Ali was special. I met her on the bus. A nice girl working with costumes at Chester Theatre. A bit of the gypsy in her. I lived with Ali in Hope. Live in Hope and die in Caergwrle, that's what they say, and be buried in Cefn y Bedd! She had a bungalow in Hope — I got my meals free, everything was free, and she even changed her insurance so I could drive her car. Aye — that's where I was when my friend called and couldn't get an answer. I was there about three weeks, living with Ali. That's why there was no light on in the house and the curtains were drawn. Nothing's safe round here.

She wanted more from the relationship than just me, and I wanted to be free. I didn't want to be nailed down. But I didn't talk to her about it, just walked out. There's too much temptation in the work, that's for sure — and that's why Debs went. Perhaps she wanted her freedom, too. I'd known her since I was fifteen. She's made up for everything she's missed now, from what I hear. In the pubs. Well, I go to the night-clubs too. She wants to go into the Navy and she's going out with some fella who's a sailor. I'm still friends with Alison, mind you — don't get me wrong — and I go drinking in Caergwrle every Saturday night, and I ring her sometimes to ask if she'd like to come out for a drink. Just for a drink. She always treats me.

I think I'll jack in working on the buses. Meeting people's alright but having to keep to the timetable and put up with cheek from the passengers is something else. I've been offered a job behind the bar in the Seven Stars. They know me 'cos I go drinking round town again now. Nice people there, but I'm not sure if I will. And I'm friends with the manageress at Benetton's — we haven't been out together or stuff like that — she's black and she asked me if I'd model clothes for her one night in a fashion show. I'll have to slip over and see her tomorrow. Tell her I will. I haven't the figure for it really, but I bleach my hair and I've tried to get my brother to nick a razor blade from school so that I can shave the back of my head like the barber does it. It's starting to go ginger at the roots. In this new job if my hair had still been brown it would have turned grey by now!

Heck, winter's here already and I've decided as it's the first of November to put up the trimmings. Make Christmas last longer.

Debs has been back with me for a month. Moved all her things back in today. Can't live without me. It's good to have her stuff about the place, 'specially after the break-in. I've forgotten about it now, really, but as Debs says — it just had to happen to me! They nicked the lot, the CD player, the video, everything, and made hell of a mess. Somehow they managed to put the back-door back into position without me hearing, though they'd kicked it down on their way in.

The people next door have moved out and the council came to board the place up after someone chucked a brick through the window. There's nothing safe round here once they get to know you've got something new. Deb's things are back now, making the place all cosy. I can't say how happy I am to see little things like her underwear drying on the radiator. Perhaps she feels sorry for me really. She's the only one who does. Some friend Craig turned out to be! I don't have anything to do with him any more 'cos he knows who's got my stuff. He says it hasn't been sold, but the sod won't say any more. Schoolfriend or no, I won't trust him again! It always happens to me.

Debs came home this afternoon saying she's got her sister's job in the lingerie factory, two days a week. She isn't so keen on the Navy now if she can get a good job round here. I'm still on the buses, signalling carefully and going slow past my old school in case I see my brother, or fast if I spot my old teachers.

I've stopped drinking now — I only drink at home. Saves money. I'm still paying for a CD player and the video that was nicked. Debs has brought her telly and stereo, and as the burglars didn't take the satellite, I was happy enough watching *Pretty Woman* tonight. Rambo was on this afternoon. I've seen it twice but it isn't quite as good as the others 'cos in the end he takes on the Russians single-handed. Pull the other!

Dyfed, my brother, has broken his toe playing soccer, so he won't be in the cross-country for Children in Need in school on Friday. I'll have to watch out how I drive on Friday in case I run someone over! I used to hate cross-country in school. I was fat, and always came in last. It's different now — I'm like Jason Donovan.

I choose to be a trendy and look how people are prepared to swallow it. Take Alison, f'rinstance. Live in Hope? No bloody hope. I've got power in my hands now, I'm not ugly any more, I'm smart, I'm smart. I'm starting to enjoy believing this, and I'm thinking of myself for a change.

Winter's here now and my Christmas tree defies the grey wastes of the Wern estate. Hope no one pinches the dish.

Another miserable evening. Nothing on satellite, only some film with that dancer, Patrick Swayze, in it that made Debs cry. I could move like him if I had his money. The film was called *Ghost,* and she said things like, 'Dean, it's so sad they can't stay with one another', but I didn't take any notice. I bought her the soundtrack of *Dirty Dancing* about a month ago, just to shut her up. She likes the song 'We had the time of our lives'. I don't. I had a bit of cash to buy the CD 'cos I'm helping a friend of a friend to take fruit and vegetables around Queen's Park, on the side, like. But I'm working on the taxis now, just for Christmas, there's plenty of call this time of year. I was glad to pack in the buses. You can please yourself more on the taxis, as long as you treat the girls in the office right.

There's two or three satellite dishes in the street now, but mine was the first. I'm a bit drowsy tonight and haven't changed out of my leather trousers, silk shirt and braces, nor taken off my earrings. You have to dress smart, tart yourself up, for the taxis. You get to know some of the punters. One or two better than others.

It's hard work, but at least I don't have to take that bloody bus up to Minera. The bleach in my hair's starting to come out and the roots are brown. Well, brown-ish. Debbie can't dye them for me tonight 'cos she's crashed out on the settee. She didn't make me supper either. I've been working all day and she's been lying there with the gas-fire full on. Every morning she's sick. The doctor's been to see her today and she's got bronchitis. She has to take anitibiotics and she gulps them down with red Corona — my bottle. The doctor asked her if she was expecting 'cos if she was some kinds of tablets would do her harm. Well, as she said, you can't be certain, you never know, do you? In this day and age! So she went to get the other kind, just in case. But she must have mentioned it to her best friend, Denise, 'cos her boyfriend told me in the Offy, 'How d'you feel now you're going to be a dad? Looking forward to it?' And I said, 'Well, 'salright. Yeah ...

'salright.'

I heard her telling Denise that I appreciate her more now, since she came back to me. Haven't got a clue why she said that. She's an old slag and I detest having her in the house, Denise I mean. At least if that's what she thinks.

I've got a new car and I leave it at the side of the house just in case someone nicks it. Seventy quid from one of the Abermorddu bus-drivers. At least it goes! Only for back and fore to work. All the way to the taxi-rank in King's Street! Well, it's better than walking, innit?

Debs talks about getting married, but I don't. She goes on about everything to everyone anyway. I'm a private person. But she will bring it up in front of other people. I change the subject. She brings her giggly mates here, and that friggin Denise like a big fat hen with them, and they rabbit on about 'Marriage'. I say, 'You take the high road and I'll take the low road,' and hold up two fish-fingers. Swivel on that!

Damn, a knock at the door! I know who it is. Mam wanting me to lay her lino and I've just started to relax. Ah well! I can't avoid Mam. She gives Debs a peck and says she's looking a bit more perky. She would if she was dressed all in white and walking down the aisle in church instead of lolling on the settee all sweaty and vomity.

I've been Dean's girlfriend ever since he was fifteen. He used to wear different things and make-up in those days. That's what was so attractive about him, he was different. Trying to recover from the shock of who his father was and who he was. I know we've been through a lot these last three years. I'm eighteen tomorrow and expecting his baby, but that's all I want out of life really. I'm used to seeing my sisters with their kids and I like having them around, and I'm going to enjoy being a mother. I'm happy living round here 'cos this is where I belong. People know me as one of the girls raised in the shadow of the Power House, they remember me as a helluva naughty girl at school, and they know I like giving

40

a bit of stick to the Pakis in the chip-shop. I go in sometimes and ask for fresh hot chips, not the ones that've been standing around a bit. And if I don't get any I say to the long queue, 'These are yesterday's chips!' But they all laugh and take it from me.

I was a bit off yesterday and stayed in my nightie all day, just lounging about the place. At six in the evening I'd finished my fags and as Dean wouldn't take me there was nothing for it but pop on my coat and walk to the Paki House in my slippers. I cracked a joke about chocolate-coloured make-up, and they laughed.

Don't get me wrong — I'm not thick. I didn't work hard enough at school, but no one can put one over on me. Now Dean's on the taxis till late every night I'm on my own. But I've started to read, so I can live in my own world then. But until he comes home I'd rather watch a film on satellite than go to bed, or an old video of *Ghost*. I always have to have the Kleenex handy. Dean likes that film too.

I've been getting ready for the baby for I don't know how long, since before I lost my job in fact. I've been putting things together for him or her. Although I've had a peek at the scan I've asked them not to tell me what it's going to be. Or the wonder of it all will have gone, won't it? I was worried I was on the small side for a bit, but now everything's alright. I've been on that machine that says if your baby is afraid and stuff. All this technology's great, but I'm certain it's not half so great as the birth itself.

'Debs, can we have a word with you in the office, love?' That's how working in the lingerie factory came to an end, after I'd been so loyal, and there'd been talk I was going to be a supervisor in our section come the new year. But they'd heard I was pregnant, and it was easier to sack me for unsatisfactory work so that they didn't have to pay for maternity leave. Well, I told them straight: 'You've shit on me.' That's the only language they understand. 'I don't want any of your fucking money.'

I had tears in my eyes and not one of them offered me a cuppa or a hankie, they just left me standing there. And they'd all been calling me Debs and saying 'Hiya!' every morning. It was all a blessing in a hard sort of way, 'cos I've got something more now.

And Dean's attitude has changed completely. He's grown up overnight, and since we've been back together he's a different person. He's promised to look for a more settled job in the new year and I'm going to help him get his dream of being in the police or a prison warder. Raise him up from being a taxi-driver. So much goes wrong with the engine it's just not fair.

I'm the only one who knows him, the only one who's taken the trouble. I know we went our separate ways for a bit. That was the time when Dean changed and lost weight, and went all trendy, not like the Dean I know at all. He bought flowers for someone else on the buses once, not for me. But that was only once. All his problems are due to when he was fat, 'cos for a while he wanted to be like Jason Donovan, and he had to prove it to himself. His hair was dyed blond, he wore earrings and a gold watch, and all he was interested in was pulling girls on the buses. He lost about a stone and a half 'cos there wasn't any food in the house. But for him losing weight was a boost to his ego.

The old Dean came back, thank goodness, and I gave Gaz the push. He was going into the Navy anyway. It was just a fling. I can relax during the day now, though I try to tidy up and do some decorating as well, and get the bedroom ready for the baby. I said to Dean when he was a bit moody one night, 'Don't worry about me losing my job. When I'm twenty-one we'll all go for a long holiday, 'cos I can get my hands on the cash then.'

To be fair to him, Dean went to the factory to see the Manager after the way I'd been treated. And d'you know what? The bugger was hiding behind the door 'cos he didn't want to meet Dean.

'Don't get your knickers in a twist,' he said. Funny thing to say in a lingerie factory! I'd like to have been a fly on the wall. Ah well, it's all over now, and Dean earns a bit on the taxis to keep the three of us.

Aye, I've got something better than all of them put together.

Reflections by a Pool

Dafydd Arthur Jones

'Of course I am,' and he heard other familiar words in his head. Once upon a time, and not very long ago either, things had been much easier. One house, a wife and child, and suddenly he recalled the happy combination and the sun shining from a blue sky, and every window wide open and Meilir's hearty laughter. One, two, three, four, and then he paused. She took it into her head to ring at the oddest moments. Not that he'd had the cheek even to mention it to her. A call at midday to explain that Meilir had been late getting up that morning, another one evening because he was flummoxed by some difficult homework. Then the child was put on the line and urged to try and explain his problem, which he did long-windedly like a little old man fighting for breath. Sometimes Mal would search for an excuse and hear himself speak sharply. But he didn't have the guts to end any conversation thus, despite the break-up. The break-up, he thought. There hadn't been much of a 'break-up' in the end; she had hung on every word, every syllable, weaving sentences neatly together until it made him prey to the most terrible guilt. After all, it was only thirty miles, he thought, no more. He stared at the blackness of the word-processor's screen. It would be so easy to fling a light coat around his shoulders and abandon the story. Mari knew as much. She'd long been used to such thoughts from a man who fancied himself as a writer. No, he wouldn't give in. He heard a splash and Elsbeth was lifting a brown arm langourously from the chlorinated water. Anyway, he'd taken the step. He put his finger slowly, carefully on the letter T. A story was on its way. He was required to make up his mind without delay.

'Who is it?' Elsbeth from the pool.

'Who d'you think?' The author from the waterside.

'And what did you say this time?' asked Elsbeth, giving the impression that she didn't care a toss.

'I said I was busy.' Mel watched the brown body slipping so effortlessly and quietly from one end to the other. She lifted one arm and then the other, like a knife slicing through the blue water.

'And are you?' He saw her head plunge deeper until her hair was one smooth brown mat over her ears.

'I'm fairly busy.'

'Have you started the story?'

'I would have if Mari hadn't rung.'

Mal imagined he'd heard his words from the other end of the pool. Talk of a decision, of taking a step ... taking another step and choosing between them, and not thinking he'd have a chance to go back, and packing his cases and slamming the door, and how he'd made her sacrifice to buy such a house with a swimming-pool, at such an expensive time. He sighed for the second time that morning. Once upon a time ... but it was no use, and stories like that no longer saw the light of day, not even in Welsh.

'Well?'

Across the cold tiles of the pool he heard that little word and found it particularly pitiless. She could plunge deeper and come up quietly like a missile and scare him, sometimes, as on those occasions in the moonlight just after he'd moved in.

'Well, are you going to make a start, then? I thought we'd have lunch out here today.'

T. And what's a letter worth?

Mal considered the question earnestly, turning over several memorable answers in his head as he followed the light dancing of her feet under the thousand silvery waves. T ... two lovers, and he knew he'd made a serious beginning this time. A short story, a gripping little tale — and then he paused. He was like that with Mair, looking for a lead and then talking and talking until things cooled down. Two lovers ... and he looked to see whether there was any light in the blackness of the screen.

Two lovers, well one actually, and two characters in a taxi splashing through large grey puddles on their way back to their snug homes. Yes, that was a lot nearer the mark. An old jalopy, a noisy, dilapidated taxi with a battered exhaust and large dents in the rear seat, and a youngish driver who'd seen all sorts, steering it with one arm resting on the frame of the window. But then there had to be people, who would sit in the rear.

Isn't it important for every author to know his characters? asked Huw A. as the taxi screeched off. But your sentences are only half-finished, your processor's full of old dialogue coming uneasily to the surface or left idle and motionless like flotsam. Why don't you put things in proper shape? It was Huw A. at it again. D'you expect me to go home like a good boy? I have a wife who's pregnant. Did you know that? The events of the night before rolled through Huw A.'s mind. The routine was from one pub to the next, from the back-bar to the front in some places, toting lagers like the town lads, and everyone giving the impression they were used to the bitter drink. Teachers and bankers, the kids with cropped hair and messy rugby-shirts, a mixture of both languages, standing around in cigarette-smoke all evening. But where are you trying to take us? asked the author quietly. Then he raised his voice, because he thought the car's exhaust was scraping the road, though he didn't want to mention it to the driver. But what was the point of dragging this into a story? He glanced at Rich in a deep slumber at his side. He was the braggart, the one who'd arrange for the lads to meet in such-and-such a place and at such-and-such a time. It was he who'd started spending money, taking a twenty-pound note from his pocket and nodding to several regulars in the bar. Words upon words, in one stream of talk about teaching and cars, the election and sport, without a fullstop anywhere. They kept together and the Welsh they spoke drowned out all the townies, pretending no one had noticed them taking up the low tables with their empty glasses. And here he was now like a corpse in a taxi, a big sack sweating profusely under the armpits. But where are you taking us? Is it going to be a story with a good-night in it? A dénouement where the characters playfully grab one another? Back in the little bungalows on the outskirts of the town proper? Back to the wife who's tucked up warm under the coverlet? But Huw A. could sense the end of the evening as it came up for nine o'clock. That was the trouble with those pushing thirty. The fun's in the talk, the pleasure in the swank, but nine o'clock is late for those who aren't used to their pint at six when the bar is three-quarters empty. He didn't have many lines to say either. He sighed again. Only the usual, in a story about sensible young men gallivanting round town and mixing with the rough lads, even if it was only at arm's length. There was talk of a late curry and a challenge to find one, or even to take a taxi to a nightclub. Rich had a lot to say for himself. But he'd spewed his guts up and had been hassling the English — again at arm's length. From a distance ... and yet and yet, Huw A. thought, turning his attention to the author. A paltry accountant deserved no better, nor a second-language Welsh teacher. Important people who go in for sports quizzes, knowledgeable men like us, who recall some eisteddfodau better than others, and can please our wives on demand. He wrinkled his nose and felt his skin crimping in the heat and tobacco smoke of the pub. He'd expected better.

He'd expected better. An author scratching his head and the weather too warm, even to think of looking at the screen. A breeze wafted the stench of disinfectant to his nostrils. He could feel the cold as he sat there searching for an ending to the piece. Take the plunge in his shorts, never mind the neighbours, that would do the trick. Frighten Elsbeth and tell her he'd decided that he'd never, never again bother even to think of Mari or little Meilir. How could he be expected to think of creating something worthwhile when he was torn between everyone? He looked at the screen and the name Huw A. Why couldn't he give him a surname instead of trying to be different? It was child's play pretending to be an author, a bit of a script-writer, half a novelist. He began questioning Huw A. silently. Not a word came from his lips; after all, he didn't want Elsbeth to suspect anything. You wanted to chat up some bird and that was quite natural. But to go home eventually would make a pleasant little ending. Mal recalled settling down in Bangor with Mair. That had been their lifestyle for years until Meilir had come along. He was let loose on Friday nights and she on Wednesdays.

He'd been able to stay at home writing. Scribbling wildly with a biro, waiting eagerly for her return, though he never let on. She'd come home about half-past ten and praise what he'd written, whatever it might be. But Elsbeth was something else again. She dipped into paperbacks and concealed her razor-sharp mind behind innocent little questions. Like an angler striking suddenly, she could be alluring, then have you hooked and landed. Her elastic body grew longer and longer in the water. She looked much more like some supple instrument as she groped for the far side of the tiled wall. But he'd better not watch her swimming like the pendulum of a clock, back and forth unceasingly. He had to get rid of Huw A. Where could he send a man like this in white trainers and blue jeans? He shook his head, taking care not to let Elsbeth see.

'The boy's a scumbag,' began Huw A., addressing the fast-asleep sack. Not that it made any difference to Rich. But for the weary driver as he screeched through the amber lights it was different. Huw A. knew that he wasn't a man to be trifled with. He boldly suggested that he stop outside the Indian restaurant, but he didn't even get an exclamation in response. But why the hell don't I get the chance to do something? asked Mal, expecting a reply. One such step and he could have spoiled everything once and for all. He could have ... and he considered it seriously. Another pint, a small glass of something, and some questioning, without burning the fingers too much. Come on, little author ... er, er, er. One step ... what d'you say?

Mal suddenly looked up. He didn't like the look of this and his finger nearly reached for 'delete' on his machine. Best start again. But Elsbeth could see him from a distance. Not even the name, Huw A., was right. To think he'd started talking to himself like this!

Huw A. was troubled only by a half-chance. He felt himself slipping slowly and comfortably into the rear seat. He could easily con Rich; he was a hero, definitely. Quite a man, able to cross the crowded floor and go straight up to her without beating about the bush. He knew the others were watching him and he was able to give them the impression that things were working out. He took a chance, and read her like a book. She was one of the town girls, he knew that from her behaviour. He'd noticed her looking for the toilet and the snug bar. But he'd have to speak English, and suddenly and without tripping up at that. Between courtship and wedlock, he thought. A terrific title! He'd had a whiff this evening of the old freedom, and the tuppenny-halfpenny scribbler had missed his opportunity. Perhaps he was the same spit as Rich with his big clumsy feet or Gwyn-next-door with his stammer. But he'd have to stick at it, bearing in mind that there were desperate men loitering in bars. But Huw A. didn't have the words, his sentences failed him at the crucial moment. He talked, under his breath, about coffee, and going home with a bold, confident step. He imagined himself sipping from large tankards and suggesting a drop of wine would be a good idea, and her going obediently to the back.

Mal was studying his partner's breasts. They heaved as she raised one arm and then the other. Things were warming up, but he'd led his characters like this before, without getting anywhere. Elsbeth, too, knew full well that he had no experience of it. Except for Mari, no one had ever been close to him, and even words like 'had been close' gave the impression that he didn't have the cheek to say anything plainly. After he'd fallen for years between two stools, Elsbeth had hit the nail on the head, plunging right in and snatching at some truth that he hadn't expected to say anything about. But for this fella to be chatting up a feather-brained bird scarcely twenty years old wasn't all that daft an idea. And to find himself in a strange bed, with her parents snoring in the next room? But he wasn't up to it, and her smile faded when she realized that he wasn't capable of much more than chatting her up in a pub.

This is an old turd of an author, thought Huw A. He almost said it straight out and gave a shove to the pot-bellied sack who was still fast asleep. But to be dragged back to Gwen. Not that there was anything wrong with that. He'd been expecting them all to make for home in the end. It would be a talking-point, and it wouldn't do me any harm either. But he could have given me one boost, one small step, seeing as she was so nice.

A drop of water fell on Mal's shoulder. The tiniest drop, because Elsbeth had taken care to wrap herself in a towel from top to toe. She breathed lightly and Mal found himself doing the same thing. She'd always hover like this after a swim, sort of half-dressed and lying at the poolside until she took it into her head to make a spot of lunch. A hard kick would work wonders, put Huw A. into the blonde's arms ... but he no longer had the energy to consider it. He'd been typing all morning, and was quietly astonished at himself for having given up so easily.

'You can't leave it like that?'

He pretended he hadn't heard. It gave him time to search for a satisfactory ending. But what to do? Drag him back? That would be most sensible. He'd had his bit of fun, just like his real self, and there wasn't much point asking for more. He nearly sighed again. He wasn't expected to do anything with her looking over his shoulder like some teacher. A man of his age and time, unable to bring things to a close. Dammit, it was time for Huw A. to drag his mate back through the estate of small bungalows, happy after a bellyful and a bit of a chat with a face he wasn't ever likely to see again. Perhaps that was best for everyone, he thought, to return to the fold after straying. I could make an ending like that for both of us. A momentary fancy, a fling just to prove something or other, and that was it, fullstop.

That afternoon Mal ventured to print out the first paragraphs. But before doing so he had a much better idea and hurled himself, feet first, and with only the flimsiest of shorts on, into the depths of the pool. Elsbeth was rather quiet. She mentioned something about a 'nothing-sort-of-ending', and perhaps she felt that Huw A. should have taken a chance and a step into the twilight for one night in his life. But Mal was the author, and in trying to warm up in a cold pool, he knew in his heart that this was the difference between him and Elsbeth. But it had been too fine a day even to mention it.

Water

Martin Davis

The tailor has found a tin of potatoes. It must have been blown out of the kitchen of the restaurant across the road during the last rocket attack. He's sitting in a corner and looking at the tin on his lap like a miser with his money, while the rest of us watch him accusingly as if we're afraid he'll scoff the lot without offering us any — although he could hardly tuck into his spoils here without our knowing. This is a cramped place and a tin without something to open it is quite useless.

All the bonhomie of the morning, when the shooting started, has died down as the afternoon sun turns this underground hideout into a furnace. The sun peeps in through the holes in the roof so that there is nowhere with any proper shade.

The old man is lying in the most shady place. He was put there at the start, when we were still concerned about one another. He watches us with his gimlet eyes, his tongue playing continuously over his liver-coloured lips. Every now and again, he laughs quietly and shakes his head.

'What's the joke, old man?'

It's the young soldier asking. He's lying flat on his back at the foot of the stairs, the peak of his cap pulled down over his eyes.

'Nothing, son. Nothing at all.'

The soldier gets to his feet, pushing the cap back on his forehead.

'Come on, share it with us.'

The old man closes his eyes and retreats into his shell.

'No. It doesn't matter.'

I can hardly hear his voice and the humour has gone from his face. He's sighing and lying completely still as if on a bier.

The next second the soldier is on his hands and knees at the old man's side and laying into him viciously.

'Come on, you old bugger. Out with it!'

The old man's eyes open with a flicker, but he's not afraid of the young soldier. He looks straight into his face and runs his serrated tongue over his lips before speaking.

'I just thought it was funny, that's all. Forty years to the day, look, it was us firing at this village. The haulm was burning on the hillside, and the barracks stable was on fire, too. You could hear the horses screeching — there was the smell of meat roasting in the air for days afterwards — and the Reds were fleeing for their lives.'

The soldier is listening to what he's saying, his mouth wide open. He looks at the old man and then, with a curse, turns back to sprawl as before.

The soldier's itching to be with his own side, fighting the enemy — not with castaways in a cellar.

'And twenty years before that,' the old man goes on, shifting his hawk eyes from one face to the next, 'my own father was defending the place against the cavalry and snipers of that rapacious Jew ... '

'He wasn't a Jew,' says the tailor quickly, forgetting his tin of potatoes for a moment, his dark eyes flashing. 'That was a lie to get you ...'

The rest of his words are drowned by loud footsteps on the street outside as a cluster of mortar bombs falls quite close to our hiding-place. Plaster and small lumps of concrete fall on our heads. Everyone starts spitting and coughing as the thick cloud fills the subterranean hideout.

Beside me, the young mother is still holding the corpse of her little girl. The child appears to be sleeping. Not a mark on her. The blast of the explosion has burst her lungs, probably. The mother stares straight ahead and hums some prayer or lullaby. When I got here at eight this morning just as the shooting started, I thought the girl was sleeping. I was amazed that children could sleep through all that and I smiled at the mother and she smiled back at me. She had a cute little gap between her front teeth. And then I saw the child had been killed.

I thought of my own children at my brother's home about fifteen kilometres from the front — they had gone there to help with the harvest, if there is one this year what with the drought and all this fighting. There's no one left on the farm. The local men are all in the army — or with the rebels, or fled with their families. It'll be a different sort of harvest this year.

By now the girl looks more like a rag-doll, as if she too has withered in the heat, her head bent back and her dark hair disshevelled; you can see the whites of her eyes, and a thin streak of blood trickling down the dust on her face, from the terrible internal injuries she must have suffered.

I've been watching that crimson thread all afternoon. It's stretched and spread as the shadows have lengthened.

I think I must have fallen asleep, or dozed off, at any rate. It feels as if I'm in for a fever. I felt a bit groggy yesterday while I was shifting stones in the top field. I thought the heat was to blame. It's hard to believe that was only yesterday.

The soldier has shared the contents of his canteen with us. There was something stronger than water in it and it didn't do much to help quench the thirst that's beginning to drive us crazy. Then he managed to punch two holes in the tailor's tin of potatoes with his bayonet while the man was asleep. But the water was salty and the soldier angrily chucked the tin away. At this the tailor woke up and began complaining. The soldier gave him a clout and no one raised a finger to stop him.

Now the tailor is sobbing in the corner and spitting blood into the dust. Night is falling and the firing has receded.

No one says anything any more. Everyone is preoccupied with his own worries. I'm starting to fret that the vegetables at home haven't been watered for over twenty-four hours.

The mother has laid her child down and folded her little arms criss-cross over her chest. She's taken a small wooden comb from her bag and she's combing the dark, matted hair. By now the blood has formed a purple stain around her mouth, as if she's been eating blackberries. The mother glances at me, smiling vacantly.

'So tiny, so pretty, isn't she?' she says over and over again, nodding at the corpse.

'Yes, indeed to God,' I say. It's a hoarse sound that comes from my throat. My tongue feels enormous and rough in my mouth.

The soldier crawls to the top of the staircase. He sticks his helmet on the end of the barrel of his automatic rifle and hoists it slowly through the hole into the half-light outside without a word to us. He waves the helmet back and forth but no one fires. Then he climbs through the hole onto the steps and disappears.

The tailor follows him and then the three lorry-drivers. I'm left with the old fellow and the young mother and the dead child. I start crawling towards the hole.

'You will fetch a doctor, won't you?' says the mother. 'I think the little one's hurt.'

'Yes, of course,' I say.

Then I'm through the hole and gulping the clear evening air into my lungs. I feel my chest expanding and think of the little lungs of the girl in the cellar like two deflated balloons.

The street's empty. Glass crunches underfoot and where rubble has been spewed over the road. Are there any people under the rubble, I wonder? It's possible, though most of the townsfolk left to join their people in the country at the beginning of the week.

Suddenly, my heart misses a beat. I can see an arm sticking out from under a huge concrete beam. Then I see that it's only a pole for holding up a canopy over a café door — the remnants of the red material are dangling from it in shreds.

Everything swims before my eyes and before getting to the top of the street I have to throw up. My throat's hurting me a lot as I try to fetch up the yellow-green bile, but I feel a bit better after that, and now I'm sitting at a table outside a café to steady my head and get my breath back before going on.

After a minute or so I get to my feet again and go into the café. The door's wide-open but it's pitch-dark inside. I stumble to the counter and climb over it. In the darkness I tread on a pile of empty bottles and cut my finger on the edge of the sink; I can feel the blood trickling down my arm as far as my elbow. I'm growling like a dog and my heart's pumping. I listen in case someone's heard the din as I stumbled over the bottles, but the evening is quiet except for the drone of an aeroplane in the distance and the occasional mortar shell like a dog barking in the yard at night.

I grab two bottles that feel like bottles of water and climb back over the bar. My finger's hurting now and I'm starting to feel sick again. Outside, with my head spinning and a lump building up relentlessly in my stomach, I lie down on the ground with my eyes closed.

I don't know how long I lie there, but gradually the lump dissolves and at last I raise myself on my elbow.

By the light of the moon I see that I have a bottle of water and a bottle of brandy. I knock back half the water and then choke on it. The whole lot comes back up immediately.

I have to lie down again. I watch the stars spinning overhead. I sleep for a while and then I'm awake again, with a cold sweat on my forehead and my guts heaving. A wave of fear and despair sweeps over me as I wake up. Suddenly, the unreal destruction all around me becomes very real. I remember that those old vegetables haven't had water for nearly two days. There'll be nothing left of them.

I must settle my stomach and make for home. This time I turn my attention to the brandy wine. It has a sour taste but straightaway I feel the knotting in my stomach being soothed.

To the north the thunder of the guns has started up again. The irregular rhythm makes me get to my feet and head for home once more. I swallow the rest of the water. It sinks to the pit of my stomach as if percolating through a sponge and I can feel it cold and heavy — but at least it's willing to remain there for the time being.

War is a messy business — literally, I mean. Tidy gardens turned into scrap-heaps, pools of oil on the road, suitcases scattered all over the place. Bodies.

Suddenly, I'm like a moth caught in the light that explodes behind me. In my fever I didn't hear the sound of the vehicle.

'Stop! Stop!'

I stand like a rabbit confronted by a viper. By the vehicle's headlamps I catch a glimpse of helmets and then I'm face-down in the dust, floored by a blow from a rifle-butt.

'Where do you come from?'

I name the district.

An uneasy muttering among the soldiers. The rebels have a stronghold where I come from. I must be one of them. They start debating whether they should shoot me on the spot.

As I hear all this the brandy in my stomach freezes and the cold seems to seep through me.

Then I hear a voice that I seem to recognize explaining that I've only just arrived in the district and that I'm not one of the rebels. In the glare I can't make out who it is.

He's still standing there, unreal. Suddenly, the thought of my being executed strikes me, and in spite of myself I feel a smile spreading across my face.

The soldiers are still suspicious, but there's no more talk of shooting me.

'I want to go home ... I have to water the vegetables ...' I hardly recognize my own voice. I'm croaking like a raven.

After taking a long time to consider the matter, they decide they have no objection to my request for a lift home. They bundle me into the back of the lorry. It's clear that they're disappointed.

I see now who it was who interceded on my behalf. A young lad who helped us out last year. He can't look me in the eye. I know that his brother is with the rebels. Brother against brother, neighbour asgainst neighbour — communal trust and co-operation growing brittle and falling apart overnight.

We have to stop twice to clear explosives from the road. But at last we reach the bottom of the lane that leads to my home.

'You'll be alright now,' the leader says as the lorry starts off on its way to the next village. 'We've walloped the backsides off the buggers around here for you.'

If they knew who my wife is, they'd probably sing a different tune.

The lorry disappears over the brow of the hill and then, silence. Almost an explosive silence. Even the cicadas have fallen silent for the time being. I lean against the gatepost, my forehead a red-hot anvil to the giant hammer of a headache; but I'm not afraid as such — I'm worried about the vegetables more than anything.

Slowly, the heavy breathing subsides and the headache grows less and I begin to make my way up the steep track leading to my home. I feel better, although I'm still a bit light-headed. A light breeze cools my brow.

Half-way up the track, I come upon the first body. An army corporal, a bearded man in his early forties. His legs lie about a metre away where they were blown off by the grenade — the litres of blood flowing from the stumps seeping into the scorched earth all around him and leaving a dark stain in the moonlight. The corporal's eyes are open and he stares at me coldly. Usually I find it difficult to look someone in the eye — but I feel no shame looking at these dead eyes.

Walking on, I see another body behind the hedge, but I pass it by. The smell of burning is in the wind, mixed with the stench of corpses. As I draw near the yard, I see that one of the out-buildings has been burned down and blue smoke is still rising from the ashes.

But the house looks as if it hasn't been damaged. One pane is broken in the window on the second floor — my son's bedroom. But I'm not worried about the house or about my son at the moment; it's the vegetables that concern me, watering the vegetables. That's the only thing burning in my head, like the thirst that's scorching my throat.

It was water that started the conflagration. Dry winters for three years. Water from the dams going to fill the swimming-pools and irrigate the gardens of the large families and wealthy farmers down in the valley while the cattle and crops of the mountain people were failing. They pleaded for a new water-pipe, but the authorities preferred to pump water to the posh hotels for the Germans and Americans on the coast, so that they could have ice in their whisky and showers every night to wash the scent of adultery from their bodies.

Because there's water in these mountains alright. Twenty years ago, we went without rain for seven months and I remember the spring in the village where I was brought up running clear the whole time. My mother and sister always had to carry every drop into the house. Compulsory provision. But now the water-table has fallen.

I'm alright here. I have a spring, an old bore-hole that goes deep down under the field behind the house and the water's still pouring from it. That's why I bought this place ...

By the vineyard wall there are seven bodies in a row, their hands tied behind their backs. One of them is twelve years old. I know one of the others too. He's a distant relation of my wife's family. Even if there weren't any shortage, the two sides would still find a pretext to slaughter one another sooner or later. We're that sort of people. It's our destiny.

Hell! If these lads were alive now they could help me with the watering. There's a lot of work to do.

There are the plots where the vegetables grow. As far as I can make out, they've escaped the conflict. The frames and canes are still standing. Even the water-pipes which spray them seem to be untouched. My heart takes a leap. I'll turn the water on and all will be well. My land will turn green again and the fruit will grow ripe. The children will come back; the war will end; the rains of autumn will return. But they won't unless I water the vegetables straightaway.

The engine of the water-pump has been riddled with bullets. I'll have to turn the wheel by hand. The wheel's slippery where the engine oil has spilt over it, but it turns alright. The pipes shudder as the air comes farting through them. The wheel feels strange. The pressure isn't right. No water comes out.

I hurl myself at the side of the metal tank which surrounds the spring. The wooden lid that usually protects the water has broken. On tip-toe, I peer in over the rim. I can see there's a body sunk at the bottom of the tank and blocking the outlet of the pump.

I run to the other side of the tank where there's a ladder and billhook. I place the stool against the tank and climb up onto the top rung but one. I try to move the body with the billhook, but to no avail. It's obvious that the heavy pack on the soldier's back is holding him down. There's nothing for it but to jump in. The water's lukewarm but colder towards the bottom nearer the source.

The body's still too heavy for me, and so I duck under the water and grope for the soldier's bayonet. For an instant our fingers touch and everything seems real and horrible, but then with my knife I cut through the straps of the pack, and the corpse starts to float to the surface. Somehow its arms are clasped around my neck and we come up together, me coughing, him uncomplaining, and embracing each other in celebration of our success.

He's too heavy for me to lift out of the tank, but I've unblocked the outlet — the most important thing is to get the water to run. It's almost dawn, I'll have to get a move on or the wet leaves will be scorching in the sunshine. I heave the load to one side and climb out of the tank.

I'm whacked and it takes all my remaining strength to get myself over the side. I half-slide, half-crawl back to the pump's wheel and start turning it, my hands slithering on the metal.

The first rays of the sun are streaking the eastern sky as the pipes tremble and fart for a second time. The water flows now, a reddish yellow in the thin light of the dawn.

I turn to the soldier draped over the rim of the water-tank just above my head. I announce my victory.

'Everything's going to be alright now, you'll see.'

But he hasn't got anything to say for himself; what's left of his face is withered away and his blood is splashing like rain all over my garden.

The Librarian

Dyfed Edwards

They're a real nuisance, these people who move books around. I arrive at the library at half-past nine every Monday and Thursday, and the first job is always to put the books back in their proper place. They do it to spite me. And they're damned lucky I never catch them at it, the buggers, or there'd be hell to pay.

Mind you, the library's a very nice place; it's in the town centre, convenient for everyone. And a small group of people causing me trouble twice a week would never keep me away. That's their intention, of course, and I do get upset when I arrive and see books all jumbled up. But I don't break my heart over it.

'Hello, Mr Jones,' the girls at the counter say as I arrive, and they're pretty, too; pretty and polite. What more can a man ask of his staff?

'I have quite a busy morning ahead of me,' I tell the girls after inspecting the shelves.

The books are supposed to be in alphabetical order, you see. But what those untidy sods tend to do is put them back in the wrong place after taking a peep at them. Trouble, trouble, trouble.

Today, for example, Anthony Burgess before Charles Bukowski, Thomas Hardy after James Herbert, and Alistair MacLean — believe it or not — among the Barbara Cartlands. And that was just one shelf; can you imagine the work it makes? It'll take all morning, as usual, just to put things back in proper order. I won't have a chance to do anything else.

But every now and then I do manage to sit down and read a chapter or two, with a cuppa and sandwich before me on the table; what better? Romances are my favourites, someone like Victoria Holt, *Mistress of Mellyn* — now there's a good book — or Malcolm Ross, *On a Far Wild Shore*, lovely. You don't often find a man writing romances. In fact, men don't usually enjoy that kind of thing at all, but I do. Some might laugh at me, but never mind about that. People have always made fun of me.

I'm at it for hours putting the books back. The assistants — there are two, usually — watch me sometimes and I can see them whispering to each other. I don't like seeing them chatting too much during the working day — there's enough to do — but I'd never tell them off. They have a lot of respect for me, I can tell that, and they probably say things like 'Isn't he a good worker!', 'He's quite smart for a man in his forties', 'He'd make some lucky girl a good husband' and 'If only I were as tidy as him' ...

I've invited them over for supper several times but they always refuse. They're shy, most likely. They think they're not good enough for me. They probably haven't told anyone that I've asked them. It's something special, isn't it, getting an invitation from a man in my position?

It gets quite hectic in the library around mid-morning with the local schools starting to come in. I've never seen a gang of kids sitting so quietly as the ones who come and read in the Children's Corner. It's a special part of the library with dinky little desks and chairs so they can read quietly. The stock's excellent and I enjoy spending part of the morning in the children's section where the books are so nicely illustrated and always in good order. Children are the only ones who put books back in the right place. Quite a few of the public drop in, too, and I've got to know some of them — like the old lady who reads thrillers; the man who returns his books in a shopping basket, as if we're a supermarket; the young long-haired couple in black leather who take out classical records from the Music Department. Real characters, all of them.

That's one reason why I've always been interested in libraries. Why I was so keen to become a librarian — so I could meet all these people, and so they could meet me.

When I was a lad my father used to bring me to the old library and put me to sit at a table with a pile of books.

'I have to discuss something with Miss Jenkins; now behave,' he would say before disappearing into a back-room with the assistant. My father was in insurance and that's what they discussed for an hour or so every lunch-time. Hardly anyone dropped in around then.

If someone asked for her, I would say, 'Miss Jenkins is discussing insurance with Dad in the back.'

'Yes, of course,' they would say, glancing in the direction of the back-room.

When I grew old enough to go to school I missed my visits to the library. But more often than not I'd play truant so that I could spend time among the books, all dusty and smelling of damp; they brought more comfort, more than anything else, to a lad without any real friends of his own.

I had set my mind on becoming a librarian there, in the old building where I learnt to read. But unfortunately, they decided to shut the place down and put up a purpose-built library on a new site. In fact, they did quite a good job of it and although I was a bit worried at the start, I've settled in well.

'Mr Jones?' says the voice behind me. 'Mr Jones, it's time to close now.' One of the assistants. I look up at the clock. Prompt as usual.

'Well done. Keeping an eye on the clock. I respect that in a colleague,' I say.

'Ten more minutes,' she says, turning on her heels.

I look around. It's time for me to choose some books. I pick up the large sports-bag that has remained at my side like a faithful dog throughout the morning, and start scanning the shelves. One. Two. Three. Four. Another. And another. There are now ten books lying nicely in my bag. Bending down, I do up the zip and smile broadly because my books are safe.

Presently I go over to the Biography section. After some reflection I take out a thick blue book from the shelf: the life of

Charles Darwin, the heretic and blasphemer, but that's enough of that. I don't intend reading this rubbish, and they can have it back on Monday.

'This will keep you quiet,' says the girl at the counter as she stamps the book. I laugh and say, 'I'll need something to keep me out of trouble. Only naughty boys have nothing to do,' and I wink at her before walking out through the glass door into the open air, which stinks of people.

I go straight home after leaving the library because I'm itching to sort out the books. Once, I was in so much of a hurry that I left my house-keys in the office. I had to get into the house through a back window, and who should spot me but a passing policeman. They always turn up at the most inconvenient times, don't they? I had a good deal of trouble getting him to believe it was my house and I nearly died when he asked me what was in the bag.

'Books,' I said.

'Oh, yes?' he said, all suspicious. So I showed him and took great pleasure in seeing him go red as a beetroot.

I usually go straight into the best room in the house. It's taken me years to collect all these books; five hundred and thirty-nine — five hundred and forty-nine after today. They're all arranged in alphabetical order, every single one of them neatly in place. And nobody comes in here to disturb them. No intruders run their dirty fingers over them. They are safe here.

The biggest problem in a terraced house is a shortage of space, and you can't imagine the hassle I had when Mother and Father were around. I had to keep everything in my room and do my best to keep the door locked all the time.

I had to get rid of them both in the end to make room for the books. At least they're comfortable in the attic. So then I did their room out as a library, my library. There's lots of room here now that I've shifted everything and put up shelves from floor to ceiling — just like in a real library.

Some day, and it's not far off now — next week, possibly — there won't be any space left. But I won't have to give up the books, and I won't be moving into a bigger house, and most importantly of all, no one else will own the books.

I've made my plans.

There's a simple wooden chair in the middle of the room with a red can and a box of matches. After I've emptied the contents of the can over the library, I shall sit in the chair and share my end with the books I've saved from the clutches of those who don't appreciate them properly. We'll make our exit together.

Don't worry, I've made sure there'll be plenty of petrol left after I've made one last visit to the public library.

I'm Sorry, Joe Rees

Eleri Llewelyn Morris

Why did you come and sit by me, Joe Rees? Why didn't you sit by the woman in the large hat in the seat behind me, or by the man with the rolled umbrella in the seat across the aisle?

I noticed you the moment I got on the bus. Fumbling in my purse for change, and waiting in the queue to pay my fare, I saw you squatting in the back seat: a man of about forty, unkempt, dirty, not having shaved or washed for days. You must have noticed me, too, because hardly had I sat down than you'd got up and come to sit by me, whispering roughly yet confidentially, 'Can you tell me when we get to the mental hospital?'

I wasn't frightened, not at all. I said I'd be getting off before then and you'd better ask the driver.

'No, no,' you said, your eyes gleaming. 'No.'

You had nice eyes, too — a bit bloodshot, but nice all the same. As I looked into them, I knew I had no reason to be afraid of you.

'What's your name?' you asked.

I had to say it about half-a-dozen times and spell it twice. 'Eleri.' You were amazed that such a name existed and found it difficult to pronounce and remember.

'I'm Joe Rees,' you said. 'J.O.E. That's easy, isn't it?'

Why did you catch hold of my hand, Joe Rees? I'd felt quite

comfortable in your company up to then. But when the bus started, I noticed you trembling. Was it the sudden noise of the engine that startled you? Or was it the thought of approaching your destination that made your stomach churn? Anyway, you held my hand and as intensely as if it had been a crucifix. It was then that I noticed for the first time the broad scar smiling on your wrist. You caught me staring at it.

'I did that,' you said, the pride of an old soldier showing his medals in your voice.

We didn't speak much after that; we just sat there hand-in-hand, and every now and then you squeezed my hand gently, and even kissed it. Then you would look at me with all kinds of emotions implied in your red eyes.

I was aware that the woman in the large hat was watching. Although she was sitting behind me, I could feel myself smarting under her stare. And the man with the rolled umbrella too; he was glancing at us slyly over his spectacles. I began to feel uneasy — not because you were there and holding my hand, Joe Rees, but because they were there, watching us. Every time the bus stopped for a crowd of passengers to get on, I thought: 'Oh God, I hope nobody I know gets on and sees me here with this man.' But at least I could have explained the situation later to a friend or acquaintance. In a way, being seen by complete strangers was worse, because they would be able to spin their own stories about us. For example, the smart, permed women in their fur coats. Did you see them as they got on the bus? I could imagine them talking after they'd sat down:

'Did you see that pair sitting by the door? That dirty old fella and the young girl, holding hands?'

'Yes, I saw them. D'you think they're courting? He's old enough to be her father.'

'Well, he was gazing into her eyes very affectionately when I went past, anyway. Aren't there some funny couples about?'

'You're telling me! I wonder what she sees in him.'

Perhaps they weren't saying anything of the sort, but what

they could have said and thought was enough to worry me. I almost felt you were well out of it, Joe Rees, beyond the range of such talk.

Why did I stay there with you, without moving to another seat, Joe Rees? Why didn't I snatch back my hand? I don't really know, unless it was that I somehow sensed it meant a lot to you to have someone's hand to hold that afternoon, and that I knew in my heart that you, just then, were the most important person on the bus. The least I could do was remain at your side until it was time for me to get off.

I walked away from the bus-stop with a sigh of relief. We had said our goodbyes and you'd whispered a warm 'God bless'. I glanced back for one last glimpse of you before the bus started off again and disappeared, but I couldn't see you at all. I saw the man with the umbrella, however, and the permed women, and windows full of other faces, all staring at me. Suddenly I turned around, and there you were, Joe Rees: you'd followed me off the bus and were standing behind me! I remember shouting at you: 'Get back on the bus, quick! You're not there yet!'

But the bus had started, and the faces at the windows were all straining to get a better look at us — all staring in the same direction, like sheep. You replied:

'It doesn't matter. I'm coming with you now.'

For the first time since meeting you, I was scared. And yet it wasn't you who frightened me, but that I might not be able to shake you off, the responsibility of it. What did you expect me to do? Take you home for tea and spread jam on your bread? What would the neighbours have thought? What would my flat-mates have said after I introduced you ?

'This is Joe Rees. He was on his way to the mental hospital, but I thought I'd bring him back for tea.'

'Well, take him there immediately, and stay there yourself for a while until you come to your senses.' Probably something along those lines.

I could have taken you there, it's true, but you have to admit that the most sensible thing, and the most normal and most acceptable, for someone in my position to do was run away and leave you. So I ran and ran, until I got home and closed the door behind me.

What happened to you, Joe Rees? Did you get to the hospital or didn't you? Do you feel better now?

I often think of you and I've mentioned you to several of my friends. Everyone thinks I did right running away and leaving you, but that I went a bit too far in sitting hand-in-hand with you on the bus. It was I, not you, who had their sympathy, of course, because I'm one of them, the normal people, who live their lives within the conventions of society, those petty rules that people make up in their heads although they've never had the heart's approval.

I'm sorry, Joe Rees. I know that it wasn't wild lightning you had in your eyes, but rather a sad sort of haze. You were more like an affectionate pet than a man off his head; I had no excuse for abandoning you. And I never knew before how warm, how likeable — and how funny — a man can be after discarding his mask and social graces. You came to me like a cat wanting to be stroked, natural and honest, with no embarrassment, and you almost purred as you held my hand. You were the dearest creature on the bus! But, you know, if we two had got up and knocked off that woman's hat, snatched the rolled umbrella from that man, tousled the curls of those permed women and relieved them of their fur coats — then, like a pair of ravens, set about pecking them clean, clean of all those symbols that hid them — I wouldn't have been a bit surprised if they weren't just as affectionate as you. And then, the driver would have tooted his horn and taken us all to the place where everyone holds everyone else's hand, and where people aren't allowed to run away.

Farewell, Frank

Elin Llwyd Morgan

It's one thing to have to tell your daughter that her father's dead. It's quite another to have to tell her he's committed suicide after killing another man.

I've been standing by the telephone for ages, staring at it and marvelling that such a gadget exists. I'm afraid of the telephone, yet without it I'd be lost. It doesn't ring very often but whenever I hear its mechanical peal my heart contracts, half out of hope and half out of fear, although the hope's receded and the fear grown since Frank left. That was nearly fifteen years ago; that was the start of a life-sentence of worrying.

But now that I've received the call I've been half-expecting for years, my heart's a lump of ice and my nerves frozen. It's the shock, probably; the ice will melt and my nerves will be all right again soon. That's why I'm so reluctant to pick up the telephone and break the silence. It'll be hectic here once I'm connected to the outside world, and I can't bear the thought of having people fussing around me at the moment. I just want to stay here like a statue, indefinitely.

Of course, that's impossible. I have to go to London first thing tomorrow to confirm that it is Frank's body, although the idea of getting up at five to catch the train worries me more at the moment. I don't sleep very well at the best of times, and I'll be whacked tomorrow. Bloody nuisance! That's all he was when he was alive and that's all he is now he's dead.

In a fit of anger I lift the receiver and dial Leah's number. Since she lives so near, she could go and identify the body, but I can't ask her to do it. Frank was her father, after all. He was only my husband.

The girl who answers the telephone thinks Leah's gone away for the weekend. Do I want her to go and knock on her door, just in case? Yes, please, knowing at the same time she won't be there. It's nearly five minutes before the girl comes back to say so. Do I want to leave a message? No, thanks, and I put the telephone down before she gets a chance to ask any more.

I don't want to ring anyone else tonight. I'll do that after I've made sure it is Frank's body lying dead in a mortuary at the police-station in Camden. It's hard to believe he's really dead and that never again will he get up and reach for the nearest bottle or rummage in the ashtray for a fag-end long enough to smoke. Good riddance, I say.

I slept quite soundly until I woke just now, in a cold sweat and the nightmare awfully vivid in my mind.

I dreamt that Frank was trying to ring me from a kiosk under a railway bridge, and a train was thundering across it. Although I couldn't see his face properly in the half-light, I knew it was him. Then a man wearing a balaclava rushed into the kiosk and hit Frank over the head with a bottle and the glass was smashed to smithereens. Frank turned around, and there was blood streaming down his face, and a lassoo of telephone-cord around his attacker's throat. The man clutched at the air wildly as the cord dug into his wind-pipe, but Frank didn't let go. After a few minutes the sound of choking stopped and the man dropped to his knees, the cord around his throat preventing him from sprawling on the ground. His eyes were bulging from their sockets, blindly staring into the void of death.

Then Frank started sobbing, the tears mingling with the blood on his face. He fumbled on the ground for a piece of wire and slit his wrists with two deft strokes. As his life-blood spurted from them he began to laugh uncontrollably. He stumbled onto the pavement with arms stretched in front of him like a blind man. An unearthly green light shone in his eyes. Before lying flat on his stomach and plunging his arms into the water, he mumbled something that sounded like my name. When he lost consciousness, I woke up with a start.

It was no wonder I was dreaming with the policeman on the line refusing to say any more than that they'd discovered two bodies by the canal in the Camden district and that my name and address were in a notebook in the breast-pocket of one of them.

I'm frightened of hearing the truth about the circumstances of his death, but I'm more frightened to go back to sleep and risk being a prey to more nightmares. It's only a quarter to four, but I'd better get up rather than lie here in bed letting my imagination run away with me.

Leah's on my mind as I wash and dress, comb my hair and put on some make-up. These things are carried out instinctively, consoling rituals when everything is else is out of control. Where has she gone this weekend, I wonder, and who with? I realize how little I know about my daughter's lifestyle since she left home eighteen months ago. We've grown apart, and I haven't made any effort to get to know her afresh. Perhaps it would be better to have a mother who's always fussing than one like me who shuts herself in and everyone else out.

Leah's in London, training to be a nurse, living in Belsize Park in a residential hall that's more comfortable than most. She passed well enough to go to university but her great ambition in life is to go nursing in one of the countries of the Third World.

'There's a Third World in this country, too,' I told her in a selfish attempt to get her to stay. Although we're estranged, I like to see her every now and again, and I enjoy my trips to London. But she'll be off eventually, I expect. There's more romance in the poverty and hardship of those hot faraway places than in this damp grey country.

For all that, Leah's more practical than her father and me put together. Frank was a writer who'd gone astray, and I'm an

English teacher in a tertiary college, wrapped up in literature most of the time.

'Too much literature stifles the imagination,' Frank said once in an attempt to take my mind off my books and get me to take more notice of him.

'Too much alcohol destroys the brain-cells, so shut up, you old soak. The most sensible thing that comes out of your mouth is nicotine drivel,' I retorted.

I really detested him by then and was dying for any excuse to get rid of him. If he'd lifted a finger against me or Leah he'd have been out on his ear immediately. But he was never violent towards us, drunk or sober, though the psychologocal strain of having to live with him was just as harmful at times.

We were no good for each other, I realize that now. Two neurotic people should never live together. Why did I marry him in the first place? Why does litter get swept out of the gutter by a hurricane? That's what obsession is like, all sense and reason blown away by a storm of crazy emotions. Obsession at its worst is more powerful than love, more destructive than lust, and no one and nothing can do anything about it. Except time.

So Leah was the fruit of obsession, rather than of love or affection or national duty. But by the time she was born that May when I was twenty-five, the obsession had already been mixed up into a mess of grief, pity, contempt and fear.

Frank spent most of his time in his sty of a study, drinking and smoking and pretending to write. He'd used to be a writer of some promise before the devil in the beer-barrel got the better of him. He won a sort of cult status with his two collections of macabre stories, but his luck ran out after a while because he was too weak to cope with his talent.

'Dylan Thomas and Bukowski used to drink,' he would claim whenever I tackled him about it.

'Don't be so naive, for God's sake! That's no excuse. And anyway, all Bukowski did was write about drinking. I don't say he didn't go on the occasional binge, but I can't believe he drank all that much, or how would he have found time to write?'

'I get time to write,' was always his answer, and then I'd shout at him to go and bury his head in the sand.

Oh yes, I was cruel alright. But after kindness failed, I put a keen edge on my tongue and grew a protective skin around my heart. In the end I gave him an ultimatum: if he refused to leave, I'd chuck him out and refuse to let him see Leah.

'You can't do that,' he spluttered. At last I'd got through his thick skin.

'Want a bet? You know damn well I could get a court order against you tomorrow.'

'Why are you doing this to me?' he asked in a pathetic voice and started whimpering like a little boy. I counted to ten.

'I won't answer that. You know as well as I do, except you're too self-centred to do anything positive about it. Now beat it! Just pack your bags and go, or I'll ring Emlyn and get him to chuck you out on your neck!'

Emlyn's a farmer who lives two fields away; a big strong chap with fists the size of his brains. He was kind to Leah and me during those troublesome years. I knew he'd have come over like a shot if I'd picked up the telephone and told him what was bugging me, but I didn't have to ask him, thank God. Once Frank realized I was serious, he packed a hold-all with his shabby clothes, told me to keep everything else, and left.

'Where will you go?' I asked, more out of curiosity than concern.

'London, probably. I've got friends there.'

Lucky for them, I thought, though I couldn't guess who these secret friends were that I'd never heard about before.

'Can I come and see Leah sometimes?'

'Only when you're sober.'

'You didn't used to be so hard.'

'I didn't used to be so sensible.'

'I love you,' he said, employing a tactic that had long lost its power. I looked at him with unseeing eyes. He stepped forward to kiss me on the forehead. He smelt of tobacco, whisky and stale sweat.

'You're not going to say "take care"?'

'Take care,' I said, the only compromise I made that day. 'Though I know that's the last thing you'll do. Farewell, Frank.'

I shut the door in his face and stood in the hall for ages, resisting the temptation to look back lest I be turned into a pillar of salt.

Frank didn't hold it against me, unfortunately. I could have concentrated better on creating a new life for myself had he disappeared from the old one. But people can't live from day to day ignoring their past. We're all the result of our past, and everything that happens is another stitch in the weft of our lives.

Nearly six months went by before Frank unexpectedly landed on my doorstep one stormy night in mid-October, reminding me of that evening five years before when he'd first come to see me, looking like Heathcliff with his black eyes and dark hair streaming in the wind. I remember thinking he was the most handsome man I'd ever seen, partly because he wasn't conscious of his good looks. But that was before his face turned blotchy and his eyes grew glazed and crazy by turns.

He looked neat and sober when he called that time, though I knew that an alcoholic's state can only be judged by degrees of drunkenness. I sensed his nervousness and felt sorry for him for once. I opened a bottle of wine at supper-time but didn't let him drink too much of it. I even went so far as locking the drinks cabinet in case he snook down to quench his thirst in the middle of the night. He left after dinner the next day on the pretext that he had to work on a script, but I noticed his hands were trembling.

We didn't get a divorce. Perhaps I'd have insisted on one if I'd met someone else, but there was no one else after Frank — no one permanent, anyway. Emlyn asked me several times to marry him, but because I didn't fancy him — let alone love him — I turned him down. I had several flings with married men, but that was deliberate on my part because I knew they wouldn't want any emotional commitment. They were just lanterns to light the darkness, that's all ...'Yes, Madi, you are a cold woman.'

The phantom in the mirror makes no reply, only stares back

at me with unfathomable eyes. My face is still attractive, but expressionless, a mask. I comb my fair hair back from my forehead, tie it in a tight knot on the crown of my head in an effort to look severe. But people with fairy faces can't look severe even when they try. Even when they discover that the father of their child is a murderer. Like God: creating one life and taking another away.

The mind doesn't give up its ceaseless turning and questioning. If I were to strike up a conversation with one of my fellow-passengers on the train, they'd be sure to think that I've escaped from an asylum. But I won't open my mouth, only sit up straight as a soldier for the rest of the journey, my mind turning and questioning all the time.

The train gets into Euston at a quarter to ten. The next step is to take the tube to Camden. For the first time ever I merge with the rest of the passengers, one more robot locked inside an armour of impersonality. It's hard to think of people in cities as human beings. Are they really more inhuman than others? Probably. You have to live by the rules of the jungle to survive in a city. Frank failed, poor sod.

The face of the detective who's just come into the room is familiar, but my memory fails me when I try and remember where I've seen him before. I've been staring up at too many faces staring down at me from the posters plastered on the walls: blurred photos of people who have disappeared: photofits of wanted men — thieves, rapists, murderers with demented eyes. A real rogues' gallery.

The detective's eyes open wide as he stands in front of me.

'Madi?'

'Geraint!' An old school friend. I haven't seen him for over twenty years.

'I'm sorry about all this, Madi.'

'It's not your fault. And anyway, we've been separated for years.'

He looks at me puzzled. I can guess what's going on in his mind: how did a smart girl like Madi get involved with a drunken tramp like this?'

'He wasn't always like that. He looked like a filmstar before the drink got to him.'

'You can still read my thoughts.'

He may have gone bald but his smile's the same. The wrinkles around his eyes when he smiled used to make me go weak at the knees all those years ago.

'How did he die, Ger?'

His face clouds over and he reaches for my hand.

'Come with me. We'd better get the worst over.'

He takes me into a chilly room that smells of disinfectant and opens the door of a huge white refrigerator. Inside there are corpses stacked on shelves, all wrapped in plastic shrouds. Geraint pulls one out from its shelf and turns back the corner of the frozen plastic for me to see his face.

'Is this your husband?'

I nod. I can't utter a word. A stone's stuck in my throat. Frank's eyes are shut and his dark-brown hair streaked with grey is neatly combed back. He looks so innocent, so pale and innocent.

'Can I see the rest of him?'

'Are you sure?' Geraint looks at me anxiously.

'I wouldn't ask if I wasn't.'

He pulls the plastic off the body and steps back for me to look at it. Every inch of him is so familiar, and that hurts. I feel an urge to embrace him, but that would be crazy. I lost the urge to embrace him when he was alive, so why should I feel it now?

Suddenly I lift his arm and twist it to look at his wrist. The flesh feels like soggy clay.

'Don't, Madi!' Geraint leaps forward to stop me, but too late. I'd seen the wound, the pale lips of the scar mocking me.

'What happened?' My voice sounds a long way away.

Geraint shrugs. 'Two down-and-outs in a punch-up over a bottle, I'd say. That kind of thing's an everyday occurrence.'

'How did he kill the other man?'

Geraint hesitates ... he doesn't want to tell me.

'He throttled him ... with a telephone cord. I don't know why he killed himself afterwards. It must have been a twinge of conscience ... '

The room's spinning about me ... I feel myself falling, being sucked into a whirlpool ... Geraint's swimming above my head, looking down at me with his fishy eyes ... I try to reach up for him, but then the darkness closes around me

I come to sitting on a hard-backed chair and Geraint's shoving my head down between my knees.

'Feel better now?'

I nod, but I'm still quite groggy.

'I'll go and fetch you a drink of water.'

'No! Stay with me. I'm scared.'

'What of, for heaven's sake?'

'Of him.' I point at Frank's body. 'Some people have souls so strong that they can enter your subconscious.'

Geraint looks at me cautiously as if he's afraid I've gone off my head.

'You look like a ring doughnut with your mouth wide open like that,' I say, and burst out laughing.

Geraint shuts his mouth, swallows hard and slaps me across the face. I look at him in amazement. I imagine him ripping off my clothes and ravaging me. I want him — not gently and not slowly but coldly and greedily on the clammy tiles with the smell of disinfectant in my nostrils.

'I'm sorry, Madi. I had to give you a clout to stop you becoming hysterical.'

I'm still looking at him hungrily, willing him to grab me.

'You're welcome to stay the night at my flat. You're not in a fit state to be left on your own.'

And then, just as suddenly, I'm ashamed of the lust that came over me, the kind that comes from sorrow. I've heard people talk of it, now I know what it feels like.

'No, no thanks, Geraint. I've got things to do, people to ring.'

'You can ring them from my flat. There's no one there to get in your way. I live on my own now ... '

'No, really. Thanks all the same, but I want to be by myself.' My voice rises and Geraint's face falls.

'Here's my 'phone-number in case you change your mind.'

Why's he so keen? Because he's concerned about me, or because he's hoping to make me something more than an old school friend who's just reappeared in his lonely life? A bit of both, probably. Though he'd hardly be behaving so nicely towards me if I was fat and frumpish. Under different circumstances perhaps I'd be willing to give it a try, but as it is, Frank's body would always be between us.

I accept the piece of paper Geraint's offering me, knowing full well that I'll chuck it away the minute I get out of here. Geraint knows that too. I'd be running away from reality if I decided to stay, postponing the pain and fuss that come in the wake of death.

It's time to open the door and let in the big world outside. It's time to disperse the calm. It's time I told my daughter her father's dead.

The Heart of Dafydd Bach

Esyllt Nest Roberts

Grasi opened her large soft lids until the night-coloured eyes were open wide, and the stars which had lit up her dream were extinguished. She opened her mouth and inhaled a breeze like cold silk in her lungs, to flush out the sour taste of waking up that had lain on her tongue like the tobacco-chewing spit of an old man. For a while she lay there completely still, listening to a silence like the din of a fair-ground, screeching and hurting her head. Her little heart kept time with the sad ticking of the eight-day clock that wept because its week was longer than everyone else's.

Throwing the heavy sheet from her body, she flung her wren's legs over the side of the bed. She pulled her nightdress up over her head and hurled it onto the untidy bed before covering her innocent nakedness with her daisy frock, its flowers winking prettily. She put on her boots and did up the laces in a slack bow but the tongue still hurt, chafing her ankle.

I don't know why I'm wearing these. I might as well be bare-footed, and they're too slippery. I stumble and fall at every step. But perhaps I shall need them today when you come to carry me off in your beautiful arms. Our hearts will be one at last, and you handsome, handsome and all loving, holding my hand, and both of us flying we know not where like the soft down of a dandelion clock, and time won't exist for us then.

Grasi opened the transparent layers of now useless curtains.

The sun's fingers were already tickling the dusty armpits of the room, but at least the fragile tweed kept the ugly darkness at bay after nightfall. She saw no one on the grey street below except the spirits of people who had been there yesterday, the day before, last week, last year, and who would be there tomorrow, the next day, and the day after that ... but she might as well have a peep through the open window in case he was there.

Suddenly, she saw a pretty cabbage-white butterfly blown like a discarded sweet-paper by the warm breeze, with no idea where it will be carried next. Perhaps it will reach the end of the earth tomorrow and understand properly the noise of people, and everyone will understand it too. Swim in their sweet wines and live off the welcome of the warm sun, before climbing the mountain in search of a brand-new sweetheart and everyone there will be tuning the vivid chords of little hearts on fire. You too will be there, dancing and singing and laughing, and all the people intoxicated by you because you fill their thoughts. But the wind will probably have dropped before then, the song fallen silent and the world dark as night, and every door locked as usual. No one will be there to hold or love, to warm or kiss.

The light, white spark landed on a bush of curly, red, untidy hair, and the head under the hair trembled uncontrollably, but the butterfly didn't move. It wasn't fear or a cold gnawing in the marrow of the bones that had caused the wild quivering but a primitive ferocity, and every now and then there came an outburst of cursing and complaint, like the steam of a small train, from the cavity in the mossy, wrinkled beard.

'What's the matter, Llasar, are you alright? You sound terribly angry. Has someone offended you?'

'Is that you, Grasi bach? Good heavens, yes, I'm perfectly alright, just a trifle ruffled. Mind you, I won't make much fuss — my conscience is almost completely clear. All I did was offer a helping hand, you see, and it's that old Huw Fudur who's to blame, dragging me after him to play some silly old tricks at Plas Meichiad. But it's come to something, you know, Grasi bach, when a man can't have a bit of fun, yes indeed ...'

'Plas Meichiad, did you say? Did you see Dafydd Bach there, walking, playing or chatting, or catching minnows in the river and bathing his feet in the cold water while the fish tickled him like shy balloons ...Did you see him? But Grasi got no reply because Llasar was already whispering in her ear about how he'd been led astray to Plas Meichian to play tricks with Huw Fudur. They'd each tried to outdo the other in stealing swedes, reaching out from the hut by the gate and thinking no one would catch them at it. But a terrible urge to pass water had come over Huw Fudur, and to do it in the rubber boots of Teil-Tomm, the owner of the swedes and father of Dafydd Bach. Unfortunately, an equally strong urge had come over Teil-Tomm to have mash for dinner. That was when Llasar was caught and accused of theft and damage, while Huw Fudur slipped like an eel between two swedes out of reach of any cruel clutches.

'But didn't you see Dafydd Bach?' asked Grasi again, her heart filled with anxiety. 'He's there every day, surely, long and amiable, awaiting his beautiful princess on the back of a silver steed, and shc'll come by one of these days and invite him to their wedding ... '

'No, I didn't see Dafydd Bach. And do you know what they want me to do for punishment? That nasty old woman, Dafydd Bach's mother and the wife of Teil-Tomm, told me I have to crush a great rock into atoms small as stardust and put it all into a tiny little box. It'll be lucky dust, she said, that'll turn wine sweet as honeycombs at the wedding of Dafydd Bach ... But just think of it, Grasi, I'll be there until the man in the moon is in his grave, and the swedes were only fodder, anyway.' He began to quake and howl, his head trembling as if he wanted to break free of his body at any minute and roll down the road to oblivion, or beyond. After that there was no point in asking any more questions about Dafydd Bach.

If the devil's smoke from the city of the Magic Grains were swirling in my head, I could live for ever on breathing the dream alone. Your words would sustain me till the planets fell asleep, and your fingers would play so delightfully that I'd have no need of food or drink. But I have to choke while searching for you.

'They're not thieves, you know, oh no, indeed. Thieves aren't able to knit stockings. They're the Fair Folk, and I ought to know because I've seen them knitting stockings by the light of the stars, and they come out only at night, anyway. But they don't like a full moon, and they'll never come out when the weather's sultry either, because that means there's a storm coming, and thunder gathering in the clouds. They play, too, and they can dance and sing, and I think they can fly because they dance so perfectly. I've seen them, you know, Grasi, like a swarm of small insects at play...' Grasi turned in the direction of the small, squeaky voice, and there she saw a feeble old woman knitting on the hot pavement. She was squatting like a long-legged, bare-footed tailor, rocking from side to side like a pendulum to the accompaniment of music that only she could hear. She wasn't looking anywhere in particular, just staring through her white, translucent eyes which were like those of a dead fish which had once swum all the rivers of the world and been familiar with them in their every aspect. But today she was a slack body and good for nothing, execrable on the edge of the earth, on a hot pavement.

'You could see them too, you know, and play with them. When you do, ask them to come and see Mari Mwm knitting stockings for Dafydd Bach.'

Grasi gasped and felt her insides trembling like petals in a whirlwind, and fireworks flashed through her body.

'What do you know about Dafydd Bach?'

'When I was a young girl, lively and vivacious, working as a maid at Plas Meichiad, I saw Teil-Tomm being born. I was there to see him entering the world from his mother's womb, a beautiful baby, and I watched him grow up into a handsome, tender-hearted young man. But a poisonous she-monster came, as you know, and stole him from me. It's hard to deal with something like that, you know, Grasi, when someone comes and steals something so precious from you, and you can never get it back, however hard you try. That's why you must look after what you have now with all your soul. All I have is memories, and the seconds steal even those now. Time is cruel, Grasi. It doesn't soothe my pain, only steals from me what comfort I have left, slowly, slowly ... '

'But what about Dafydd Bach's stockings?'

'In due course, the poisonous she-monster had a lad of her own, and he was as perfect as his father. I know, because I saw him one morning at his mother's breast, and he was the prettiest little thing on the face of the earth. She doted on him, and all that mattered thereafter was the life of Dafydd Bach, and everything had to be perfect for him. My task in life became to knit for the little fellow's wedding the best stockings ever made, and it was only by becoming one with my task I could manage that, she said. I was sent for thirteen years to tend the fire at the forge where the silver shoes of Dafydd Bach's horse were being made, and there I lost my sight completely. The glow of the fire had stolen it, you see, and that's why the forge of that blacksmith is hotter by far than any other blacksmith's in the world. Then I could devote my whole life to knitting stockings for Dafydd Bach because there was nothing else to distract me. The she-monster thought that blinding my eyes would also deprive me of my memories. Nor was I the only one to suffer under the lash of that miscreant, no indeed...'

'Where are Dafydd Bach's perfect stockings, then?'

'As I've said, Grasi, not all the memories have been stolen by the glow of the forge, and that's why the silver shoes of Dafydd Bach's horse will never be done, you see, because faint memories linger there still ... '

There is nothing more perfect than the one who is the breath of my life. You will come tomorrow and hold me tight, tight, so that nothing shall part us. You will be the rain and the sun which will germinate me and raise me higher than anything that has ever been or will ever be. I'm waiting, until tomorrow ...

As if the devil's smoke were whirling in her head, who should Grasi see coming towards her and dragging his feet like a ghost but Dafydd Bach himself. His smile was lovelier than even in her dream. But Grasi's little heart sank under a leaden weight when she saw a shadow like a scorpion's tail following him — his old bitch of a mother coming after. Dafydd Bach flashed his bewitching eyes at Grasi, but the scorpion extinguished them with her poisonous words.

'It's you who wants the heart of Dafydd Bach, is it not? I demand three things as payment for his heart: a man who loves a girl from Lly^n, who cares not whether she's kind or mean, who across the mountains a'courting goes, yet never gets mud on his brandnew hose. Go to Cork at crack of dawn and seek a wise one that fine morn; buy some beer when the weather's fair, from a gull who keeps a tavern in the harbour there. But what I want most is that you bring me a harpist to be my heart's darling; the strings of his harp will sweetly play though I wake by night and sleep by day. Then you can have him. Agreed? A smile lit up her face and the pair disappeared like a snuffed candle. Only a thin blue ribbon of mesmerizing smoke remained in Grasi's head, but the flame was rekindled when she recalled the marvellous eyes.

The silence of the place was like crystal The air stirred not, nor was there any sound. Suddenly, the white butterfly rose with supernatural force and flew far, far away over river and mountain, nor guided by a warm breeze this time, for she knew full well whither she was bound. She would come, tomorrow, to the end of the world, understanding the speech of people and all folk would understand her. Swim in their sweet wines and live off the welcome of the radiant sun, before climbing the mountain to her new-found sweetheart, playing on the vivid chords of the little heart on fire. There he would sing and dance and laugh for joy, and all the people would be spellbound by him as he filled their thoughts.

The customers were roaring drunk in the Faoileán pub when Grasi left the marshy beach of Corcaigh with her little casket of black beer. She left the place with its unfamiliar din still reverberating in her head, and the friendly laughter still tickling her. Nor would she ever forget the harpist. He would remain in her memory while there were waves on the sea, his enchanting words preserved in the phial of her memory for ever. He had flown over distant Garn Fadryn to keep a date with his sweetheart, but since his sight was poor he'd found himself on the Corcaigh estuary. There he had remained, prinking and singing until the wee hours of the morning, until he'd seen Grasi and her casket of black beer, and, observing her pain and grief, consented to be the beloved of Dafydd Bach's mother on condition that there was a full moon exactly a year after Teil-Tomm died.

And that is how Grasi won a share in the heart of Dafydd Bach.

Dafydd Bach and his wondrous eyes. The only thrilling thing about him were those eyes, and Grasi knew that full well, after she'd seen him pick his nose one morning and hoard the mess in a tiny box in his pocket. (Something to do with a wedding-cake, he said.) He was also in the habit of cleaning between his toes with a teaspoon, and did a host of other unpleasant and unhealthy things with his little pink slimy hands.

Suddenly, the pretty white butterfly rose up and was carried by the warm breeze. It knew not whither it would be carried next. Its trust was that it would reach the end of the earth next day, better to understood the speech of folk and that everyone would understand it. Swim in their sweet wines and live off the welcome of the radiant sun, before climbing the mountain and finding its new sweetheart tuning the vivid chords of some little heart on fire.

Imperceptibly, the wind dropped, the song ceased. The whole world turned to night and every door was locked. The butterfly fell slowly, through the open window and the brittle curtains. There was none to hold or to love it, to warm or kiss it, except for the sad ticking of the eight-hour clock, and that too was weeping.

The Window Mender

Eirug Wyn

When night falls the vultures will return, and there will be no hole for the fresh air — thanks to the window mender.

It is the dead of night, darkness calling to darkness, and the bedroom is an oven. It is unhealthy. The heat spills out of the radiator and Seanchan cannot open the window for fresh air. Coat after coat of paint has jammed the wooden frames. He is aware of this whenever they return. They come at dead of night. Scratch, scratch, scratch. Scratching a sore. Scratching a scab. Ripping the flesh. Tender flesh. Scratch, scratch, scratch. Scratching to the quick. Scratching until the blood flows. They will not leave him alone. They are on the windowsill. He can hear them.

Seanchan is in bed. Sweat on his forehead, on his upper lip, on his throat. Sweat in the darkness. Sweat preventing him from sleep. Eyes in the half-light, saucers in the darkness, listening. Listen to the sound they make. Scratch, scratch, scratch. They are at the window. They are sharpening their beaks.

Seanchan can hear them. Scratch, scratch, scratch. There is nothing between him and them but curtains and glass. Curtains, glass and darkness. A soft curtain of darkness. A hard pane of darkness. Seanchan gets up slowly and goes over to the window. He can hear them. He is within inches of them. He can hear the scratch, scratch, scratch. He takes careful aim. His fist is within a quarter of an inch of the curtains. He takes aim. He draws his fist back eighteen inches, and screams:

'Bastaaaaaards!'

The fist whips through the curtains, strikes and smashes the pane into smithereens before meeting cold air. Cold, healthy air.

Far below, the glass richochets onto the concrete yard near the front door. Lights go on. A dog barks. Seanchan is on the fourth floor, with his fist still through the window. Suddenly he realizes. The vultures have gone.

There are inquisitive rabbits in the window holes. Voices asking questions. Throats stretching as they interrogate the night about a broken window. He pulls his arm back into the bedroom as if it is red-hot. His wrist is caught in the shards and the blood flows warmly. He feels a fool as he washes the wound, watches scarlet froth whirl down the plug-hole.

It is not easy to find a window mender in London, but having flicked through the yellow pages, Seanchan discovered a treasure. 'Stanley Hook — Glass Merchant.'

'No bovver, mate. Be vere at one o'clock. Fourf flowa? Jesus! Might need scaffoldin', mate ... dat could be ... two hundred quid ... if not, call it seventy foive evens ... and ... AND ... ,' he emphasized it twice, 'if you pay cash, fuck de Vee Aye Tee.'

Four hours to go before the window mender arrives. Four hours of doing nothing but looking out of the window. The rain is falling without respite, soaking everyone and everything. Seanchan has moved to the kitchen window. It is too cold in the bedroom. It is cold because fresh air is pouring through the hole in the window.

Below, people are hurrying, people going about their business. People flowing ceaselessly. Past the oblique wall of Folden Road, a lilac umbrella is combing the pebbles on its peak. Before long she will come into view. A small woman, bent like The Sleeping Bard's bramble that hath both ends in the ground. A plastic cap on her head and she drags a shopping trolley, which apes the rhythm of her walk.

From the other direction comes a a wild-looking man half-carrying and half-pushing a moped. The look on his face says it all. He is talking to himself.

A young girl is standing at the corner of Folden Road. She lingers in the rain under the bright sign of the Studio. She could be thought suspicious; she is waiting for someone. She leans against the wall, one foot indolently raised. Her exposed knee shows under her raincoat, which is pleated, so that she can put her heel tight on the wall about a foot from the ground. She smokes one cigarette after another and, after exhaling, tilts her head as if she is going to scream, but it is only a cloud of smoke, not sound that comes out.

The screech of sirens freezes the bustle. Everyone pauses to watch as a police-car, an ambulance and paramedics whizz past. Someone is waiting for them. Someone expecting to be saved.

Suddenly Seanchan fixes his attention on the trio. There is something about them. Three boys walking quickly along the pavement and, an old hen behind them, a stout woman waddling from side to side, like an aged sheepdog stalking a flock. She talks to them ceaselessly, but Seanchan is too high up and too far away to hear. Every now and again, she throws her head back, in hallelujah to her god. There is a wild-contented look in her eyes as if she has been fetching her first pension, but she keeps one eye on the naughty lads.

They know she is there. They can sense her. They are taking her route. She is leading them from behind.

Eventually they pass the window. Seanchan has to move nearer to the window because they are almost disappearing from the frame, but not before he sees them begin to run. Running on nimble legs ahead of the stout woman. Nimble, athletic legs like the legs of vultures.

What will they do without her?

Two hours to go before the window mender arrives, and it is still raining. Seanchan lies down on the bed. He closes his eyes. He needs to sleep.

But it is cold. It is cold here. Cold because there is a fist-sized hole in the window, and the March winds are roaring and tearing the curtains to shreds against the glass. The heat from the radiator is not enough to warm the room, but the wind is like a healthy breeze. The vultures have gone and fresh air has poured into the room. His lids are heavy with sleep. Deep sleep. Sleep until Hook arrives. A cold sleep washing over him, flowing through the hole in the window. Vultureless sleep ...

'C'mon, mate! Open this dawer ... for Chrissake!'

The window mender has arrived to stop the hole.

With a hammer and chisel it took Stanley Hook half-an-hour to repair the window. Seanchan hands him seventy-five pounds. He gratefully stuffs the notes into the back-pocket of his overalls.

'That's blood on that carpate, mate. Got to get it cleaned, you know ... leaves a stain ...'

Seanchan is back at the window. He is watching Stanley Hook walking contentedly to his van. He places the palm of his hand on the new glass. It is cold. The smell of putty fills his nostrils, and the fingerprints of the window mender are all over the pane.

Seanchan looks again at the street below. The van is almost out of sight. When night falls the vultures will return, and there will be no hole for the fresh air, thanks to the mender of windows.

The Referee

Alun Ffred Jones

Arthur Picton was not a religious man. Heaven and hell, angels and devils, hardly figured in his thoughts. And yet, occasionally, in the small hours, the manager would wake from a nightmare in a cold sweat and the apparition was always the same. A horde of black and white demons were attacking him, like Batmen (if that's the plural of Batman) dressed up as referees, each with a whistle in his mouth and sounding like a hundred screaming fire-alarms. He'd wake up like a man demented shouting for his wife, Elsie, to rescue him.

The truth of the matter is that in Arthur Picton's sub-conscious referees had turned into demons. It was they who stood between him and success and praise. It was they who conspired to punish his beloved team for offences they hadn't committed, while allowing others to get away with murder. A psychiatrist, perhaps, would have said that Arthur Picton was suffering from paranoia. For Arthur, on the other hand, this was simple common sense. Every referee was either blind or stupid, and a high proportion were both blind and stupid.

But when the 'phone rang on this particular afternoon these nightmares were far from Arthur's mind.

'Hello, Mr Picton,' said the voice on the line. 'The Reverend Huw Davies here ... .'

Instinctively, Arthur leapt to defend himself from the

expected reprimand.

'Aye, well, I've had a hard time of it recently, Mr Davies. You see, I often have to work on Sundays — but mark you, I pay the subscription every year.'

After a slight pause the voice started again — rather nervously this time.

'No, you misunderstand me, Mr Picton. I'm not your minister.'

The manager cast around for something sensible to say.

'Oh! Oh! Sorry — you had me confused for a minute. Davies is the name of our minister too,' he said. Adding under his breath, 'I think.'

Fortunately, things got better after this. The Reverend Huw Davies was to referee the game between Bryncoch and the Groes on Saturday, and he wanted a lift because his car had broken down. Arthur Picton was too confused to do anything other than agree, but as he put the phone down his nimble, devious mind was already at work.

'The Reverend Huw Davies,' he whispered, and then, like one who has seen the Light, thundered, 'Sandra! Go and ask your mother where she keeps the Bible and hymnbook! Sharpish!'

Sandra came out of the bedroom with a very suspicious look on her face. But years of living with her father had taught her that this was neither the time nor place to ask obvious questions.

On Saturday afternoon at one o'clock prompt the Bryncoch team's bus was waiting on the village square. It should be explained at this point that the team didn't usually travel to away games by bus, but on the previous Thursday evening the manager had had four 'phone-calls from players who owned cars, and every one had the same message. The car wouldn't be available on Saturday to take the lads to the game. The wife of one needed the car to go shopping; another had forgotten to get it taxed, another was taking his for a service, and the last claimed that a pound of butter had melted on the rear seat in the terrific heat and he couldn't get at it without a gasmask. Arthur Picton knew enough about human nature to realize that it wasn't just the butter that had stunk but, for once, he couldn't say precisely what. Anyway, he had his own scheme, and to go to the match by bus suited his purpose down to the ground. And so it was that the bus came to be standing on the square that Saturday afternoon. But, as usual, some were late.

'Does Tecwyn have to be late every week?' Arthur asked wearily.

'She's very hard to handle,' replied Wali.

'Who is?'

'Jean!'

Arthur Picton had known full well what the answer would be, of course, but it was less hassle and quicker to bring the conversation to an end like that than have to listen to a long, zany spiel from Mrs Thomas's son. A moment later Tecwyn came into view.

'Where've you been?' enquired Arthur, more out of habit than any interest in the answer.

'I had to take … '

'Jean, yes, I know. Come on. Who's missing?'

'George, Graham. Wili Bryngo and …' but before Wali could finish the list five of the lads arrived noisily.

'Where've you been?' said Arthur again, even more wearily.

'It's my birthday and you know what the lads at the Bull are like when someone has a birthday … '

Arthur turned away with a look of despair. Wali watched him trying to decide what sort of response would be most appropriate. Tecs stared out of the window. George tried to make up for it by explaining that he'd only had five pints. Arthur ignored him. He had more important things on his mind. He had a plan and the whole team was part of it. He explained that he'd arranged to give a lift to the match referee and that Mr Huw Davies was a minister.

'Now listen,' he said, ' this is what we're going to do. For a start, open the windows, it's like a brewery in here. Next, we're not going to drink. Are we, George? And we're not going to swear. Are we, Graham? And we're not going to ask daft questions. Are we, Wali? And we're definitely not going to play about with that, are we, Harri? I want the minister to feel he's on the Moreia Sunday School trip. So no dirty songs. Alright?'

'Cor, Arfur, it's like being in a bloody convent,' remarked George.

'George, I wouldn't let you within a hundred miles of a convent. Go and sit at the back. And don't bring out those cards. Away we go, Eric.'

When the bus came to a halt near the Pen Lôn houses, the referee and minister — two in one, as it were — leapt onto the bus into the open arms of Arthur Picton, who welcomed him with the enthusiasm of H.M.Stanley coming across Livingstone in the Congo years ago.

'I'm most grateful to you,' said Huw Davies.

'It's a pleasure to do a good turn, Mr Davies ... What does it say in the Good Book? "And he went to him, and bound up his wounds, pouring in oil and wine, and set him on his own beast, and brought him to an inn, and took care of him." The Good Samaritan, wasn't it, Mr Davies?' Arthur had been carefully swotting up for this day. The minister raised an eyebrow.

'You seem to know your Bible, Mr Picton.'

'Oh, I dip into it from time to time,' said the manager, lying nonchalantly through his teeth.

Across the aisle and one seat back, Wali had been placed under Tecwyn's supervision out of reach of the referee. But Arthur's comment had hurt Wali Thomas.

'D'you think I ask daft questions?'

For Tecwyn this wasn't so much daft as difficult.

'He didn't mean it, see.'

A pathetic answer like that wasn't going to keep Wali quiet.

'I'm not as stupid as some people think. And I'll tell you something, Arthur only went to the central school. He reckons they lost his eleven-plus paper, but I know the truth. He drew a picture of a pig instead of doing his sums.'

After confiding this amazing fact, Wali obviously felt his

honour was satisfied. He settled back in his seat, staring defiantly at the manager's ginger nape. Tecwyn looked in the same direction, a grin flickering across his face.

When the bus reached its destination, Arthur Picton felt that all his plans were working and about to bear fruit an hundredfold. What with the noise of the bus and George, Tecwyn hadn't heard much of what had passed between manager and referee, but when the driver had stopped to let a car overtake he'd heard Arthur talking.

'And I'm sure you'll agree with me that Christians have to stick together on the field of battle — and the football pitch, if it comes to that. Take the game this afternoon, for instance ... '

The rest had been drowned by the roar of the engine, and Tecs thanked Providence for that. He was beginning to feel quite ill.

It was pandemonium in the Bryncoch changing hut. George, a jockstrap on his head, was squatting on the floor, looking very groggy.

'It's my birthday, isn't it?' he murmured between fits of laughter.

'You'll be hearing more of this, my lad!' bawled the manager.

'I've got a Victory V he can have,' ventured Wali.

'Don't talk so daft. He's not ill — he's pissed!'

Wali bristled.

'The Christian spirit didn't last long, did it?' he said provocatively, staring straight into Arthur's eyes, about a foot above him. Tecs was about to pour oil on troubled waters when there was a knock on the door. It was the referee, come to wish the team good luck. He couldn't help noticing George on all fours.

'What's the matter with our friend, Mr Picton? Is he ill?'

'No, no.' He didn't know what else to say.

'He's praying!' Wali said.

The Reverend Huw Davies looked at George, then at

Arthur who hadn't moved a muscle for all of ten seconds. If there was suspicion in the mind of Huw Davies, he kept it well hidden.

'Very interesting. A most unusual sight.'

'Indeed it is.' Arthur found his tongue at last.

'Well, I won't interrupt his meditation. I'll see you all on the field.'

He closed the door. The players looked at one another. Arthur rushed over to George and picked him up like a sack of potatoes. 'Wake up, you idiot!' he bawled. 'Praying? Pull the other one!'

Seeing Arthur's clenched fist, Wali rushed over and offered to take George out into the fresh air, to sober him up. The team followed. All except Tecwyn, who cleared his throat before venturing to speak.

'Arthur ... '

'What is it?'

'Wali.'

'What about him?'

'You've upset him. Saying he asks daft questions.'

'Well, he does, doesn't he?,' replied Arthur, patronisingly.

'Aye, but he isn't as stupid as some people think he is.'

'Stupid? D'you know what he did in his eleven plus?'

It was Tecwyn's turn to look astonished.

'What?' he asked.

'Drew a pig instead of doing his sums.'

Arthur made his exit thinking he'd won the argument. Tecwyn followed shortly after, not knowing what to believe except that people could be very odd. And he'd known that for years.

The game was going well for Bryncoch. George, after starting out like a lost sheep, had scored two smashing goals. Then he suddenly received the ball in midfield from Arwyn Plas and kicked it straight past the other side's number four. The defender tried to trip him but George kept his balance and shot magnificently from the edge of the box, and the ball was in the back of the net. The referee blew his whistle. There was jubilation on the field and the touchline. Arthur's cup was full to running over.

But it wasn't a goal. The referee was standing on the edge of the penalty area indicating a free kick for Bryncoch.

'What's up, ref?' George was the first to catch on.

'I'd blown for a foul before the goal, unfortunately.'

'Un ... f ... ortunately ... Too true, mate. I've scored and a perfectly legitimate goal, you areshole.'

'Less of the language or I'll have to book you.'

'You can report me to the Archangel Gabriel if you like,' George hissed, demonstrating an unexpected acquaintance with his Bible.

'Cool it, George!' Arthur's voice could be heard in the distance, but to no avail.

With George's face within six inches of his own, the ref couldn't help noticing.

'Have you been drinking?'

'What's it to you, pal?'

'I can't allow a drunk on the field. You're a danger to yourself and to the other players. You'd better get off, please.'

'I won't,' was the number nine's only verbal response, whereupon the referee took a decision that was to have unfortunate consequences, to say the least. He raised his hand and shepherded George towards the touch-line.

'Take your paws off me!'

The referee was starting to lose his cool.

'Off!'

'Watch it! Don't you push me!'

'Listen, I'm not going to ... Aaah!'

No one found out what the Reverend Huw Davies was not going to do because George head-butted him and he fell to the ground in a heap.

'Warned you, didn't I?' said the number nine, as if that were any excuse.

Arthur strode over to try and prevent more mayhem. Wali followed him.

'The cat's gone and pissed on the thingamejigs — the matches — now alright,' he said.

'Shut it, George! You idiot! Go and sit on the bench out of the way — and stay there!'

The poor refereee had managed to get back to his feet. The blood was streaming from his nose onto the notebook in his hand.

'Mr Picton,' he said in a quiet voice that showed that he hadn't read his New Testament in vain. 'In fifteen years as a referee, I've never come across a man so intoxicated and impertinent on a football field.'

This slander of his boss was too much for Wali.

'Mr Picton hasn't touched a drop,' he said. And then he added, 'Ever!'

'Shut up, Wali,' said the boss gratefully. 'The Reverend Davies wasn't referring to me,' and he tried to smile.

'And in twenty-five years in the ministry I haven't been as disappointed in anyone as I am in you, Mr Picton.'

The smile vanished. 'No one's perfect.'

'What's the lad's name?'

'Ann Griffiths,' said Wali.

'Shut up, Wali.'

'George Huws.'

The referee made a note, adding, 'It's only fair to tell you I'll be making a full report to the League committee.'

This was too much for Arthur Picton.

'And it's only fair to tell you I'll be reporting you — for bringing the game into disrepute, Mr Davies.'

'Remember the mote and the beam, Mr Picton.'

'And you remember Lot's wife,' said the manager, walking away.

It was an angry manager and team who climbed into the bus at the end of the afternoon, having lost by three goals to two. Of course the ref was to blame, and if he hadn't changed sharpish he'd have missed his lift home as he was now persona non grata.

'Send him to Birmingham, that'll learn him,' said Wali.

'Eh?' asked Tecs.

'Don't speak to him.'

'Coventry, you mean, you dimwit,' said Arthur.

'Oh aye. I knew it was in the Midlands and there's a soccer team there.'

Although Wali's sense of geography was weak, his observation had put an idea into Arthur Picton's head, one which would confound the referee's plans and cause him embarrassment, since tomorrow was Sunday. That's why the bus stopped outside the Cross Foxes on the way home. 'For the lads to relax,' as the manager put it. The referee was left on his own in the bus, like a pelican in the wilderness.

'Hell's bells, did you see the ref's face?' Arthur was delighted.

'Like a fiddle,' chuckled Wali.

'Yehudi Menuhin, Wali,' added Tecs, very cultured.

'I probably will be by eleven o'clock,' replied Wali in response to what he thought was a question.

Apart from the referee, there was one other person who didn't appreciate the Cross Foxes, and it was George, strangely enough. The whole afternoon, the game, and particularly the head-butt had given him a splitting headache and he had to leave the post-match revelries for some fresh air in the car-park, where he struck up a conversation with the referee. The minister wasn't long in Coventry and within five minutes he was offering George some advice. The latter was reluctant to take it until he learned that the Reverend Huw Davies was an ex-international. The young forward was full of admiration.

In the bar of the Cross Foxes, too, the conversation was about football, and George's abilities in particular. Tecwyn reckoned that the lad had potential. Arthur was of the opinion that he would have put him in the shade if he'd been playing against him, because he'd been one of the best centre-halves of his day. This without any hint of shame. Tecwyn must have looked a bit doubtful, as usual, because Wali leapt to defend his boss.

'Mr Picton got his cap for Wales, didn't you, Mr Picton?

1957 against England, and you scored, didn't you?'

'Quite right, my boy. Won two-one, if I remember right.'

'You've never mentioned it before,' said Tecwyn.

'Not one to swank, am I, Tecwyn?'

Tecwyn didn't say anything.

'Nonsense. You're embarrassing me just by talking about it. Come on, the next round's mine.'

Arthur got up and went to the bar — an unusual occurrence. Tecwyn, turning to Wali, asked, 'Have you ever seen the cap?'

'No. Someone stole it from his bag on the train, so Arthur says.'

'How do you know he got one, then?'

'He said he did, when he was applying for the manager's job. It was a toss-up between Dic Ty'n Pwll and Arthur, and Dic was the favourite until Arthur mentioned the cap. He got the job then.'

Tecwyn looked up at the ceiling, but before he had a chance to make further enquiries George came back in, accompanied by the referee. In the twinkling of an eye George was bragging that he'd been discussing football with an ex-international.

It was true that the minister had won an amateur cap in a game against England at Aberystwyth in 1957, and he'd scored two goals. Wali's eyes were like saucers.

'That was the game you played in, wasn't it, Mr Picton?'

Arthur Picton went ashen-faced. There was a stunned silence while he fought to regain his self-composure.

'Well, of course I remember you now. Scored two goals, didn't you? That's it. I had an idea it was you. How are you after all this time?'

But the pieces hadn't fallen into place neatly enough for Tecwyn.

'If Mr Davies scored two goals and the score was two-one — how come you scored, Arthur?'

'What ...? Ah ... well ... I never said it was me who scored...'

Arthur Picton didn't sound very sure of himself, but Wali

was quite definite.

'Yes, Mr Picton. I heard you with my own eyes.'

'If I can put in a word at this point ... ,' said the Reverend Davies. Everyone turned, all ears. He didn't want to embarrass Arthur, but it was only fair that everyone knew the truth.

'It was like this, friends. Although it was I who scored the two goals for Wales, there was another goal in the game — the one England scored. And who do you think scored it?'

'Mr Picton?'

'Exactly, Wali. Eh, Arthur?'

'Mmm?' Arthur's mind was far, far away, but he managed to get a few words out.

'You see, Tecwyn, when I said I scored I didn't say at which end, did I? Ha ha! What'll you have, Huw?' And he turned to the bar for the second time in five minutes.

But the referee didn't need a drink. Indeed, he was in something of a hurry and he looked expectantly at Arthur. Within ten minutes the Bryncoch bus had set off again with a rather subdued manager in the front seat at the referee's side.

'Er ... . thanks for rescuing me just now ... that is ... for telling a ...'

'A lie, Mr Picton?'

'Aye ... um.' A silence followed until the Reverend Davies asked why Arthur had chosen to brag about that particular game at Aberystwyth.

'Well, as it happened, there was a chap working with me down south who was playing that day. His name was Dic Nicholas — inside right he was. You probably remember him?'

There was a slight pause before the referee replied that yes, he had a faint recollection of him. Arthur noticed nothing. His mind was flashing back over the years.

'I wasn't there myself but I remember Dic saying a mate of his from Llanelli had scored ...' Arthur Picton turned to stare at the Reverend Huw Davies. 'Hold on. You said you scored ...'

'Ah, yes, well ... that wasn't exactly true.'

'But you were playing?'

'Not quite. To tell the truth, I was linesman.'

'The truth? Don't talk to me about the truth.'

Arthur was about to explode. But the minister hadn't finished.

'I said it for George's sake. It's obvious he looks up to international players and, well, it was an innocent white lie, after all.'

'And making me look a fool at the same time. I feel like stopping the bus and telling everyone you're a liar and a cheat.'

'Would that be wise, Mr Picton? After all, we're both in the same boat, aren't we?'

'And in the same bus, Mr Davies. You owe me one.'

'I'll pay.'

'I don't mean money. The sending-off this afternoon. I can't afford to lose George.'

'But Mr Picton, I'll have to report him. How can I explain it to the Referees' Association?'

'God moves in mysterious ways, Mr Davies, in mysterious ways. Number 58 in the hymnbook.'

With that quotation ringing in his ears, the Reverend Huw Davies walked out into the darkness that awaits all referees. And Arthur Picton went home feeling that, after a day of deep disappointment, he'd scored a small victory.

The characters in this story were created by Mei Jones and Alun Ffred Jones for the radio and television series 'C'mon Midffild!'.

Down and Out

Goronwy Jones

I'm down and out. Been turned out of my flat, if you could call it that. The sort of place where the whole bloody caboodle except the bog's been stuffed into one room. I had to pretend I was a student to get it when the dole boys stopped paying the hostel for me in Richmond Road. I was told by Frogit, the only nice student in the world, to go and see some bird in the college, give her his name and ask for a cheap flat in Roath. Seven quid for one room makes a bit of a dent but the place was handy for the Ely, the George, the Claude and the Crwys, so an alco like me wasn't complaining, was he?

To tell you the truth, I'm glad I left. Hellish funny people living there. The Paki next door wanting to borrow things all the time, and the closest you ever saw to a monkey living overhead and saying nothing except 'Cool it, man' every time I complained that his record-player was on too loud.

'Bloody hell! Some of us got to work in the morning, mate,' I says. 'Not go to Joe Coral's like some.'

But it was alright for him in that attic 'cos the old bitch who owned the house lived on the ground floor and couldn't hear the noise. If she knew what was going on, she'd have been up there like a shot. No women after ten. One bath a week, but you had to ask her to put the immersion on beforehand. No straining cabbage in the bathroom sink. If there wasn't a wash-basin in your bedroom and you were daft enough to boil cabbage, where the hell were you supposed to strain it?

I'd had a hell of a good sesh on the Saturday night, on a pub-crawl with the lads, from the Claude to the Crwys and ending up in the Ely for a singsong. It was only natural for us to go on to Casa Martinez in St. Mary Street afterwards. I don't like admitting it, but I haven't had much luck with the birds since I've been down here in Cardiff. I'm too scruffy for these tight-arsed Welsh pieces, I suppose. But this one comes up to me while I'm knocking back the wine with Stan Crossroads in the Casa.

'You want dancing?' she says.

Hellish funny way of putting it, I thought to myself, but I'd be bonkers to turn her down. It was a slow number and this bird just clings to me, and it suddenly dawns on me — Jesus, you're in with a chance by here, Gron! She was licking my ginger locks and saying she liked the kiss-curls behind my ears. I didn't know I had any. After one or two more glasses and some more kissing and cuddling, I tell Stan we're leaving — the bird and me, I mean.

'Good luck,' says Stan, 'but you don't need much.'

This bird was a nurse, like. Ginger, same as me. Birds of a feather, aye? But she says she can't go back to the Heath this time of night — they'd give her a hell of a bollocking. I knew the old bag of a landlady would be sure as God to catch us, but where else could we go?

Next morning, about seven o'clock, we were tip-toeing out of the house and I was feeling great as I went to fetch the *News of the World* after putting the bird — her name was Freeda — on the bus. I'd managed to get past the guard at Fort Knox, aye? I didn't think no more about it, but when I comes home from work on the Monday evening, there she was — Mrs Wilcox — looking daggers at me at the foot of the stairs. Without a word, she gives me this piece of paper.

Notice to quit.

If I'd thought I'd hoodwinked her, I'd another think coming. Mrs Wilcox hasn't had a whole night's sleep since she lost her husband four years ago. I felt real sorry for her, honest, and I used to bring her spare pieces of carpet from work. Bits that would be alright to put on her hearth, aye. But all the Axminsters in the world wouldn't save me now.

Not only did she know Freeda had been there all night, but Mrs Wilcox also used to go through the rooms of the four lads in her house every day, cleaning and emptying the bins and moving your things around. A good excuse to snoop, I think it was, aye. And what she found on the chest-of-drawers in my room made her go up the wall.

'I don't 'ave a son, but if I 'ad, I 'opes to God 'e wouldn't be'ave the way you do,' is what I got.

And then I saw red. At work in Howell's all day, you've got to smile and pretend and suck the arseholes of the crachach, and say sir to the bosses, although you can't stand them, but there's not a snowball's chance anyone's going to tell me what I do in my own time, let alone go through my things and push their nose in.

'Stuff your notice,' I says, 'I'm leaving now!'

And up I goes to pack my cases and a minute later I'm out the door with a case in both hands.

'And a Merry Xmas to you too!' I says, leaving the woman staring at me gobsmacked. I banged the door hard as I could.

It was only after I'd walked about a hundred yards down the street, sweating like hell and muttering under my breath, I realized what I'd been and done. Where would I go? I've always said beer solves all problems so down I goes, by open-tap, to the New Ely. Luckily, who was there, bent over a Guinness as usual, but Jero Jones the Welsh-learner.

'Hello, Gron,' he says in Welsh. 'Wanna pint? I am speaking splendid now. Bad Welshman who is thinking in English.' He likes to get that bit over with before we have a proper chat in English. I tell him my story and every now and then he chips in with 'Hope so' and 'Can't do it'. By nine o'clock it was up yours, Mrs Wilcox, and everyone in the Ely knew about my problem.

'Hope she chokes on her Horlicks this very night,' I says.

'Hope so, anyway. Hope so,' says Jero.

'An old bag like that can't slag me off.'

'Can't do it,' says Jero. 'Can't do it nowadays.'

'Come to our place tonight, says Frogit. One of the lads will sure as God be staying with his bird.' They live in Albany Road, they're always taking in strays like me. A lad from Brittany's been staying with Connolly this last month. Came to Wales to dodge being drafted into the French army. His hair's down to his waist and it'll be a long time before it's safe for him to go home.

Dai Shop, who's just got his driving licence back after being caught by the breathalyser on his way home from the Eisteddfod at Cricieth, lives with them too, and he gave us all a lift back. Everyone, that is, except Frogit, who's a bit of a lad for the ladies and after some new bird every month.

'A student, are you?' I says to the fifth lad in the car.

'Hell, no,' says he, 'I work at St. Fagans.'

'Where?'

'The Welsh Folk Museum.'

'You know, Gron,' says Dai Shop, who's a teacher, 'where they rebuild old houses that've been knocked down in other parts of the country.'

I'm not much the wiser, aye.

On the way home we happen to go past the street where Mrs Wilcox lives, and I wind the window down, stick my head out, raise two fingers and bawl like a wild man, 'Stuff your bloody house, you bitch from hell!' As if she could hear me.

The lads were pissing themselves and they laughed even more when I started to get a bit sentimental later on and said if there was such a thing as Good Samaritans it was them, giving a helping hand to lads like me when they're down and out in Cardiff.

The handy thing about Cardiff is you can get more booze after the pubs close with no trouble at all. In Caernarfon when I left you had no choice — it was either the Cash Club or the Chinks. Now they've closed the Cash and there's a punch-up in the Chinks every other Saturday night. That's one reason why this city suits a young fella like me who wants a bit of life — for a while anyway.

Usually the lads from the Ely go to one of two places — the Casino down in the docks or Papajio's in the city centre. The Casino's hellish dark, dirty and noisy, and you have to get a taxi down there. If I had a rise I'd buy a small car. But the price of beer in the Casino isn't too bad. Wine, halves and shorts is what you get in Papajio's, as I discovered the other night.

'Pint of lager, please,' I said the first time I went in there. They don't serve mild in any of the clubs, I've found. It doesn't cost enough and they want to skin you alive, aye?

'Only do halves. Lager's off. Wine or shorts?' says this bird all off-hand like. What's it matter if they're pretty when they talk like that?

'Bottle of wine, then,' I says. Cheaper than by the glass.

'What kind?'

'Any kind,' says I, not knowing much about wine.

'Red?'

'Aye.'

'Two pounds please.'

'I only want one, aye,' I says, but the bloody stuff was two quid a bottle! Paying through the nose. At the off-licence in Howell's it's just over a pound a bottle.

I peer through the dark and cigarette-smoke to see if I know anyone. I see Sabrina from *Pobol y Cwm* dancing with some bloke. I wouldn't have minded an autograph to show them back home I'm meeting the big names on the Cardiff scene, but I was too scared of going up to her. I saw Wayne Harris there too but that's not who he really is because he also sings with Edward H. Davies.

None of the Ely lads were willing to come with me 'cos this was Thursday night, the shits.

'Come on, Stan,' I says. 'You all but live in that place, and you've boasted about it often enough.'

'You won't pull a wejen there except on a Saturday,' says Stan. A wejen is a piece of skirt and a sboner is her boyfriend. They're not all there down here in the south.

'Well,' says I, 'I've been lugging a pile of bloody Axminsters from the stores to the showroom all day and I need to wet my whistle.'

By the time I reach the Papa I've decided to ring Mr Huxley, the boss, in the morning to say I'm a bit groggy — it's my back again, honest. So down goes the booze ...

'Martha Morris!'

'Do I know you?'

Jesus! This one's got a memory like a sieve, aye.

'Gron bach, I didn't recognize you with that ginger moustache.'

'Like it? Trendy, aye?'

Martha was in the same class as me in the Sunday School at Moriah. She was in the grammar school and I was a bit lower down, aye.

'Where do you hang out, Gron? Your mam told my father in the shop you were down here.'

'I live in Roath, don't I? And I go to the New Ely just about every night. Never see you there, though.'

'D'you like it there? Bit of a dump, isn't it?' she says, wrinkling her nose. There was I gazing at her in her long flowery dress, her hair just-so and a lot of make-up and black mascara, and thinking she wouldn't fit into the Ely either.

'Sunday School and Band of Hope turned you against the booze, aye?' I says, not letting on.

'Oh no. We go for a bit of a drink one or two evenings a week. Don't mention it to Dad, though, will you? Down the Conway — been there?'

'Aye,' I says, but I don't say what a hellish boring night I had there once.

Then Luned and Gwenan and Siân bounce up to us. Teachers, living with Martha in Llandaf. I didn't fancy any of them but there they were standing in front of me like the Daughters of the Dawn.

'Gron comes from Caernarfon, too,' says Martha.

'Oh yes, where do you teach?' asks Luned.

'I'm not a teacher,' says I. Why the hell do they all think

I'm a teacher?

'Oh,' says Gwenan, 'where do you go for some Welsh life?'

'Don't worry, love,' I says, 'I've got the lads.'

'He plays cards in the pub every night,' says Martha, and they all laugh and go tut-tut.

'What do you do in the evenings, then?' I ask, a bit embarrassed, like.

'Well,' says Gwenan, just about dying for someone to ask her, aye, 'we're in the choir. The Urdd Choir and the Godre'r Garth choir two or three nights a week. D'you sing? No?'

'Jesus Christ!' I says to the DJ. 'Turn that bloody noise down, aye.'

'Hey, what's this guy want?' he says. 'Victor Sylvester?'

Everyone's laughing at me and Gwenan's saying, 'And two of us run an evening-class for Welsh-learners, don't we, girls? And Siân's Secretary of the local branch of Plaid Cymru, aren't you, Siân?'

Siân says nothing but smiles shyly and fidgets with her handbag. No need for her to be nervous, 'cos what about me having to listen to a gang of clever birds like this telling me how they're keeping Welsh alive in Cardiff? Made me feel hellish queasy, they did, 'cos I haven't got a talent for anything apart from playing a fair game of darts or round of snooker, aye, and what's the use of that?

'Christ, girls,' I says, 'I thought I'd done quite well to find a gang of Welsh lads for a bit of fun in Cardiff just like I was home in Caernarfon. I'm just not good enough for the places you go, like.'

'Come on now, Gronw,' says the auburn one, Luned. Gronw? Why the hell's she calling me that? 'Anyone can go to the Urdd!'

The Urdd, like hell! I've never belonged to the Urdd. But I don't want to say anything 'cos I know Martha Morris has been a member from when she was so high. But she lived up in St. David's Road with the crachach, and that's who the Urdd types were in Caernarfon. Children of deacons and teachers and the like.

They went in for folk-dancing and daft things like that. Cissies. Can you see the Sgubor Goch lads putting up with that? I remember Miss Jones Welsh giving out some comics to the class. 'Only for the Urdd children,' she said, and John Ty Nain and me pulled faces at each other. And I remember a busload of them leaving the Maes in town for camp in Llangadog and singing stupid songs as they set off. 'Down by the riverside,' aye? John Ty Nain and me chucked stones at the bus as it left but I don't want to upset these birds so I keep my mouth shut.

I ask Martha what she's doing on Saturday night, but she's going to a wine-and-cheese party up Rhiwbina way. And next week? Very busy, something on every night.

'How come you can spare time to come here?' I ask her sarcastically.

'It's good here on Thursdays,' she says as if I'm not there.'A good crowd from the BBC comes here.'

I knew then Martha Morris was waiting for a chance to get off with someone, and not one of the local lads. There wasn't much to the shy girl, Siân, but I go over to her, put my arm round her waist, and wasn't doing too bad when, damn it all, a draught of the red piss I'd been drinking goes down the wrong way. I nearly choke on it and it sloshes all over the floor, half through my mouth and half through my nose. The girls scarper to avoid getting it on their long dresses. Just as well, but none of the bitches raise a finger, either, when a sod of a bloody big bouncer comes up and grabs me by the scruff of my neck.

'Out, you!'

'Not fuckin' likely, mate,' I says.'I've just come in after paying ten bob at the door, and two quid for this plonk ...'

But he was determined, and 'cos I was too things started to go haywire, didn't they? Before you could say Jack Robinson I'm out on my backside on the pavement with this big bastard kicking the life out of me. I was all black and blue, aye.

While I'm still groaning on the ground two blokes comes out of Papajio's — the manager and Gareth Connolly from the Ely. I didn't know any of the lads were in there. They were quarrelling like hell.

' ... and call your bloody animal off,' shouts Connolly. 'I'm in the CID and I could get this place shut down tomorrow if I wanted to.'

The manager turns all nice then and helps me up, brushing the mud off my coat. This was round the corner from a club called the Revolution, where some swine of a bouncer did for one of the local lads about a month ago. The place has got a new name now — Smiley's.

Connolly and me walked home through the city streets sharing the bottle of wine he'd brought out with him.

One Lettuce Does Not a Salad Make

Bethan Evans

Suzanne, the German assistante, had a splendid French accent; the words flowed from her lips in a velvet, perfect stream. But when Iola first spoke to Monsieur le Directeur, the staff at the Lycée St. Exupéry just smiled at one another. The difference was awesome. The Welsh girl persevered, but her accent grew more and more lumpen, more harp-playingly Welshcake and cowpat with every syllable. Monsieur le Directeur, an ape of a man with amber teeth, insisted on calling her *la petite Anglaise*. She responded with, *'Mais non, Monsieur, je suis galloise.'* But *la petite Anglaise* she remained for the rest of the year. Fortunately, she didn't see him all that often. Only rarely did he turn up in the English department. He didn't have much respect for *les Britanniques*, particularly now that *les imbéciles* were involved in the Falklands fiasco.

Suzanne's English was also impeccable, but she and Iola decided from the outset that they would communicate in French, and this meant a good deal of the time because they had to share a house.

It was in a terrace and had unfetching calf-shit beige walls, a bathroom in the cellar and no central heating. They had tossed a coin to see who would have the larger room with a double-bed. *'Pile,'* said Iola. *'Face,'* said the franc. Iola moved her things into the small room with a very single bed, brown carpet and pink curtains, the window of which seemed to amplify the noise from the street outside in stereo. Whenever the refuse-lorry came by, the bed shook.

Suzanne's bed rattled every night. It bounced, creaked and resounded to the accompaniment of the strangest French vocabulary, words that Iola couldn't find in the dictionary, try as she might, although the context was quite clear through the Rizla-paper walls.

Despite having a good-looking boyfriend back home in Germany — a tall, dark-haired man who drove his BMW all the way from Heidelburg to see her every fortnight — Suzanne seized every opportunity to extend her knowledge of every aspect of *la vie en France* and the French language. There was never any shortage of students to help with her research. She had long shapely legs and an ample supply of short skirts to show them off to full advantage. Another useful weapon was her hair-style: she had a blonde mop which concealed half her face but which she tossed back with a seductive flick whenever she set eyes on a prospective research assistant. It was Iola who always had to answer the door, and offer an apéritif to a remarkable array of men while Suzanne was brushing up her vocabulary with one who had arrived earlier. Iola, too, had offers to broaden her vocabulary when some of them grew tired of waiting, but she preferred to keep to a more basic one and to writing daily letters to her faithful boyfriend at home in the old country.

One evening, while three young men were having their third glass of wine in the salon, one of them asked her whether it was true that *les Britanniques* were a cold, emotionally undemonstrative people. She explained quite readily that the Welsh were even worse than the English when it came to kissing and touching anyone apart from babies and lovers. She used as an example the fact that she had never even kissed her own mother. Unfortunately, since she had not yet mastered the language's more vivid vocabulary, she used the verb *baiser* for 'to kiss', which is what her second-rate dictionary had said it meant. She was unaware that the word's meaning had changed over the years and that it now signified something much more than just the touching of lips. She stared with a sinking feeling at the young men, who were helpless with laughter. She blushed to her toenails when one managed tearfully to explain that she had just declared that she had never fucked her mother.

Her French improved dramatically from then on, and she threw herself wholeheartedly into the French way of life. She got used to the taste of red wine, despite having sworn after her first bottle of Bull's Blood at the Padarn Rock Festival that she would never touch the stuff again. She learned how to appreciate at least one glass every evening. After years of molar wrestling with beef cooked to the consistency of concrete in traditional Welsh fashion, it came as quite a shock to be confronted with a raw fillet floating in a lake of scarlet blood. But her new friends were patient, and Iola soon realized that she was very partial to raw meat after all. She tasted cheeses which looked putrid and smelt even worse, and fell head-over-heels in love with them. She loved *les îles flottantes* and binged on *crème brûlée*. She ballooned like a pregnant whale and had to buy new clothes with elasticated waists.

Suzanne, however, stayed as slim as a thread, because she didn't like cheese, and her nocturnal research was hard work and remarkably physical. Iola learned to write love-letters with a Walkman plugged into her ears, and often took a leisurely stroll to the phone-kiosk to hear his voice.

'Hiya. It's me.'

'How are you, gorgeous?'

'Better now. I miss you.'

'I miss you like hell and I want you.'

'I want you madly and I love you.'

'I'm nuts about you and I'm coming to see you.'

'What?'

'I'm taking a week's holiday and I'm coming over by train.'

'Honest? Oh, Wyn! When?'

'Next week!'

'Yes! But can you afford it?'

'No, but you're worth every penny of my overdraft.'

'Oh boy, I'm all excited now.'

'Save it. For me.'

The rest of the conversation became quite bawdy and then Iola floated back to the house.

Next day, she went to Hypermarché Leclerc during a free period to buy some sexy underwear, but trying it on when she got back, found it was a bit tight on her. Her flesh flowed over and under the two egg-cups of the bra. The shiny knickers kept on rucking up under her navel, but if she breathed in deeply, it would do. She gave up her *mille-feuille* with afternoon tea and put up with cottage-cheese and a potato every evening, but by the fateful morning the button of her jeans was still inches out and her stomach was thundering its discontent. She hoovered, dusted, washed, shaved, dried, and scoured her teeth until her saliva turned pink. She put on the shiny black underwear, pulled a large black sweatshirt over her head, and squeezed into her black leggings. Wearing the loose raincoat she had bought with her first salary-cheque, she looked quite smart. She dragged a chair over to the mirror and stood on it to try and see what her lower half looked like. It was all wrong. She flung the high-heeled shoes into the depths of the wardrobe and found a pair of black boots. That was better. A bit wintry, perhaps, but definitely more chic. A thin layer of make-up, half-a-ton of rubbish kicked under the bed, a quick shake of the bed-cover, and off she went to catch the bus.

The weather was cold and wet, and the factories were spewing their smoke invisibly into a soup of fog. The station looked like a black-and-white film-set, with a solitary man in a Bogart raincoat taking a drag on his Gauloise. She hurried over to the public toilets to tidy her hair. The stench was like a fist in her face, but she wrinkled her nose and wiped the mirror with her sleeve. Damn! She should have had her hair cut. Her fringe was falling over her eyes, but it was too short to stay obediently behind her ears. She tried to wet and twist it into curls around her fingers, but without success. She settled for tossing the rats' tails back over the crown of her head and holding her chin up in an attempt to foil the laws of gravity. She rubbed her teeth with her finger before standing back with a smile. She would do.

When she returned to the platform it had started to rain.

At last, she heard the Brussels train rumbling into the station. She bit her lip. Endless rows of windows went slowly by, grey faces staring vacantly out of their smoke-filled confinement. What seemed like centuries later, the train came to a halt, and a door opened here and there. Young men in military uniform leapt noisily and heavily laden from the steps, rushing home to squeeze every possible second out of their few days of freedom. Then came two businessmen, and a young girl struggling with her baby and all the obligatory equipment. Someone was helping her and handing her yet another bag. A long, strong arm with musician's fingers. The long legs stepped down onto the concrete platform and he looked up. Seeing Iola, he smiled.

Iola was dying to run towards him, but was restrained by shyness and a Methodist upbringing. She walked slowly with knees of blancmange. He was so incredibly beautiful; over six feet of hard muscle, light-brown hair curling over warm blue eyes, and a smile like a god's.

He opened his arms wide and hugged her tightly. He felt so big and solid. She felt so big and soft. He cupped her face in his hands and kissed her with a passion that had been building up for months. She ran her fingers through his hair and over the nape of his neck and kissed him wildly. Fists beat on the windows of the train and the applause radiated through the glass. The couple smiled at the audience of acned, shouting squaddies, blushed a little and embraced each other again.

After the initial shock on reaching the house, Wyn went for a quick pee. The lavatory was in the cellar, of all places, and had been built by a dwarf. What had been so large in the bus now shrank to nothing in the cold. Ducking his head, he made his way over to the sink and bent low in order to inspect his forehead in the mirror. He was glad to see that the pimple which had been worrying him all night had subsided. The water was cold. Christ, she'd put on weight. He had better not say anything, he didn't want to spoil the week, but bloody hell, she was like a balloon, a barrel, a real Big Bertha. And why hadn't she described the house for him in her letters, instead of letting him imagine a white-washed cottage on a beautiful hillside, looking down over acres of green vineyards? This place was a dump. He filled a glass with icy water from the tap and held it to his lips before quickly pouring it back down the drain. French tap-water probably wasn't fit for human consumption.

She was sitting on the bed, having taken off her coat, shoes and socks, but that was all. Why hadn't she taken everything off and lain naked to welcome him as she had done in his dreams?

She'd intended to lie back, sensual and naked, on the duvet, but she knew that he had noticed she'd put on weight, although he hadn't actually said anything, fair play to him. It would be so much easier to hide it all under the warm, dark refuge of the bedclothes.

He sat down beside her and the groping began. Items of clothing flew through the air. As she took off her bra, she switched off the light.

'What did you do that for?'

'For us to be in the dark.'

'But I want to see you.'

'But ... Oh ... Alright, then.'

She fitted like a glove, she was so lovely, so supple, doing all she could to please him.

He was gentle and aggressive in turn. She worshipped him. The wooden headboard of the bed kept striking the wall and the banging was deafening, but he couldn't stop now. The noise was getting on her nerves but she couldn't ask him to stop.

'Coming?'

'Almost.'

He couldn't hold back much longer.

There was a crescendo of groaning and squealing and then a huge crash. They had fallen through the frame of the bed and the headboard had collapsed on top of them.

'What the hell ...?'

After a moment's silence, Iola began to laugh, quietly and nervously at first, then loudly and uncontrollably, until the tears were streaming down her face.

'I don't see what's so bloody funny.'

She couldn't speak, her stomach was hurting so much.

'Give over, will you?'

'I'm trying to!'

'And shift your leg, it's hurting me.'

The bed was in pieces and every one of the flimsy wooden slats which had supported the mattress was neatly broken in half.

'Bloody cheap bed! Can't these Frogs make decent furniture?'

She let him put his mechanic's mind to work amid the pile of wood and bedclothes, and went to make a cup of tea. It was half-past ten in the morning; they would have a late breakfast. She warmed up the expensive croissants she had bought specially for the occasion, large golden ones pregnant with a heavenly mixture of almonds and sugar, topped with white icing and toasted flaked nuts.

Wyn came into the kitchen shivering in a woolly jumper.

'I'm freezing. I thought France was supposed to be a warm country.'

She smiled and drew up a chair so that he could place his bare backside on it.

'This cuppa'll warm you up, look.'

He glanced warily at the small square of paper hanging over the rim of the cup.

'What's this?'

'The teabag label. They don't make teabags like we do.'

'Why not?'

'No idea. They usually drink coffee.'

'What are those, then?' he nodded at the plate of croissants in front of him.

'Breakfast.'

'Eh?'

'Special croissants. They're gorgeous. Try one, they're nice and warm.'

'I don't like them.'

'How do you know if you haven't tried them?'

'I always have bacon and eggs for breakfast, you know that.'

'But ... you're in France now, Wyn.'

'So? Don't they have pigs here?'

'Well, yes, of course they do, but they don't make bacon like we do.'

'Typical. All that fuss about French chefs being so bloody marvellous, and they can't even make bacon.'

'Try one, just to see.'

'No. I'll have cornflakes. I suppose they make cornflakes, do they?'

After three days of sleeping and making love on the floor, with huge steak and chips for supper every night, Wyn grew a bit more contented. But he didn't think much of that German tart. Stroking her thighs and making eyes at him in front of Iola, indeed. Who did she think she was? But she did have a terrific pair of legs, fair play. But no tits. A girl with no tits wasn't much good. And Iola's were fantastic. He really loved her, and wanted to hold her all the time. Perhaps she was a bit bigger than usual, and kept prattling on in French all the time with her friends, but she hadn't changed; she was still his sexy, affectionate Iola.

Iola put the phone down with a smile.

'We've been invited out to supper tomorrow night!'

'Who by?'

'Evelyne, one of the English teachers. She's great, you'll like her, her and her husband and another friend.'

'Do the husband and friend speak English?'

'The husband speaks a bit, but I'm not sure about the friend. He's Greek, I think. We can stay the night, she said, and you don't have to worry about the food, I've told them how fussy you are, and they're going to burn a steak to ashes for you!'

'Great. Thanks. What about the lush?'

'I've told them you can't stand wine, so don't worry.'

She was looking forward to talking to someone else for the first time since he had arrived, and was glad of the excuse to get out of the house. He'd shown no interest whatsoever in going for a stroll or seeing the town or going to a bar with her friends or anything like that. Naturally, she'd been delighted to make love for hours on end after months of having to rely on letters that had bordered on the pornographic, but she really needed a break from the claustrophobia of her room.

He didn't fancy going out to supper with some bloody teacher and her foreign friends, but it was clearly important to Iola. Perhaps he could have a pint of bitter there, instead of the tiny bottles of cat's piss he'd bought in the duty-free.

'Welcome, Iola. Welcome, Ween!' Evelyne and Iola kissed each other on the cheek, twice, and Wyn got the same treatment, though he didn't know which cheek to kiss first, and he came close to giving her a nasty headbutt. She was a stonking woman, considering her age. Thirty-five, Iola had said, but she looked ten years younger. Evelyne showed them into the living-room and introduced them to Patrice, the husband, and to Stavros, the friend. Iola received the ritual two kisses and Wyn began to sweat. But Patrice held out his hand, thank God, and shook hands with a good, firm grip, too. Stavros's handshake was a bit limp, but he looked quite normal. And yes, they had some large bottles of Stella. Nice one. They weren't great drinkers; but he was talking less than them. Jesus, he was starving. Would they be eating before midnight? he wondered.

'You have hungry, Ween?' enquired Patrice.

'Aye, like a horse,' he replied. 'Those flamin' croissants aren't a patch on bacon and eggs, are they? Wouldn't fill a flea, man.'

They went through into the dining-room, which was large and green and, like the rest of the house, full of beads and baubles and other hippy things and pictures of sand-dunes and Arabs.

'Why does the whole place stink of cat's piss?' he asked Iola as he followed her in.

'It's patchouli.'

'Makes me want to throw up.'

119

'Behave!'

Why was she so angry with him? He was doing his best, wasn't he?

There was a large bowl of lettuce in the middle of the table and baskets of unbuttered bread near by.

'Help yourself to ze salad, Ween,' smiled the sexy Evelyne.

'Aye. Right.' He glanced at Iola for assistance. She just scowled back at him.

'It's right in front of your nose.'

Lettuce? Only lettuce? What about pickled onions, cheese, ham and sliced boiled eggs? Where were the tomatos and crisps and salad cream? Call this salad?

He lifted a small limp leaf from the bowl and dropped it unceremoniously onto the edge of his plate, then handed the bowl to Iola. Her cheeks were flushed. Too much of that red wine, no doubt. She piled her plate with the greasy lettuce, as did the others.

Stavros smiled at him.

'You are not like salad?'

'Salad, yes, lettuce, no.' He flinched as Iola crunched his toes under the table.

'Aw, give over,' he said to her in Welsh.

'Stop being so bloody rude, then.'

'I was only telling the truth. I don't like bloody lettuce.'

The three others were quietly eating the green leaves, trying not to notice the tension in the strange language their guests were speaking.

'More *bière*, Ween?' asked Patrice after a short silence.

'Aye. It's really good, thank you.'

At long last the steaks arrived. Iola had begun to relax after drinking the wine. He was doing his best now, and starting to smile, fair play, and come to think of it, he wouldn't have noticed that the salad was only the first course. His single leaf had been waiting for the steak — 'well done — very well done — cremated, please' — while the others were eating and mopping up the vinaigrette with their bread.

It looked great, despite being a good deal smaller than the T-bone he had hoped for. He plunged his knife into it with relish, and then stopped dead. It was bloody well red inside, and blood was oozing from it. Looking up, he caught Evelyne staring at him.

'Is there something wrong, Ween?'

He glanced at Iola, but she was looking away, her forehead buried in her left hand. Surely she didn't expect him to eat raw meat?.

'Well, yes, actually, it's not very well done. It's bleeding still, look.'

'Oh. Sorry, I forgot. English people ... '

'Welsh.'

'Sorry, yes, all British people like their steaks like cardboard, *hein*! I will cook it some more, *pas de problème.*'

The second attempt was much better, but there was something seriously wrong with the sticky, creamy potatoes.

'Iola, my spuds are honking. What are yours like?' he said to her, again in Welsh.

'Lovely. Just eat them, will you? They're perfectly all right.'

'Like hell they are!'

'There's garlic in them, alright? That's all; it won't kill you.'

'Garlic?'

The others looked up again. Patrice chuckled.

'You are not like garleec, no?'

'Am I like garlick? No, I smell nicer.'

'But, for we in France, eet ees ze most wonderrful zing, everybodee love eet.'

'Aye, and don't we know it? We can smell you a mile off, man.'

'Qu'est-ce qu'il a dit? J'ai pas compris.'

The rest of the meal was muted, and because there was no Cheddar cheese among the runny, putrifying, disgusting array of cheeses, Wyn had two more bottles of beer while the others silently stuck into their *fromage*.

Iola managed to apologize while Wyn was emptying his bladder at great length in the toilet, but everyone remained very polite, denying that he had upset any of them. But they all went to bed unusually early.

'Hey, nice bed, isn't it? We're going to have fun on this.'

'No chance.'

'Eh?'

He did his best to persuade her they should take advantage of the size and quality of the bed and of his desire to transport her to heaven and back, but it was like kissing marble. She turned her back to him and slapped him off like a pestering fly. He tried to put his hand between her closed legs, but received a fist between his own instead. When his voice returned, he too turned to face the wall.

'Be like that then, you bitch.' And within seconds he was snoring.

Iola failed to fall asleep for hours, and when she woke next morning her eyes were like red marbles and her head felt like a swollen, throbbing ball of lead.

Wyn was sleeping like a baby, his arms around the pillow. Her body and heart wanted to embrace him, like a warm duvet, but the brick wall of the previous evening lay firmly between them. When Wyn opened his eyes and smiled at her, a few bricks fell but when he let loose a deep, resounding burp in her face, they immediately cemented themselves back into place.

'Come on, get up. We're going.'

'What? Now, this minute?'

'Yes.'

'Aw, come on, help me wake up first ...'

'Like hell I will.' She leapt out of bed and flung Wyn's clothes into his startled face.

He coughed himself awake. What the hell was wrong with her? PMT, it must be. He groaned and dragged himself into a sitting position. Jesus, he had terrible wind. Bloody foreign food. His head wasn't a hundred per cent, either.

Iola insisted that they leave without even a cup of coffee. Wyn combed his hair as she scribbled a note — in French — to Evelyne. Within minutes they were out in the cold grey street, and apart from the old man driving the street-cleaning lorry, there was no sign of life anywhere. Anyone with a brain would still be in bed on a Saturday morning.

'What's the hurry, Iol?'

He received no reply, only a Medusa look enough to freeze a man to death on the spot. She strode ahead of him, hands thrust deep in her pockets, her backside hardly moving. Wyn looked up at the clouds and reluctantly followed her, only just managing to leap out of the way before the lorry sprayed water all over his new trainers. He had a thumping headache now.

They had a coffee that was more like treacle in a rather dubious café, but there wasn't much conversation there either.

'Are you going to talk to me some time?'

A sheep-like grunt.

'What the hell have I done?'

Eyes flashing silently.

'You're being bloody stupid now, Iola.'

He followed her out into the street again. There were shoppers about and the pavements shone now that the mist had cleared.

'Do you fancy telling me what we're going to do today, then?'

Iola turned to face him.

'I had plenty of things arranged, up to last night.'

His forehead creased.

'Eh?'

'But I don't want to do any of them now, and I haven't the bloody faintest what we'll do. What do you fancy?' Her lips were ominously thin and there was an odd ring to her voice. God only knew what had bitten her, but he knew her well enough to be aware that neither her voice nor her eyes nor her lips were normally like that, and he didn't want to go on rowing with her like this, out here, so he tried to mention a few things that he thought would please her.

'Um, what about a bit of shopping?'

'Shopping. You?'

'Yes.'

She eyed him suspiciously.

'Okay. There's a shopping precinct through there.'

'Great. Shall we go, then?'

They wandered from one window to the next, hardly speaking to each other. He walked hesitantly because her lips were still tightly drawn. She felt like a fiercely boiling pot inside and was fighting to keep the lid firmly in place. Having reached a kind of crossroads, with a fountain playing in the middle of it, they came to a halt.

'Which way now?' asked Wyn.

'I don't mind. You decide.'

'You're the one who knows the place.'

'You're the one who wants to go shopping.'

'I thought that's what you wanted to do.'

'Well, I don't. And it's a bit late to think like that now, isn't it?'

'How do you mean?'

'Doing something just to please me.'

'Oh, come off it! Everything I ever do is to please you!'

'Ha! You hardly ever please me, mate.'

He took a few seconds to understand.

'You can be a real little bitch sometimes. What the hell's the matter? What have I done that's so bloody awful?'

'You're not that stupid, Wyn.'

'What do you mean?'

'You're always doing this, aren't you? Pretending you don't understand so that you don't have to face up to something you don't like.'

'You're talking a load of bollocks.'

'I am not. Last night was important for me, Wyn. Those people are my friends, and I wanted them to like you. But you didn't even try, did you? You were deliberately trying to be rude, sneering at everything that was offered you. You just haven't got any respect for people, have you?'

'Don't talk daft. The food was shit — that wasn't my fault!'

She was crying, bloody hell, she was crying like a baby and her voice was getting more high-pitched with every word, and everyone was staring at them. He wanted to apologize, but she wouldn't let him touch her. She was like a windmill, arms flailing.

'I'd been looking forward to it so much. I'd been going on and on about you, telling them how wonderful you were, and look what you've gone and done! You've taken no notice of anyone since you've been here, you've been a bloody embarrassment, and I can't understand what I ever saw in you. I must have been off my head. And I was so sure that I was in love with you!'

'Iola ... I came here to see you, not your — '

But she had gone. For a big woman, she could certainly shift. There was no sign of her. He ran after her. Well, in the same direction, anyway, but she had completely disappeared. Having poked his head into every shop, and feeling a real bloody fool doing it, he decided that she would be sure to come back after she'd had a chance to cool down. He went back to wait near the fountain. She was taking her bloody time. What if she had had an accident, got run over by a car or something? He felt like crying. There was a café on the corner and the bread smelt wonderful, but he had no money. He had insisted on Iola's carrying the French currency from the start. She was used to the stuff. He fumbled in his pocket and found an odd-shaped silver coin. Would this be enough for a cup of coffee, at least? He tried to decipher the tariff but was unable to make head or tail of it. He went to the counter and tried to attract someone's attention.

'Oh, see voo play. You. Aye. Coffee? This enough?' He held out the silver coin. The man looked at him stupidly, and shook his head with a disdainful '*Non*' and pursed his mouth like a chicken's arsehole before going back to polishing glasses.

'Stuff you, then. You fuckin' wanker!'

He went and sat down against the wall of the fountain and waited. Was that Iola in the blue coat? No. A middle-aged woman, not much to look at, either. Oh, come on, Iola, where are you? I'm sorry. I didn't want to go for a meal with your friends, did I? I just wanted to be with you. I've been without you for months, and

I wanted to spend all day and every day with you. I thought that was what you wanted, too.

Iola had reached the second floor and could see all this from the balcony. For an instant she felt a strong urge to drop one of the flower-pots onto his head. She took a cigarette from the packet she had just bought and lit it. She never smoked when he was around. He had no idea that she smoked. She stared down at him. He looked so pathetic and sad and completely lost. She saw him standing on tip-toe in an attempt to catch a glimpse of her in the crowd. He of all people, all six foot of him. She couldn't help smiling. He was straining his head from side to side like a cross between a cockerel and a giraffe. There was a lump in her throat and strange things going on somewhere in her stomach. She would go down to him soon. She inhaled deeply and flicked the ash into the flower-pot.

When he saw her walking slowly towards him, he ran to her and enveloped her in his arms, and kissed her — long, lingering kisses that made her toes curl up. When they separated at last, a small crowd of smiling shoppers who had stopped to watch them began to smile and applaud.

'Well, what did you expect? I'm a Welshman in love. *Chanson d'amour!*' he shouted at them, and then, in English, 'I love her!'

That night, back in the house, after hours of making such passionate love that Suzanne had to shout at them to keep the noise down, they shared two fried-egg sandwiches and a bottle of wine.

Falling

Gwenan M. Roberts

It was all so confusing. Yesterday, everything was crystal clear, like the glove on her hand, but today ...

How quickly one flows through the shadows of the mind. Alice stepping inquisitively into the rabbit hole — floating through the light air with the images flashing past her, all mixed up like food in a processor. The electricity stirring the parts into a thick liquid and that little note, 'Drink me!'. Floating, flirting, feeling. Warm, naked bodies touching and filling the moist entrance. 'Drink me!'

'You have no conception of time, do you?' asks the Mad Hatter scornfully. And poor Alice having to swim through the salt of her own tears.

How quickly one flows through the shadows of the mind. Or was she mistaken?

'Are you at college?'

'Yes.'

'Tom never went to college. The snail-shearing was enough for him, staying at home like his father and grandfather before him.'

'Enough of your nonsense now. It was you who got careless, expectant with the little colours, wasn't it?

'Would you like some more tea?'

'Haven't you any coffee?'

'Oh no, no. Time, you see, it's frozen. It's tea-time, don't you understand?'

Warm, naked bodies in a tight embrace and time frozen.

The liquid blends, bubbling away and the sparks flying in all directions, leaving nasty little stains. You must remember the trial. Twelve little creatures writing on their slates — 'Guilty. Not Guilty. What is your relationship to this case?' And her, poor thing, growing and growing.

And the Queen of Hearts, where was she? Off with her head! Off with her head! Criminal! Her words like a fist on an open palm. Such treachery. Still seeing the little red hearts in pieces on the floor.

'It's got nothing to do with me. It's someone else's.' The Queen of Hearts was nowhere to be seen.

Red. Red flowing over the paper, over the seats. His copper head lowered. In shame? Red like mouldering blackberries flowing before her eyes. But not a stain from within her. Nothing. Not a single drop of scarlet hope. And time pressing relentlessly onwards.

How quickly one falls ... 'I'm late, I'm late ... ' and the watch on its chain tick-tick-ticking. 'I don't care how late you are. It's no concern of mine. Have you no shame?' Shame? How could something so lovely be shameful? Warm bodies pressing and aching, full of wonder, into the hole. The entrance to the den. Or was it coming out? ... Confused, blended and mixed, like the warm sludge served on a spoon at supper... And yet. Ugh! Take a quick breath. Was she about to be sick again?

'Come along, Mrs Lewis. Aren't you well? Eat up now.'

'But I'm expecting.'

'Expecting who, Mrs Lewis, dear?'

'No, expecting. And everyone's turning their backs on me.'

'They'll come and see you next week, I'm sure. Here, let me empty the bedpan.'

Everyone turning their backs. The cards, the strange-looking Hatter. And the Queen of Hearts, where was she? She was nowhere to be seen, you know. Nowhere to be seen, no indeed.

I can hear their whispers now. 'You're confused, my dear.

Come on. Confused, muddled, all mixed up now.' But how could she be muddled? Everything was so clear, like a glove on the hand ... and the moment so perfect. Hold me tight. I'm falling. I'm here, don't worry, I'm here inside you, you inside me. Swaying so sweetly. Rock a bye, baby. Flirting and falling, swaying and suckling, warm and inviting. 'Eat me. Eat me.' And you, suddenly, becoming such a small, sweet, innocent thing. In need of your mother.

'You can't have her. Bring her back.'

Aching all over, all that swelling and slackening. All that shouting and screaming. Until there was nothing left. Relief. Regret. Remorse. Nowhere to turn. Nothing to fill. And life insisting on pushing at the walls, but failing ... And time just slipped through my fingers somehow.

'How old would she be now? Eighteen?'

'Who?'

'The little one.'

'Your granddaughter's twenty-one, isn't she?'

'Not my granddaughter. Alice. The little one.'

Why does she look at me like that? It's Alice's birthday, or is it the Hatter's? There'll have to be a tea-party. But you're far too big for that sort of thing. Eat the cake and be small again, petite and pretty. Firm warm breasts and shapely legs. Secret entrances slipping open, and throbbing passages. Instead of slowly wasting away, wrinkled and tired, like a shabby old womb of no use to anyone.

'I never had any children, you know.'

'Of course you did. You must be confused, dear. They come to see you.'

'Not my children. Adopted. Punishment for losing the little one.'

Praying every month that the bleeding would stop, but the familiar cramp announcing that the scarlet curse was on its way again.

'Just like little fragments of heart. I remember it so clearly, you see. So clearly. I'd been fucking when I wasn't supposed to, you see.'

'Mrs Lewis! You're confused. Muddled, mixed up. Let me take the bedpan. Eat your soup. Let me take the bedpan.'

It's they who're muddled, not me, carrying the old secret like a guilty fable in the memory. I wonder what happened to my supper? Maybe Dad will be here presently and read a story before I go to sleep. The old watch is ticking loudly tonight. He's late. Or is it me that's late? And these old gloves keep slipping off my fingers.

'Nurse, could you help me with this bedpan, please? And play some cards while I wait for the children?'

By the Waters of Babylon

John Emyr

As our feet touched gravel we heard a shout. We turned round to look. If they hadn't guessed who we were and greeted us thus, we should certainly have ignored them completely and chosen another spot.

'What made you so late? Detlef was right — the Celts are asleep on their feet half the time.'

Everyone laughed. They seemed a mixed bunch, sitting close together in a shallow dip in the gravel. Before hearing the shout we had been intending to make for one of the other groups, near one of the largest bonfires.

We'd seen the fires as we crossed the bridge, the lovely smell of their pine coming in through the half-open windows of the car. Our guests had not yet lit their fire.

The spot chosen for the barbecue was on the bank of a wide river. The previous week's beanfeast had been on the edge of a wood near a house up on the mountainside. The atmosphere this evening was just as awkward for us, and just as unexpected.

On this side of the river the bank was long and flat under our feet. Gravel and pebbles, white as limestone and just as dry. On the other side there were bushes and fields, and behind us, on this side, a cluster of tall trees which drooped their branches over the undercut bank.

Here was the bridge. On one side, huddled close to road

and river, stood the inn with its old-fashioned windows wide open to the noise of cars and the murmur of water and the laughter of guests at tables under the trees.

But what first caught the eye were the fires.

The colours of the evening were unusual and striking, it is true. The clear, clean greenish-blue that is to be seen on summer evenings when the birds burst into song for the last time before retiring for the night, the sun gone down but not yet having quite dragged its glow after it, and the wings of bats weaving their aimless patterns and the air filled with their squeaking.

The chain of lights around the eaves of the inn and under the branches of the trees above the tables were also exceedingly lovely.

But it was not these which gave the place its special and unfamiliar character, it was the fires.

They smouldered and crackled and flashed before us now all along the river for a mile or two, perhaps three. We could see them getting redder and redder, and then yellower, as night came down. A bright and untidy row, like beads falling loose from the river's bare arm. This was a good place for a barbecue, Tecwyn had said.

I heard a scream. Before it was completely dark a gang of children had decided to play trains. They moved in a chain from group to group, from fire to fire. They danced around the bonfire like wild things — delighted to be disturbing the games of the adults.

'Caught in the traffic, were you?' someone said in German.

'It took ages, you know. An accident on the road.' We let Tecwyn do the explaining. They were his friends, after all. We were on holiday. Best not to rush into conversation. But I noticed one of the others watching me surreptitiously.

'A bad accident?'

'I counted four ambulances.'

I could still hear the sirens wailing in my ears. I could see the blue lights whirling, and the crowd staring.

'Ah well, that's how it is. We don't want to be gloomy tonight, anyway.'

The feasting began. There were quite a few of them — a young crowd from various countries — scoffing and devouring the food and laughing.

'Who the heck — ?'

Some nutter in the vicinity of the farthest fire had taken it into his head to provide music. And the instrument? — a trumpet, of all things. There was a murmur of gentle protest. And more laughter. The notes of the trumpet mingled with the smoke from the fires.

'You're Welsh, aren't you? Come and meet Mel. She's Welsh, too. She can speak the language.'

By now our bonfire was at its height. It was difficult to say how many people were present. Everyone came and went as they pleased. The faceless shadows of bonfire night. Impossible to recognize anyone until they were close up, until you could smell the meat they were chewing.

'Rob! Shame on you for saying such a thing.' Mel didn't look me in the eye as we shook hands.

'My Welsh is pretty rusty now, I'm afraid.' But she was speaking the language.

She was a woman of about thirty, showing the first signs of age. The green make-up plastered around her eyes didn't conceal their weariness.

'On holiday, I suppose?'

'Yes. You too?'

'No. This is my home now. This is the ninth summer I've spent here.'

We chatted. She was eager for news from Wales. I mentioned various people. Her eyes lit up as I talked about them. For a moment she was wide-awake and enthusiastic. Then the eyes flickered and the weariness returned.

'How old were you when you came out here?' I asked.

'Nineteen. I worked as a secretary until I married. I'm homesick sometimes.'

'Homesick?'

She laughed. 'I'm a romantic, you see. The mountains. The

language. The people. Ah, they are what I miss most! More than that, too. It's hard to put a finger on it. I can't help feeling that I've broken away from something more significant. Do you understand? I've turned my back on something larger.'

A burst of laughter came from near the grill.

'A song,' said one of the lads. 'It's time we started singing.'

Someone began to strum a guitar. Two or three pop-songs were sung in desultory fashion.

One of the Germans was watching us over a slice of meat.

'Mel, what about a Welsh song?' he said, with his mouth full.

'Yes. A Welsh song from Mel,' said a friend at his side.

A good deal of urging and thumping and shouting in English and German.

'On your feet, on your feet!' Everyone was clapping wildly. Mel's face was calm. Everyone was staring at her. She was like a little girl about to say her verses in chapel. She swallowed and looked at the circle of familiar faces around her, each gleaming in the light of the flames. And then she looked at me — the stranger from Wales.

'No,' she said quietly.

'On your feet, on your feet!'

At last Mel got up. She couldn't remember any Welsh songs at the moment, she said. Instead, she would sing a fairly well-known, light-hearted German song. She sang it in a beautiful voice in the minor key, a voice that vibrated and trembled charmingly.

'Splendid! Splendid! Bravo, Mel!'

There was a wild round of applause from the gathering. The people on the edge of the circle didn't know whom they were applauding. Mel, overcome with shyness, smiled. She had sat down as soon as the applause started. When she stopped smiling her eyes were sad.

'Splendid,' I said to her in Welsh.

'That's enough now, kids.' She scowled at one of her children, a little chap who had been earnestly trying to steal fire from the adults. She spoke to the child in English. He took not the slightest notice of her. The mother glanced back at me.

'It's impossible to keep them in order,' she said, again in Welsh.

'When did you come to live here?' I began questioning her most unimaginatively, and like a tired traveller unloading her luggage, bit by bit, item by item, she gave me the story of her life.

She had met her husband in London, of course: Gregory, a businessman from Minneapolis. Had gone back with him to the United States. Her husband had wanted to travel and she, probably, was dragged along with him. First to Italy. Started a business there — in the car trade. Then moved to Austria. The business had gone bust. Greg tried again, putting all the money he had left into opening a factory which retreaded tyres, on the other side of the border. Pleasant days. Plenty of profit, plenty of demand. The venture had flourished.

They had had enough money to buy a house and bring up children. Oh yes, they had been very happy in those days — they had more than enough. Plenty of friends, and enough people of the same sort from other parts of the world, all speaking fair German and fluent English, and sending their kids to the best American international school.

While we were chatting, two of the children came up to the mother and caught hold of the hem of her shawl. They had been rolling with laughter a minute ago, Now, in the presence of strangers, they were completely silent.

'Kevin and Martin, here's someone from Wales. Do you remember me telling you about Wales?'

Not a word from either of them. The younger of the two looked at the older one with wide eyes, then glanced back at the mother.

'How does it go, Mum? Is it a good story?'

Mel chuckled. 'Oh, these kids have memories like sieves.'

'Hey, Mel. What about another song — a Welsh one this time.'

The sadness leapt back into her eyes.

'Don't be silly, Detlef. I don't remember any Welsh ones.'

'Surely these Welsh people can help you to remember.'

'Come on, Mel.' said one of the others. 'How about a hymn?'

'Yes. A Welsh hymn, Mel,' pleaded the crowd.

Mel's eyes seemed to be stricken with grief. Detlef had his supporters. He was a man of about forty and he'd had enough of the barbecue, and wanted entertaining.

'Enough of your shouting now, Detlef.' This from a friend at his side. 'I'm sure we'll have another contribution from Mel before the evening's over.' The friend, too, like Detlef, was rather tipsy.

'Come on. Why not, Mel? You've got a terrific voice. Come on. Just one Welsh song.'

Mel looked up and stared at them for a long while. Then she looked at me. I was unable to see the men's faces. By now they were standing outside the glow of the flames. But the woman's face was clear, perfectly clear, and gleaming white.

'Don't ask me to sing again tonight,' she said quietly.

'Ha! ha!, did you hear that, lads? The Celts have become too sensitive to sing. Don't be so sensitive, Mel, please.'

Sitting beside me now was a tall figure in a dark coat and wearing a cloak. I had happened to look at him while the others were talking. There was an oblique slant to his shoulders under the cloak. And his face, like Mel's, was extremely pale. He had been picking at his food, and when he got to his feet to reach for something or other, I noticed how tall and thin and bony he was. His forehead was yellow. From his upper lip there hung traces of a smile.

'Good-evening,' he said hesitantly. His voice came out of the darkness and it struck me that he would be in his grave soon.

'I'm a friend of Mel's,' he said, 'or rather, of Greg's, her husband.' This in a rush, wheezily, without much breath behind it.

'How are things over there in Wales? I was on a business trip to London six months ago. Things were in a bit of a mess, I must say. Quite a mess. What sort of a place is it now? Getting worse?'

He looked at me with his sooty black eyes. He bent forward expectantly. He had the habit of moistening his upper lip with the tip of his tongue between sentences.

I told him about 'the crisis'.

'Disastrous,' I said, summing up. He dampened his upper lip.

'Is it, really?'

'Yes, really.'

The children returned to disturb us. One of them said, 'Come and play cowboys.'

Once more I noticed the gang of children. The children of the various families. They had left their own families and had gathered in one happy, menacing group. Now they began to band together and were standing on the other side of the river. The reflection of the bonfire was clear in the water between us and them. They were not standing quietly, either, but running and leaping about and chanting. And dancing energetically with one another and waving straight branches like spears in their fists. Challenging the adults, that was for sure. A tribe of Red Indians screeching and laughing at the grey adults. The savages sang their own strange songs at the top of their voices.

The phantom in the cloak frowned and moved over to the grill to look for something else to eat.

Mel chuckled.

'Those kids,' she said to me. 'I'm not a real Welsh woman, you know. Not any more. Why they press me to sing now, I don't know.'

'You were born and brought up in Wales,' I said.

'Yes, but fair play. I've been a real expatriate now — for almost ten years.'

'Have you?'

She caught her breath and looked back at me for a long moment. Then it passed.

'This is my country now. I still think of Wales sometimes, though.'

'Come on, Mel. have you remembered a song for us yet?'

The flat, English voice was persistent.

I looked at her. The make-up had run on her eyebrows. Her lipstick was dark red — a clotted purple. She sat down on the gravel, her hand playing with the pebbles. She looked up and smiled guiltily.

'Come on, Mel. Don't be so shy. One little song for us now, just one. Surely you don't want to disappoint your old friends, do you? Who ever heard of a Welsh woman refusing to sing? What do you say, lads?'

There was a yell of agreement from the crowd.

I fancied I saw a muscle twitching in Mel's face, just above her right cheek. She turned away and looked into the shadows. There were signs of strain under her eyes. She turned back and mumbled, 'Don't ask me to sing tonight.'

When I saw her turn her head like that, I thought for an instant that she was about to say something more. Her lips were tightly pursed.

But no. She took a long, deep breath. The children were laughing in the distance. The sound of their strange chanting was being carried clearly across the water. The notes of the trumpet called out through the air and drifted slowly after the smoke in the direction of the sea.

The Coat

Lowri Angharad Evans

Robart Jones farted. Loudly. Then regretted it. It wasn't much fun any more. Martha had used to go on at him whenever he let off wind — opening windows, the lot. It was worth it, just to see her cheeks puff like a bellows and her bosom heave. Then, chuckling to himself, he'd give her a kiss and say sorry.

But today there was no one to sniff the foul smell. Just himself and the cat, and she was too lazy to catch a cold, let alone be bothered by a fugitive fart. He got up from the sagging sofa, stepped over the dinner-dishes that were fast becoming stuck to the dirty, threadbare carpet, and went out the back to fetch coal. He'd got as far as the shed before he remembered that for the last two years he'd had a gas-appliance and coal was no longer used to make fires. It was Martha who'd taken a fancy to it, having seen next-door's.

-Easy to manage, aren't they?

-And clean.

-Pretty, too.

-And expensive, he thought, but didn't say so.

It wasn't yet four o'clock and it was beginning to get dark. The clocks had gone back and the nights were drawing in. Nothing to look forward to but a long, dark winter. Rubbish on the box, idle chatter on the wireless, and none but the cat to care whether he got up in the morning or not.

He'd thought of going to the surgery — not for treatment, but for someone to talk to. He'd had enough of people speaking at him as if he wasn't all there.

-How are you?

-Champion.

-Keeping alright?

-Champion.

-Getting chilly.

-Yes, it is.

-There we are then.

-Aye.

-Aye indeed.

At least it would be warm there. Plenty of magazines to look at, the receptionist to tease, and people to strike up a conversation with. After all, everyone likes to complain about their health and it would help to pass the time. The only snag would be thinking of something to say when his turn came.

-But my dear Mr Jones, that's a woman's complaint.

-Good heavens, is that so?

Or even worse:

-Undress, please, Mr Jones. Come along now.

-Champion.

-No, the whole lot, please, Mr Jones. Come on now.

-The whole lot?

-That's what I said.

It was too damned cold for all that. He would give the surgery a miss.

He took off his slippers, scratched his big toe through the hole in his sock, and came to a decision. Go out for a stroll. Do something, anything at all — that was it. He'd been cooped up between these four walls far too long. They'd brought him solace at first, all these things cluttering up the place. Things Martha had chosen or received as presents, making room for them on the oak dresser and polishing them until she could see her face in them. Now they were cables, binding him to a past that could never return. He took the teapot from the mantelpiece and fished a five-pound note out of it. There's no pocket in a shroud — that was what Martha used to say. And for the first time since he could remember, he decided to do as he was told, despite her not being there.

He put on his best shoes — flimsy things, but at least they were clean. Then his cap, and his scarf, and his grey raincoat. He went on for his stroll. The cat stirred, then went back to sleep — the good-for-nothing scamp.

He didn't know where exactly he was going, so he did what he usually did and followed his usual routine. It had been good enough for him so far — why change now?

-So where are we going this summer, Robart?

Whenever she called him Robart and not Bob he knew she was nagging him. She was the only one to call him that, and his mother didn't like it all.

-I christened him Robart.

As if his father had had nothing to do with it, let alone the minister.

-What d'you mean?

He knew full well that she'd have loved just to pack a suitcase and leave a note for the milkman that she wouldn't be back for a fortnight.

-Are we going to have a break this year?

-Alright, just a short one.

-What about the Lakes this time?

She wouldn't have known what the Lakes were if she'd fallen head-first into them, except that the woman down the road had been there and never stopped swanking about it.

-Too crowded.

-What about Scotland then? Plenty of room there.

-Too far.

The Parry-Robertses had been there. Both of them, in their small car, with their leather suitcases and fat pension. Martha would have liked to send them a postcard.

-London? To see the sights?

-Too expensive. Too many foreigners.

-Where then?

-Well, let's go to Blackpool, shall we? At least we'll get a good breakfast there.

An enormous breakfast, swimming in fat and shimmering on the plate. Leave the pink nylon bedroom behind for a whole day, paddle in the sea, have chips on the way home — what could be better? It wouldn't have suited Mrs Parry-Roberts, but he and Martha had a grand time. At least, he did — and she didn't go on too much about it.

He hadn't been anywhere for ages, and if you don't do something for long enough, you forget how to do it. That's what Martha used to say when she was nagging him to take a bath.

-Robart.

-How are you, Mr Rees?

-Nights drawing in.

-So they are.

-Keeping alright?

-Champion.

-Getting chilly, too.

-Aye.

-There we are then, I'll be seeing you.

-Aye. Aye indeed.

Turn the corner. Go past the chapel. He couldn't bear to look at its front door. Enough of his upbringing survived in him to stir some small smick of shame in the pit of his stomach every time he set eyes on the old place. He went past.

He walked on. Stopped. Crossed the road and went into the second-hand clothes shop that stood next door to the Employment Centre. He had no idea why. He'd never been in there before. Just a whim, and there was no one to tell him not to.

The bell rang so loudly as he stepped into the pool of light that he nearly jumped out of his skin. He remembered now why he always thought it better to do as you've always done. Much more sensible. But he was in the shop now, so he started to have a look around. There was no one there except him. No one. Only a scruffy room full of old clothes, old toys, old shoes strewn on a shelf, and some old, mouldy, much-thumbed books — they had all seen better days.

-Hiya.

-Good grief! Where did you spring from?

-I was squatting in the back there. Just been given two bagfuls to sort. Can I help you?

-Only looking, thanks.

-For something special?

-No.

He remembered now why he detested shopping. Too late.

-What size collar are you?

-Pardon me?

-You're a sixteen, I bet!

-Aye, you're right ... I think.

-I thought so. Don't move.

He was rooted to the spot. What the dickens did she want? She was no older than the girl next door, but he knew he had to do what he was told.

Then he noticed the smell of the place — the smell of other people, a nice smell.

-Now then, take off your mack.

-Take it off?

-Well, yes. So's you can see what I've got for you. Get your skids on!

He might as well have gone to the doctor's. At least he was a man.

-Now then. It's getting colder, isn't it?

-Yes. It is.

Obediently, quietly.

-And you'll need a top coat.

-Well ...

-You won't find a better one than this. Feel the weight.

A black Crombie, with a mauve lining, and yes — it was a heavy one.

-Perfect fit!

-Is it?

-Perfect. You've got to take it.

-Got to?

-Yes, got to. Fits like a glove. Tailor-made for you.

-Where did it come from?

-A good home. We're not supposed to say from where.

-I won't let on. I never talk to anyone anyway.

-Mr Parry-Roberts.

-Ty Uchaf?

-That's right, Mrs Parry-Roberts brought it in this morning. That's what I was doing when you came in.

-Poor dab.

-Went sudden in the end, didn't he?

John Parry-Roberts had been a bully if ever there was one, and he'd done extremely well for himself, too, once he'd sold Ty Uchaf off. Ended up a bank manager. Highly respected. Lot to say for himself. Used to go to Scotland every year in his small car. Could afford to buy as many Crombie coats as he liked.

-I'll take it.

-Course you will. Can't leave it here gathering dust. You look real cool in it!

-Cool? I thought it was a winter coat.

-It is. Looks smart on you.

-Alright. How much do I owe you?

-Five smackers.

-How much?

-Five quid.

-Five pounds?

-That's it.

-Right.

-Champion.

Martha would never have dared set foot in such a place. Too proud to accept charity, let alone wear other people's cast-offs. But there it was — Martha wasn't here, and he wasn't doing anyone harm. He'd got a bargain and anyway he needed a top coat. He kept it on and had the grey raincoat wrapped in a plastic bag. The door-bell rang behind him as he stepped out into the murky street.

As he made for home it started to rain. Not real, wet rain, but a fine drizzle, the kind that sticks to your face like a mask. He pulled the new coat about him, doing up the top button. It was warm, and heavy. The girl had been right, and he felt his shoulders broadening to take the weight. He wondered how it felt to be wealthy. To be a bank manager, when you'd been brought up in Ty Uchaf of all places. To count other people's money and have some of your own. A nice little car and holidays in Scotland.

He turned the corner. What would Martha have thought, seeing him in John Ty Uchaf's coat, swaggering his way home like this, having spent five pounds in as many minutes, not to mention being out in the rain?

-Shift your backside!

The cat skedaddled out of his way, back to the fireside.

He put down the plastic bag and his old raincoat on the table, letting beads of rain that were dripping from it soak into the dirty tablecloth. Then he went upstairs and stood in front of the long mirror on the landing.

He hardly recognized himself. He looked taller in the new black coat, and broader in the shoulder. Upright, and more dignified, somehow. He drew cold fingers through his white hair and patted it into place on his forehead. Then he thrust his hands into the coat's deep pockets to see himself properly. He'd once owned a coat like this, a long time ago, when he'd been a young man, with a job in the quarry, and courting Martha. He had no idea what had become of it. Probably eaten by moths by now. But this one was like new. And it had belonged to John Ty Uchaf. Who would have thought, in the schoolyard all those years ago, that Robart, with his socks around his ankles, his nose running, and his jampot glasses, would get to wear the coat once worn by John, with his big hard fists and golden hair, his leather football and regular pocket-money? Who would have thought that the little boy who'd been beaten and shamed, scolded and punished on account of the malicious tales carried by Ty Uchaf's eldest son, would get the better of him in the end? He was very pleased with himself.

The following morning, the cat didn't know what day it was. He washed her plate, opened the curtains, made a cup of tea in the teapot and scraped margarine on his toast. He didn't sing, but came close to it. He turned on the radio and laughed for once at an old joke. Even the constant chatter and thumping music didn't get on Robart's nerves this morning. The weather wasn't fine or warm, nor was it Friday. He was in a good mood, that was all.

Time passed quite quickly. He'd polished the brasses on the mantlepiece and soon it was time to go out for milk. The collar of his new Crombie was turned up warm around his neck.

-Mr Jones.

-Hello, Alun, how are things?

-Very good, thanks. And you?

-Champion.

-You're looking well.

-I'm feeling well, thanks.

-Looking younger, somehow.

He laughed to himself and went on his way. As he passed the Co-op he saw Mrs Evans, Chapel View, coming towards him. Seeing him, she dropped her shopping and it spilt all over the pavement.

-Good heavens!

-What's the matter, Mrs Evans?

-I thought for a moment ...

-Are you alright, Mrs Evans?

-Yes, I just couldn't believe my eyes, that's all. Just for a second. The way you were walking, and everything. Don't take no notice of me.

-You're not usually one to get upset, Mrs Evans.

-Sorry. I thought you were someone else.

He didn't go home till it was time for dinner. He had a bag of chips under his arm — fat, greasy ones, like he used to in Blackpool with Martha. They tasted good, too — of laughter and silly hats and sunburnt arms. He could have done with more of that. As he came in, the cat opened one eye, then went back to sleep.

That evening Robart Jones sat in front of the gas-fire as usual. He wasn't watching telly as he usually did. He was playing the fiddle. He'd got it from an old uncle. It was a bit out of tune, but that didn't matter this evening. Although he hadn't touched the instrument for ages, he still knew how to play it. He was in great form, completely absorbed in the music, when someone knocked on the back-door.

-Hello?

-Mr Jones?

-Mrs Parry-Roberts?

-Can I have a word?

Mrs Parry-Roberts was a stout woman, with a mop of untidy hair and a black necklace at her throat. A woman enchanted by coffee-mornings and annual meetings, a woman who loved to be seen doing things.

-You'd better come in.

The Crombie hung on the back of the kitchen door, its mauve lining agleam like a new shilling in the light of the gas-fire. Robart moved to stand in front of it, blushing up to his ears. He felt as if he'd been caught in bed with another woman. As if he'd been caught pinching sweets. He felt as he had at school when Mr Ifans bawled at him for tripping up poor John Ty Uchaf and tearing his trousers. He'd known then that he was being blamed unjustly. He knew now that he hadn't done anything wrong. There was no law against playing the fiddle after ten at night. Yet his face was scarlet.

-There's been a misunderstanding.

-Oh yes?

-Yes. I understand you've ...

-What?

-You've been and bought Mr Parry-Roberts's best overcoat.

-Have I?

-Yes, you have — and I want it back.

-Her words struck him like a bolt of lightning.

-But ...

-A misunderstanding, as I said. John promised it to our eldest boy, you see. And that daft cleaning woman put it in a bin-bag by mistake. You'll get your money back, of course. Here ...

And before he could say another word she'd gone, with the coat under her arm, and there was a five-pound note in his hand. The purring cat was rubbing against the calves of his trousers, asking to be fed. He grabbed the fiddle, shoved it back under the stairs, switched on the telly, and put on his slippers.

He'd forgotten how to live. You only have to stop doing something long enough to forget how to do it. That had suited him fine in the past. Now he knew what he'd been missing. It had all come back to him.

Yes, John Ty Uchaf was a bully — always had been.

Cuddling

Manon Rhys

Heno, heno, hen blant bach ...

I can't stop shivering. It doesn't matter what I do, I'm shivering so much, the bed shakes...

'Thank goodness you're here to keep me company, Pwten. It's nice to feel your warm weight on my feet and to hear you purring away. But I have to keep perfectly still because if I move you'll wake and sulk and run away with your tail sticking up in the air.'

And leave me here on my own ...

'Fair play to Auntie Nans, isn't it? She was only pretending, you know, just now, when she came in to say good-night. Pretending she hadn't seen you at the foot of the bed, just as she's done every night this week. 'Turning a blind eye' Miss Bowen called it in the Welsh lesson yesterday, and John Richards said his grandfather had one after losing his proper eye in some war or other. Lots of people turn a blind eye to things, Miss Bowen says.

'Why d'you think Auntie Nans wouldn't tell me a story? I begged her to tell me the one about when she and Mam were little and they stole peas from the garden and had belly-ache, and Mamgu sent them to bed early. She didn't feel like telling that story tonight, she said, or any other story.'

Not tonight ...

'That was a whacking big kiss she gave me before leaving! I'm sure the lipstick mark's still there. When she put her arms around me and cuddled me tight, tight, I could hardly breathe.

'I liked the smell of her scent. She promised to dab some behind my ear when I call on her after school tomorrow. And we're going to make Welsh cakes, and I'll be allowed to flip them over on my own, without any help.

'Her cheeks were soaking wet when she got up and went to the door. She turned to me and tried to smile, but she was crying...'

And then she was gone ...

She's been gone for hours. Now everything's dark. Everything's dark and cold, and I just can't stop shaking ...

'Come here, Pwten, for me to cuddle you and stroke you. You can come under the quilt with me. We'll pull it up over our heads and pretend we're in the little white tent under the apple-tree.'

It's always warm in the tent, warm and safe, and no one knows you're there, as long as you stay perfectly quiet ...

'That's it, lie still now, and behave. Do you realize how lucky you are? I could chuck you out of this bed any time, remember! And then you'd have a kick in your backside right out into the garden, wouldn't you? But I wouldn't do anything like that. Because we're friends, aren't we? You and me, warm and safe together ... '

But I can't stop shivering ... And I'm nearly crying ...

I'm the best in class — out of the girls — for sticking it out without crying. I'm better than some of the boys, even. Alun Wyn had hysterics yesterday morning when he caught his finger in the door of the girls' toilet. Cry-baby! He had no business to be there in the first place, Miss Bowen said. I know why he was there. He'd been peeping at Lynwen Evans's knickers. At playtime she'd been boasting about her posh pink ones with lace on them, and he'd gone to hide behind the door to get a peep. I could have told him he was wasting his time. She always wears ugly navy-blue knickers full of holes — ragged old ones after her sister in the County

School. Yuck — I wouldn't wear them if you paid me. It's no wonder she tries to kid the boys. But Alun Wyn was the only one daft enough to believe her. And he was caught fair enough.

I felt sorry for him when I saw him crying and sucking his finger like a baby. But everyone else was laughing at him.

Only once I've cried in front of the others. That was the time of the big fight with Robert Stevens behind the Unit. I was winning easily, and that was why he started shouting nasty things. I got angry then, so angry that I flipped. He was making fun of me because I'm a girl, and all the boys were shouting with him, and the girls were taking my side. It was a shambles, just like that daft wrestling you see on the box.

But what put the kibosh on it was feeling the wet running down my legs. Suddenly they all went quiet. Then Robert Stevens pointed at the puddle between my feet and started laughing again. Everyone started laughing, the girls and all, and there I was with my shoes and socks sopping and I couldn't stop crying. I wanted to run away and hide for ever ...

Miss Bowen's seen me crying — in the cloakroom, after everyone had gone home. She came and sat down by me and asked what was the matter. But I was crying so much I couldn't say anything. She put her arm around me and I started crying all the more. I was shaking all over, and choking, just like when I had whooping-cough and couldn't go on the Sunday School trip.

I cried and cried till it was dark. And all the time Miss Bowen was cuddling me and her hand was holding mine tight. She gave me a hankie, a white one with a red rose at the corner and the letter C under it. It was a very pretty little hankie.

I stopped crying at last and said I was feeling better, though my head felt as if it was splitting. We sat there together, quietly, for a while ...

Then she promised never to mention it to anyone that I'd been crying, but she'd like to know what the matter was. She'd been worried about me for weeks, she said.

I took a big breath and closed my eyes. At last I was going to be able to tell someone. But when I started to try and speak, nothing came out. I just couldn't say anything ...

She smiled and squeezed my hand, and told me not to worry, that she knew what was on my mind, and that she was going to help me.

I looked at her, surprised. My heart was pounding because I just knew she had no idea. She *couldn't* know — and yet, maybe ... Did she?

'Your mother's ill, isn't she?' she said, 'and you're worried about her, and have to help a lot at home, I'm sure ... '

That was when the phone rang. I had a chance to splash some water over my eyes. They were all red and swollen.

When Miss Bowen came back she was smiling.

'They didn't know where you were. I've promised to take you home straightaway.'

I remember thinking how I'd be able to swank next day that I'd been in Miss Bowen's car. Lynwen Evans would be very cross.

I didn't budge when we got to the house. I just sat quietly in the car, not taking my eyes off the front-door. I knew that Miss Bowen was watching me, but I just couldn't budge.

At last, she got out to open the door for me, and put her arm around me before taking me up the path.

And then the front-door opened ...

And then he was standing there.

He smiled, bent down and put his arm around me. Then he put my hand to his cheek. He hadn't shaved.

Suddenly I noticed Mam standing at the window. I turned and ran in and thew my arms around her. I was glad to see that she'd got up from bed. I was so glad that I started crying again. And there we were, the two of us, Mam and me, crying and cuddling each other.

He was still talking to Miss Bowen out by the car. I could see them through the window, their mouths moving, but I couldn't make out what they were saying.

Miss Bowen smiled and waved, then got into the car and drove off.

Then Mam squeezed me tight, tight.

Then he came in and gave us an odd look.

And then he closed the door ...

That was the night Mam and me cried all night ...

'I wasn't crying this morning, Pwten, though everyone else was. Mamgu, Auntie Nans — even *he* was crying, and I'd always thought he couldn't cry, and that men weren't supposed to cry. But there he was, making funny little noises in his throat, and hiding his face in a big white hankie. It started in the front-room, in front of all the strangers. He was crying all the time in chapel and the cemetery and later in the vestry, and his cup and saucer were rattling. It went on and on! I started to think he'd never stop and would be crying for ever!'

Can people cry for ever? They say some people cry when they want attention ...

Mam always used to cry on her own, when she thought no one could hear. She'd lock the bathroom door and cry and cry. But I could hear her. Every night I could hear her. As soon as he came home she'd come out of the bathroom all smiles, although her eyes were red and swollen ...

'I can hear you dreaming, Pwten. Are you having a nightmare? Or is there something worrying you? That old robin making fun of you, perhaps, or has that ugly old tomcat been stealing your food?

'That's the News at Ten music, Pwten. We haven't much time. Mind you, perhaps we'll be lucky again tonight. Perhaps he's asleep; perhaps he'll sleep all night in his chair. Perhaps we two will go down tomorrow morning and there he'll be snoring in his chair with *The Sun* over his face. Perhaps, Pwten ...

'Perhaps we'll wake up in the morning and go downstairs together ever so quietly, and he won't be there. Perhaps he'll be fast asleep in his bed and we'll have Frosties together in the back-kitchen, and we won't see him. Perhaps I'll be able to go to school without seeing him at all ...

'Perhaps, Pwten ...

'But I don't think so ... I don't think for a second we'll be so lucky.'

He's opening the back-door and dragging himself out to have a pee. He's kicking the bin on his way back and the lid clatters and rolls on the ground. He's swearing. The whole house is shaking as he slams the door ...

Milk-bottles out on the front-step ... Locking the door ... A tap on the barometer ... Winding the tall clock at the bottom of the stairs ... Putting the landing light on ... And he's starting to climb ...

'If only you could stay here with me, we'd both be safe. If only we stay perfectly still, perfectly quiet ...You and me together, Pwten ...You and me safe together under the quilt ...Warm and safe ... I'll look after you ... You won't have any more nightmares then ...'

He's humming as he shaves in the bathroom ...

'Pwten, don't be afraid ... I've told you, I'll look after you ... You don't have to move ... No need to open your eyes nor prick up your ears nor shake your tail ... You're safe with me ... Don't worry, I won't let him touch you ...

'I'll hold you tight ... That's it, stay still and lie down ... Don't budge ... Stay still, I said. You must ... Pwten, don't wriggle like that ... Stay with me, don't go. Please, Pwten, don't go ... Please, Pwten, don't leave me here on my own ... Pwten, why did you scram me?'

Get off then, you little bitch!

He's coming across the landing.
He's putting out the light and standing in the doorway.
Everywhere's dark but I can see his face.
He's smiling.
It's cuddling time.
Pwten, why did you leave me on my own?

I can't stop shivering.

Next Door to Avalon

Mared Lewis

She drummed her piano-player's fingers impatiently on the scorching black plastic of the car's dashboard. The traffic in this town was getting worse, no doubt about it. Meriel wondered whether, if she came out in the car at three in the morning, she'd find the same long caterpillar of vehicles sniffing restlessly up one another's backsides.

She would have to keep an eye on her blood-pressure, whatever she did, or the pretty little nurses in their film-set uniforms would tut-tut over their expensive equipment, the tasteful wallpaper framing their scorn. Not to mention what Lana would say.

At last, Meriel managed to turn left for Ralph's, an enormous supermarket that sold everything except human organs. The parking lot was full to overflowing, and the heat was a white glare off the concrete. Los Angeles in summer — when the shine of tinsel city curled up at the edges. With the temperature of the San Fernando Valley reaching 100 degrees Fahrenheit in mid-summer, everyone with the means to do so fled eastwards to the cooler states, or else they 'did' Europe.

But most of the Valley's inhabitants didn't have the means, as this parking lot demonstrated today. Coloured mothers in old clothes dragging children of all descriptions by their necks out of large, dilapidated cars. A couple of little men with beards like Rip

Van Winkle's squatting tailor-fashion in shop doorways, sheltering from the heat with a big piece of cardboard saying 'Vietnam Vets. Hungry and homeless'.

A Hispanic-looking old man edged the wide nose of an old Ford Mustang into the only parking-space that was left, the one Meriel had been waiting for. She cursed under her breath. But there was no point in getting worked up in this heat. Why should she, anyway? She was pregnant, not old. In two months' time she would be exactly as she'd been this time last year when she first arrived, standing pale in the huge reception lounge of LAX and not believing her good fortune.

She eventually found a place to park and turned off the air-conditioner. She got out of the car with some difficulty, her thin cotton dress sticking to her body. The heat came like a smack in the face.

It was good to be back in the small flat and close the door on the world outside. Meriel had a whole hour before Gareth and Lana arrived. Plenty of time to prepare a light snack and chill the bottles of mineral-water that had started to boil in the boot of the car.

Lana didn't eat much — her vital statistics were too important to allow her to eat candies and popcorn, she'd told Meriel. And what was the point of struggling to lose weight in the gym with the other pony-tailed women if you scoffed all sorts of junk afterwards? 'It's real important to keep healthy,' she'd said, putting a motherly hand on Meriel's chubby, red arm. 'Especially in your condition.'

The flat's kitchen had its back to the afternoon sun. It was a downstairs kitchen, so the lemon-tree that stood guard at the entrance to the block lent its generous shade. Meriel spent all her time in this small flat nowadays.

She had bought new red gingham curtains like the ones she'd seen on the television programme *Little House on the Prairie*. When they were closed during the afternoon, the large palm-tree cast its shadow onto the flimsy material. Meriel liked the effect, glad again she'd taken the decision to move to California.

A wind-chime made of small shells that she'd bought in Venice Beach hung from the ceiling. She'd almost broken her leg putting it up, wobbling on the chair, but no one had got to know about that. The warm light breeze caressed the shells, making them tinkle slowly and melodiously. It was a smelly old red-headed whore who'd sold her the wind-chime from her doorstep in one of the dirty narrow streets that led from the carnival atmosphere of Venice Beach. She had a Chinese dragon tattoo on her arm, in memory of an old lover, she said — 'A mean sonofabitch'. She'd taken no notice when Meriel mentioned the Welsh Dragon, and Meriel blushed slightly and was sorry she'd ever brought it up. 'Ya'd do fine here,' said the old woman. 'But get rid of that lump first.'

'Lemons outside the window!' her mother had written in a letter, admiringly. 'And they're so expensive in the village shop!' It was strange how a lemon-tree could awaken such admiration in a woman so begrudging of her praise.

Meriel reached for a large black shiny growth — Lana called it an egg-plant, but you never saw anything so unlike an egg in your life. Lana had been proud to introduce Meriel to the wonders of Californian life. And of course, she'd been a keen pupil, eager to become part of it all, to blend in.

When Gareth and Lana opened up the flat for her seven months ago, she'd known that she'd found the ideal place. She could tell it wasn't much to Lana's liking, but the American had begun to have enough of traipsing round the flats belonging to Gareth's friends, especially as some were close to the 'bad' districts, others too high up for Meriel to climb to several times a day, and one or two were a bit too nice ...

'Kinda cute,' she'd said, looking round as if inspecting a chicken-coop. Every house is like a chicken-coop, probably, when you've got a great big white mansion with a garden big enough for an eisteddfod.

'Like it, Meriel?' Gareth had whispered, his eyes devouring her.

'A great place to teach Welsh to the Invisible Man,' she'd replied with a grin.

Gareth had glowered at her, Meriel remembered that much clearly. Well, fair play. He hardly knew her at the time, did he? How was he to know that she wouldn't swindle them both and do a bunk to San Francisco or beyond — quicker than you could say 'Green Card'?

The contract had been quite specific, and the broud-shouldered attorney, with a filmstar's grin, had asked Meriel to sign two copies under the signatures of Gareth and Lana. Meriel had been taken on to teach Lana Welsh and to help clean the big house three times a week with Celia, a large fat girl who lived in one of the derelict squats near the Dodgers' Stadium in one of the poorest downtown districts. But Meriel's main duty would be to teach Lana Welsh, the piece of paper said. Teach her Welsh, and so carry out a function of which Angelino was incapable.

Bare-faced lies.

Documents passed to and fro. Meriel also had a visit from two men with paunches from the INS office, one of whom interrogated her and Gareth about the nature of her work, while the other snooped about the room pretending the whole business was a real turn-off. A charade. One huge silly piece of play-acting, with no one caring a toss for the part they played in it.

The social security number arrived in due course and then the flat in her own name, and the right to open a bank-account into which the regular little cheques would be safely deposited. Then she waited for the all-important green card.

It was all a scam. From a legal point of view. But it couldn't be all that bad because they'd been able to accomplish it so easily, with broad grins on their faces.

'You haven't done this before, have you?' Gareth had once asked her. He was doing up his shirt buttons as if he had all the time in the world, and the hairs on his chest were golden in the gap of daylight between the curtains.

'Done what before?' she said, turning over to look at him mischievously.

Gareth smiled despite himself. The sound of a siren could be heard passing by and the old dog in the next flat started baying. Meriel would listen for him in the small hours, howling as if for his own pack somewhere out there.

'All this business. What's a nice girl like you doing messing around with the authorities of a foreign country? Couldn't you marry some little Welsh teacher and live happily ever after ...?'

'And have a houseful of kids, is that it?'

His smile vanished.

'I can think of worse things,' he said quietly.

'It wasn't good enough for you, was it?'

Silence. That rare, lovely silence you get in a hot, scruffy city, with the desert wind pressing its nose against the window for a moment and gently shaking the frame. And the whole world holding its breath.

Meriel noticed the way Gareth's hair flopped over his left eye, the way he bit his lip and then turned to look at her, his eyes taking her all in, up and down ...

'You'll make a good father, Gareth,' she said tenderly, and the desert wind caught her words and urged them across the room.

'Think so?' he said immediately, and came to sit down by the bed. His eyes were sparkling. Meriel said it again, whispering it as she held his head between her breasts and ran her fingers through his hair.

'Lemons growing outside the window!' Meriel lifted the large shiny egg-plant and stroked the smoothness of its dark skin. It was amazingly, innocently smooth and soft as she squeezed the flesh for an instant. Her palm closed around it lovingly.

The bell rang and the knife sliced into her finger. Damn it! They had a bloody unpleasant habit of turning up too early. It had probably been Lana's idea, hoping to catch her standing one-legged on the table clutching a bottle of whisky.

She sucked her finger vigorously, but was too late to prevent a poppy-shaped drop of blood from spilling onto the whiteness of the delicate full moon on the plate in front of her.

'Meriel!'

Lana was all over her in a trice, brushing back her hair from her face and studying the black shadows under her eyes. Meriel heard herself answering like a robot:

'No, I'm not doing too much. Yes, I've had a lie-down today. Yes, I'm keeping out of the heat.'

You couldn't help liking Lana. But the maternal instinct in this tall, glamorous woman was somehow most inappropriate. Meriel had been dead scared of Lana when Gareth had taken her to meet her, shy as a teenager introducing his first girlfriend. That had been the afternoon after they'd first met, barely a week after she'd replied to the ambiguous but intriguing advertisement in *Y Drych*, the newspaper of the Welsh community in America.

Lana was forty, golden-maned and sexy, her fingernails were highly varnished and her clothes stank of money. There was such authority in her voice as she questioned Meriel that the younger woman felt like beating it back home, to the green fields of Anglesey and her mother's thin, uncompromising lips. But as Lana went on to explain how she'd been unable to have children, and how Gareth wanted a little Welsh child to bring up and love as his own, Meriel couldn't help feeling sorry for them.

The bargain — or rather, the contract — was sealed there and then. Lana's word for it was 'lending'. Meriel would lend them her womb, and she'd be given first-class care during her pregnancy. And after the birth, everyone would be happy. Gareth and Lana would have a brand-new little Welsh baby, with care instructions in the folds of its nappy, and Meriel would have the documents entitling her to stay and work for Lana and Gareth. To teach silent Welsh to a baby she wouldn't ever see again after it was an hour old.

Lana was stretching her arms out wide now on the bright little sofa in Meriel's flat, her fingers still glinting in the light that stole through a gap in the curtains.

Gareth sat at Meriel's side, his legs comfortably stretched out, the top of his shirt open, his tie dishevelled. It was his lunch-hour and the old red open-topped Cabriolet had once again found its way to the flat, to the melody of the shells clinking in the breeze.

'I've been thinking ...' said Lana, her eyes dancing like a little girl's. 'What if we arranged a visit to the Hollywood Bowl before the baby arrives? It's a great night out, you'd have plenty of fresh air, and it's a good place to sit without having your back hurt. What d'ya say, Gar?'

Gareth stirred, as if his mind was far away.

'Er ... yeah. What d'you think, Meriel?' His eyes were burning, piercing her, searching.

'Oh, you guys are as bad as each other, you bums! It's something in the blood, must be! No wonder you Welsh never won any battles — too busy trying to arrange who'd take the first step!'

'Lana went to see *Rob Roy* three times. She knows everything about us Celts, see,' said Gareth, and Meriel laughed with him.

Not for the first time Meriel sensed that Lana was out of it, and she knew it too. It was a good feeling.

'Laugh as much as ya like. It's always like this, Meriel. Lucky it was me who made the arrangements for you guys to make a baby, or where would we be?'

It was all a big joke. Meriel turned away. 'If only you knew, if only you knew!' went a little song in her head.

And in the distance Lana was taking charge, as usual.

'An occasion to remember ... A real farewell ... before you get your body back and see the last of Gareth and me!'

The diner was busy and people were standing in an untidy, impatient line near the door. At last, Meriel found a comfortable seat by the window, and the red Waltzers plastic of the Menai Bridge Fair was scorching against her shoulder as she sprawled there waiting for Gareth.

This particular diner was alive with music and chatter night and day. Meriel came here often just to watch the world go by, observe the starlets who frequented the place in order to be seen and catch the eye of a film-producer. Things had moved on from the toady days of Hollywood & Vine in the 'twenties. You could sit down with a cup of coffee now or earn tips as a waitress.

He was late. Meriel had to turn the girl away three times. She'd stuffed her biro back into the deep pocket of her apron three times, the customer-is-always-right smile wearing off more quickly each time. This woman was taking up a table and the film crews from Burbank were pouring into the place like crazy. Eventually Meriel ordered a pretzel and a cup of English tea, so that she would have a better claim on her corner of the diner.

A bald man wearing a jazzy shirt louder than his personality came up to her. He asked whether she'd mind if he sat at her table. She smiled, and made melodramatic gestures, just in case he was someone important. But all he was doing was trying to pick her up; his bald head was plastered with oil and his eyes had an expectant look.

Eventually she managed to get rid of the jazzy shirt, by using the two handy monosyllabic words that never failed to work. Perhaps he thought she was a whore. A whore and an ambitious young girl could look much the same: the same bearing, the same twist at the corner of the mouth.

Meriel stirred the brown liquid in the cup into a whirlpool. What Lana had said yesterday had been a real slap in the face. Farewell. Fare well. Like in a film. Like on Bangor station with her parents receding further and further away from her as the train slunk slowly, relentlessly into the first tunnel. It was a word pleated between two hands, pressing, pressing, before they started slowly to be prised apart. A word that was like a kick in the teeth. Farewell.

'You're in a dream!' was what her mother usually said. And yesterday afternoon she'd woken from the dream, in a stifling little flat with the light streaming in through a gap in the curtains, splicing her in two.

Once she'd given birth, she would have to say farewell. It was down in black and white, it had been decided beforehand. She would hand over the small bundle, shake Lana's ringed hands for the last time, and slowly extricate herself from Gareth's firm, manly grip.

Then she would step out onto the sidewalk and off she would go, the blood trickling down her legs. No one would know. No one would notice. She would avoid the Vietnam Vets in all their hirsute splendour, step over the kids playing poker on the hot asphalt pavement, along the empty pavements, in a city full of cars with other people in them.

Meriel had to see him. She glanced at her watch. For someone who was always punctual, Gareth was late. Very late, in fact.

The big white limousine was waiting patiently in the well-kept cemetery, its wide bonnet dignified under the shade of a large tree.

The small cluster of people stood like crows around the neat oblong hole in the ground. From where she was standing under the tree Meriel could make out Lana's trim figure elegant at the graveside, leaning on another smartly dressed woman. Out of the corner of her eye she saw other groups of mourners like blackberries here and there, acting to the same script, and the gravediggers slogging away in the midday heat.

She turned her attention back to the first group. The minister was speaking in Welsh, and even from where Meriel was standing, the language sounded stiff and inflexible, as if taken out of a box, all dusty. The words hovered in the warm breeze for a moment before sinking back into the green artificial grass of the cemetery.

The door of the limmo opened with an expensive clink and the chauffeur got out, deftly lighting a cigarette with his right hand and smoothing the front of his suit with his left. He scanned the fine blue sky as if searching for a cloud. At last his eyes alighted on her and he walked over, and stood under the tree.

'Ya knew the guy?' he asked, the peak of his cap nodding towards the mourners.

Meriel shook her head.

The man took a drag of his cigarette and the tip glowed for an instant. He stared at her through half-closed eyes. For a moment he said nothing. Meriel was aware that he didn't believe her.

'I guess he came from England,' he said at last. 'Garry. Did well for himself — married Lana Mackenzie, the producer. D'ya know her?'

No. She'd never heard of her.

Muffled singing could be heard from the direction of the grave, and a Welsh hymn came wafting its way towards them.

'He had it all.'

'Is that so?'

'Everything ya could want. Big house in Brentwood. Large real estate business. A wife like Lana Mackenzie ... And now this...' The chauffeur took off his cap. He ran his fingers through his hair like a film-star before replacing it on the back of his head with style.

'And now this,' said Meriel to herself.

'Heart-attack ...' said the driver authoritatively. 'It's kinda hard to understand some things, huh?'

There was a breeze from somewhere and an earnest whispering in the leaves of the large tree.

'Yes,' said Meriel. 'It's hard to understand some things.'

And as she spoke, she was certain she could feel the little Welshman stirring in her womb.

Going In

Meg Elis

The worst thing is the waiting. Once the initial shock and sheer panic are over, you have a chance to think. And that's when it gets tough. While you're waiting. Oh, not waiting to see how your commitment and determination will stand up during the months of imprisonment — that's not what I mean, though that's the face you show to the world. What hurts are the little things. Silly things, like what'll you do about subscriptions to magazines, and what'll happen to your bank account, and what the hell will you do about your period if you can't use tampax in prison, only those old rags you gave up when you were fifteen? Nobody mentions the little things. All you hear is how people feel when they look out through prison bars in the direction of Wales — and that's daft, anyway, because Meurig's cell was facing east, so when he was homesick he was staring in the direction of Manchester. No one would have admitted that, though, it would have made him look a fool. No, he was someone special, set apart: he'd been in gaol, so people respected what he had to say.

What'll I tell people when I come out? It's stupid to start worrying about it now; I've got so much to do and finish before going in. But I'm worried all the same — will people think of me differently, expecting some great truths from me? As if prison changes your character - just like that. Do they expect me to become introverted, a girl like me who enjoys a bit of fun, is rather lazy, and has fits of worrying about the language — and come out a determined creature, resolute and still active? That's silly. But is that what they're expecting?

'You sound as if it's the end of the world,' said Huw when I rang him with the news.

'It's the end of my freedom.'

'Think so?'

'Almost certainly. I broke a suspended sentence, and only about three months after it was imposed. And this offence is quite a serious one.'

'So it's six months for you, is it?'

'Quite possibly. Are you surprised now that I sound as if the world's coming to an end?'

'Afraid you won't be able to stand it?'

'Nonsense. What I'm afraid of is missing the Eisteddfod.'

'Oh.'

All at once he began laughing, and hearing him at the other end of the line, I began to do the same, until both of us could hardly speak, and the conversation which was to have been so serious and sensible was collapsing in giggles and laughter.

We just about managed to arrange to meet; we couldn't say anything else because we couldn't stop laughing. As I left the kiosk, the smile was still on my face. Then suddenly I paused to consider the matter; I stopped to think about it. It was ridiculous — well, seriously, I hardly had cause to make a fuss, expecting to go in as I was. Be sensible, girl, be sensible. I tried to sober up by thinking about horrible, unpleasant things in prison — the childish, monotonous work, the screws, the regulations, the food ... but it didn't work. Hearing Huw's voice on the 'phone, and knowing that I'd be seeing him soon, had raised my spirits above all that, and made me feel that the commitment and heroism and everything else the *Cymdeithas* went on and on about belonged to someone else, and I had no part in it.

Afraid of missing the Eisteddfod, indeed! Was that a proper thing for a language-activist to say?

Well, yes, it was, possibly. I'd be deprived of one of the high points of my nation's culture — and there I was, off again. What I regretted missing was boozing with the gang, not the chairing of the bard. And feeling as if a year, instead of a week, had been stolen from my life, because I wouldn't be seeing those old friends I never see except at the Eisteddfod. And things weren't the least bit better when I realized that I'd be out of prison a fortnight after the Eisteddfod. A hell of an anti-climax. If I were to be released in the middle of Eisteddfod week now — but there was no way I could arrange that ...

I woke from my reverie and found myself almost home. If my intention had been to come to my senses, I'd succeeded — by now I felt quite downhearted. But the reason for that was thinking of missing the fun, not giving serious thought to what imprisonment entailed. I'd better not try to think like a martyr — I'm me, myself, that's who I am. I closed the door of the flat behind me and sighed as I thought of the pile of work I had to finish before the trial.

Real martyrs wouldn't fret about how to find time to wash underclothes before going to court ... I flung a pile of dirty things into a corner and moved on to the next mess. And do heroes manage to answer every letter than needs answering, and do they tidy all their books and put them in order — ? My letters slid in an avalanche from the kitchen table and I tried to save them, but only managed to cuff one of them back into the butter-dish. Ah well, it didn't require an answer, anyway. But the others ... . I'll never have time ...

I sit down on the only empty chair and look around the kitchen. It isn't much comfort to know that all the other rooms are in the same state. If only there were someone to give me a hand. I've got plenty of mates who'll be prepared to interrupt the court proceedings for my sake; if they were a bit readier to do the dusting for me, I'd appreciate it ... Now I'm being ungrateful, and martyrs / activists / heroes aren't supposed to be ungrateful ... I'd be glad to have someone to lend a hand —

The doorbell made me jump, and as I went to answer it I was stuffing the worst mess into corners and cupboards, kicking a clear path to the door. As I opened it, there was Huw.

'Hello. You didn't take long.'

'Glad to see me?'

'Of course. But don't expect a grand reception, will you? Look at the state of this place.'

He follows me through the passage and into the front room, and it's worse there than in the kitchen. I glance around the room, then at him and then I smile, and he hasn't noticed the mess, and by now I'm not worried about it either, nor thinking much of all the chores awaiting me. I smile, afraid that we might burst out laughing again, like we did over the 'phone. That's one of the funniest things about this whole business, but it won't do, because martyrs have to be sensible and serious. He came here to have a sensible chat. But he's still smiling. Then I thought it would be best if I started things. Without smiling. Sensible. I don't look at him.

'I've got so much to do.'

'How d'you mean?'

'Well, look around you. I've got housework to do. Cleaning, tidying up, and so on. Not to mention packing.'

'Oh. Oh, yes.'

It's obvious that he hasn't given it a thought. Does Huw, too, think prisoners for the language — or even prospective prisoners — live in a world apart where there's no such thing as housework? I'm gradually losing faith and thinking the authorities should have got hold of someone more suitable to imprison. I don't fit the pattern at all. Huw's still looking at me without understanding. Farewell to the sensible chat. It looks as if it's farewell to any sort of chat now. But Huw's looking as if he's thinking seriously: he's looking around and even starting to pick things up off the floor and put them in drawers. The wrong drawers, but what does it matter? He turns to me, about to speak, about to have a serious talk.

'You're busy.'

'Looks like it.'

'Mm.'

End of sensible chat. He's not doing much at all now — fidgeting, picking things up, then letting them drop to the floor, the table, wherever they happen to fall. Suddenly he turns to me:

'Haven't you got other things to do?'

'Like what?'

'Well — all this housework, clearing up like this. Are they important? Do things like that matter now you're going in?'

'What do you expect me to do? I have to get my things together.'

'Yes, of course, but — well, there are other things, aren't there?'

'What do you mean?'

'Aren't you going to say something in court? A speech?'

'Yes, probably. I'll write something. Nearer the time.'

'So you're not in any great haste to do it?'

'Should I be?'

'Well, hell, girl, you're up in court for what you did on behalf of the language — it's highly likely you'll be locked up. Don't you want to say something to convince people?'

'Oh.'

So now I know. I sink into a chair, first brushing a pile of books out of the way. He thinks like that as well. In his eyes I'm no longer myself, not Bethan his girlfriend, but Someone Who's Going To Prison For The Language. Damn him! Damn the language! Damn everyone for not letting me go to gaol in my own way. I explode, lose my temper amid all the mess, and pace about the room like a lion in a cage.

'So why don't you go to gaol? Why don't you try to convince people with your terrific speeches, and let me be, why don't — '

'Hey, hang on, what's the matter?'

There's no anger in his voice; he's genuinely concerned. I stand there facing him —

'Afraid of going in, Bethan? You?'

'Why do you say You like that?

'Well, I know you're so keen on the language. You always

have been a stalwart. Now you're ready to go to prison, and I never thought you'd be worried about it. Not you.'

'I'm not worried. Not about going to prison. I'm not worried at all about that.'

My voice sounds much more firm than I'm feeling. But Huw's looking like a pilgrim who's been relieved of his burden.

'Oh. That's what I thought. That you wouldn't be worried. Not like me.'

'You?' My turn now.

'Well, yes. If I had to go in, like. I know how I'd be. Nervous, worrying about this and that, about small unimportant things.' He laughs. 'I'd never make a martyr, see. Martyrs don't worry about what's going to happen to their bank-accounts and their cars if they go in — Bethan?'

He falls silent and is looking at me. Because I'm laughing. Looking at him, and at the mess in the room, and laughing. Still laughing, like on the phone. Now he's starting to smile. And I'm not worried any more about going in.

Striptease

Meleri Wyn James

Jed unbuttoned his jacket very slowly, first revealing the soft hairs on his throat and then, bit by bit, the golden tangle of his incredible chest. The jacket, a cream-coloured imitation Armani, would of course be ruined. Each one had to be thrown away after just one performance.The material was as thin as toilet paper and the oil-less oil on his body left a permanent stain. This was a dreadful waste but Jed could only blame the material, comforting himself that the screams demanded the suit be part of the show.

He smiled icily at a woman who had pushed her way to the front. She stood agog. He was sure he could make out her tonsils — not a pretty picture. As he stared at her, Jed felt the tickle of a mild electric shock go down his spine. He had to admit there was no kick quite like the one he got from seeing hundreds of women lusting after him as they did.

Of course, their husbands — perhaps quite naturally — scoffed at his line of work. To them he was nothing but a 'poof' and it was all too easy to dismiss such a girly lump of flesh. His professional name — his real name was Colin — only added to the merriment.

He couldn't care less about the jibes. It was only self-defence on their part. They just couldn't handle the idea of men putting on warpaint every day like so many women. Prinking, pruning — soap, oil, moisturizer and body-lotion, shampoo and top-of-the-range conditioner, and just a smidgen of make-up to hide the blemishes when a man wasn't feeling at his best. Creating the next best thing to the perfect form of Michelangelo's David.

It was hardly surprising that middle-aged men were so ugly. Those who didn't believe him only had to look around and observe the ageing men with their crusty hides riddled with red veins, their lank thinning hair and flabby beer-bellies — and then take a look at their wives.

To some extent, Jed had to be vain. It was part of the job. Women didn't want to see Mr Average taking his clothes off. Was it any wonder that at middle-age women insisted on making love with the lights off? Watching ordinary Joe display his orange-peel skin and beer-gut before the highlight — the yanking down of aged grey Y-fronts to reveal a lard-coloured arse — would be more of an anti-climax.

Looking as good as someone like Jed required hard work and sacrifice. He didn't drink. Evian was tipple enough for him. The morning-after headache would be enough to interfere with the exercise routine that secured him a place at the front of the Dragon's Dreamboats. First an hour with the weights, shoulders, chest, legs, arms, and then the sit-ups, press-ups and thirty minutes on the running machine. He didn't want to over-do it, though. He didn't want the body of an Arnold Schwarzenegger clone. There was nothing uglier, in his opinion, than fourteen stone of flesh and blood moulded into peaks of hard muscle. Such men weren't normal — they were like something from outer space. A shudder shot through his carefully toned torso.

Despite the hours of preparation, the last thing he wanted was to look abnormal. That was probably why he refused to shave all his body-hair — although he did trim his eyebrows once a fortnight — or to lie too long under the sun-lamp.

Jed let his fingers caress the hairs on his chest, playfully. The oil felt hot on his fingertips and it excited him. He grabbed manfully at the top button of his trousers and popped it open. He'd had a guts full of games. He paused a moment, listening for the deafening roar of the squealing women. Then he slid open the zip. In a second the stage was as dark as night.

That probably surprised those who'd never seen him at work. They thought he took all his clothes off. He sipped the Evian in an effort to relax. He couldn't help himself, this attitude enraged him ... even to think he was that sort of man! Every man among the thirty dancers agreed that stripping naked wasn't going to excite women. They were too smart to lust after a man's body just because it was a man's body. You only had to look at the rows of magazines on the top shelf of any newsagent's to see at whose groin the basest desires were aimed.

The show was no more than a tantalizing kiss - a tease of chest, a fondle of leg or arm and then the climax: ripping off his trousers to reveal a taut backside in a red G-string.

He'd first begun to despise the idea of revealing all after seeing a young girl stripper in a London night-club. Curiosity ... and randiness, that's what drove him, and a gang of others, to watch 'Let Lucinda ... ' The very name was full of promise and five pairs of eager eyes watched Lucinda strut onto the stage. But the smile had soon waned from his face as he watched his friends ogling and drooling over the girl. She might have been pretty with less eye-liner around her panda eyes and had she allowed her hair to grow back to its natural brown. But what had extinguished the flame in Jed was the look on her face. She just wasn't interested. Her eyes yelled: I'm bored!

The women's screams showed the Dragon's Dreamboats hadn't disappointed them. It was impossible to dismiss their frantic screaming. Every night the clubs were full for the performance, and even the most bashful housewives — those who had never got rid of their shyness in the bedroom — were standing up screaming and clapping and chanting to see more, more, more.

'Oy, gorgeous!' one woman had shouted as he walked to his motel one night. Jed turned to see a greying head, not unlike his Gran's, flashing her Red Dragon knickers at him. He almost ran for his life. The thought of this wrinkled prune rubbing randily against his ripe young skin sickened him. Thank goodness this wasn't for ever, that it was merely a break — a lucrative break —

between college and a career.

There it was again, the tiny something which niggled and wriggled inside him, constantly reminding him that he could never be satisfied with this. Despite the scores of women, of every shape and form, who offered themselves to him daily — and this was no boast — they never looked up long enough to see that there was a head attached to his magnificent body. That disturbed him.

Gerald

Twm Miall

Gerald stands in the same place at the bar every night and always buys a packet of nuts with his fourth pint. He never touched a drop until his wife left him a few years ago.

It was Bart introduced me to Gerald.

'John speaks Welsh,' he said.

'Fuck the Welsh,' said Gerald. 'They only talks it when they wants to take the piss.'

For a while after that, Gerald used to sort of bark at me, until one night when he started chatting quite pleasantly. He told me he'd once passed through Blaenau Ffestiniog and the place had left an impression on him, though he couldn't say why.

He also said he thought his grandmother had come from Anglesey, but he wasn't certain. She could speak Welsh, he said, because he always called her Nain and, anyway, he could remember her speaking the language to the chickens in the back-yard at Llanbradach. That was the evening Gerald bought me a pint, and then I bought him one and we were drinking solid then till stop-tap. As we were walking out through the door, he said:

'I knows I'm not one 'undred per cent Welsh, like, 'cos I'm from Cairdiff, but d'you think I'm fifty per cent 'cos of my Nain, like?'

'You're as Welsh as you feel, Gerald,' I replied.

'Aye, s'pose I am,' he said, and disappeared round the

corner into Broadway.

One Saturday soon afterwards, Gerald came into the bar carrying a shopping-bag. He took out a brand-new camera and showed it to Bart and me. He insisted on taking a photo of us. He was holding the camera very carelessly and I was afraid it was going to fall onto the floor. He went through the most complicated motions as he took the shots, turning the camera every which way, crouching down, and so on.

He finished what he called his 'aerial shot' of us standing on one of the tables. As he tilted the camera back, I noticed he had a half-full bottle of whisky and a Welsh dictionary in his bag, but I didn't say anything. Nor did he.

Some time that summer, it occurred to me that I hadn't seen Gerald around for a few days and I asked Mike the barman if he knew what had become of him.

'He's gone on 'oliday, our kid — North Wales,' he said.

'Aye, think he said he was goin' to Blaenau Ffestiniog — that's all slate quarries round there, innit? Went by train he did, aye. Takes about five hours from Cairdiff— change at Crewe. Gone for a week, I think he said.'

Bart started laughing when he thought of the lads in the Blaena pubs having to put up with Gerald, but I somehow couldn't make it out.

Next time I saw Gerald he'd just come home from Blaena. He was pissed as a newt. He threw his arms round me and said, 'I've been to Wales, John, I've been to Wales!' Just like that, over and over.

He'd walked over Bwlch Gorddinan in the rain, he said, and somewhere near Roman Bridge he'd picked up a small yellow plastic duck from the side of the road, and put it in his pocket before going on to the castle and the Gwydr pub, where he'd dried his clothes.

'Here it is,' said Gerald, putting the little yellow duck on the palm of his hand. 'That's got to mean something, 'av'n it? Got to mean something.'

The following afternoon, he'd come out of the Queens in

Blaena at about three o'clock and hopped on the bus for Caernarfon. While chatting to the driver, he'd decided the man was talking with the same accent as his Nain. The driver was from Porthmadog and by now Gerald was almost certain his grandmother was from there, not Anglesey as he'd previously thought.

He'd gone up onto the top deck of the bus, sat down, lit a cigarette, and looked out at the grey slates shining in the rain. Then he heard half-a-dozen school kids talking Welsh, and he started to cry.

That night I went with Gerald to the door of the pub to make sure he was steady enough on his feet to walk home. I watched him heading for Broadway. As he crossed Blanch Street, I saw him waving and heard him shouting, 'I'm a'undred per cent Welsh! I'm a'undred per cent Welsh!'

The following summer Gerald went to Malta for his holidays. I didn't hear how he got on there, but Bart said he'd been drinking for ten days solid and regretted going.

Whenever I see Gerald these days, he shakes my hand and greets me with 'Shw'mai, John? and takes his leave with 'P'nawn da' or 'Nos da'.

If it happens to be raining, he rummages in his pocket for the duck, and then he remembers, quite suddenly, that he lost it somewhere a while ago.

Tea with the Queen

Mihangel Morgan

I received an invitation to have tea with the Queen. The card read:

Dear Sam,

Will you come and have tea in Ianto at two o'clock in the afternoon on Thursday of next week? I've been thinking of you often recently, especially when I make tea or coffee in the cat.

So until next week.

Kind regards,

Your majestyesty

Postscript. Phone from the station.

Her handwriting was remarkably fine. An italic hand. I had a card like this almost every week, always with the inevitable postscript and the instruction to phone from the station, despite there being no station in the vicinity and, moreover, her having no phone. Anyway, I could walk from my house to where she lived in a quarter of an hour.

As far as I knew, she lived in a hut or shed down near the old factory on some land where houses had once stood but which now belonged to nobody. The place was derelict, all rubble and stones and rubbish and weeds, but it had a remarkable view of the sea (that is, if one ignored the factories and ugly old houses and the various kinds of filth strewn all around). Despite her surroundings and dilapidated circumstances, the Queen could maintain an uncommon dignity. She dressed in clothes which had seen better days, usually old long velvet frocks with flowers on them, fashionable at the beginning of the twenty-first century, in the 'thirties perhaps. She also wore long earrings, bracelets, rings (at least one on each finger and on her thumbs too), a necklace and a tiara (everything in diamante and with many of the worthless glass gems missing). It was her coronet which gave her the idea that she was some kind of queen.

The weather was extremely hot the day I went to see her but inside her hut it was dark and chilly.

-Come in, Sam, come inside Ianto.

Ianto was the name of her hut, her home.

-I'm glad of your company, glad to see you again. Sit down.

-Thanks.

Her little old narrow chairs were rickety, and so was her small table. On the table were tea things.

-I've made tea in the cat — your cat — your present to me.

I had given her a teapot in the shape of a cat last time I was here.

-Will you have a cup of tea, Sam?

-Yes, please, Queen.

-Lapsang souchong, my favourite.

She lifted the cat-teapot and poured into the pretty little flowery cups on the table. Not one drop came from the teapot.

-Milk? she said, picking up a small jug with no milk in it.

-No thanks.

-Sugar?

-No thanks.

There was no sugar in the basin either.

-You take your tea exactly as I do, don't you? No milk and no sugar, she said, and of course everyone who knows what's what drinks Lapsang without milk — but I've put milk out just in case. You never know with some people. But obviously you know better, don't you?

-Queen, may I ask you a question?

-You may.

-Why do you always mix up *ti* and *tithau* and *chi* and *chithau*?

-A linguistic question, oh, I love questions about words, and to tell you the truth, I was hoping you'd ask.

Her face was like yellow vellum, old and shrivelled, but her smile was child-like, a lantern.

-I mix up the singular, *ti* and *tithau*, and the plural *chi* and *chithau* or *chwi* and *chwithau*, for a bit of fun. I like the variety.

-I've also noticed that sometimes you say *rwy* and sometimes *rydw* and sometimes ...

-Sometimes *yr wyf i*, sometimes *wy i*, too, and sometimes *dw i*. The answer is again that I like the variety. But in this case I also like the different speeds. *Rydw i* means something different from *dw i*, the feeling's different. Apart from that I like to rape language, I like to screw it!

-To screw it? Why?

- Because language is an old bitch, an old harridan who likes to be used. She's a witch, and an angel. She's music and din ... (she was starting to go into the *hwyl* now) ... language is a deceitful old devil. Language is a beneficent spirit. When I woke up this morning I realized that language was in the room with me before I'd even opened my eyes. Language was on my bed, she was in bed with me, she was everywhere. In the light streaming in through the window, in the curtains, in the mirror; in the cracks of the glass. When I looked out across the sea this morning I could see that language was on the sea and in the sea, in fish and water and the salt of the sea. I looked back over the city and saw the great buildings and there was language on them and in them and no one in the city can escape from language. And there was mist on the sea and the mist was stealing across the sea towards me like a monster. And I thought the mist was like language going over and through and into everything — that's what language is like, too. Language is everywhere. I get the feeling sometimes that everything's intertwined with language. I get the feeling that everything that exists is made of language. I get the feeling sometimes, believe it or not, I get the feeling that I myself am nothing but language — nothing but words and sentences. I shouldn't exist if it were not for language.

She raised her empty cup to her lips and took a draught of her imaginary tea.

-Let's go for a stroll in the garden, Sam, said the Queen getting to her feet. Her long old frock caused a breeze as it swished over the dusty floor and its folds rustled against the small table, making the dishes tinkle. She opened the door of the shed and the sun and warmth came in like an apparition. We went out among the stones and weeds — that is, into her Majestyesty's 'garden'.

-Have you heard that they've discovered the body of God in a coffin on top of a rubbish heap in Brazil?

-No.

-Oh, yes! They have! she said ferociously as if I had doubted her.

-Yes, she said again, and when I heard the announcement on the radio I remember thinking of them knocking down the houses that used to stand here where we and Ianto are standing now. The houses had been empty for years and they came and demolished them because they'd become dangerous. And they came and knocked down Nurse Reynolds's house. I remember her living there. She was a respectable old woman. There was a cupboard in the house and when the walls fell in the cupboard was opened — and do you know what was in it?

-No idea.

-A skeleton.

-A skeleton?

-Yes. A little skeleton. A child's skeleton. Her own child. As a young girl that old nurse had slept with some man and pretended to be ill for a bit and gone back to work at the hospital without anyone suspecting she'd had a child and concealed the birth, battered the baby about the head and stuffed the corpse into that cupboard. Just think of it — and she was a nurse!

-Ugh.

-Things like that happen from time to time. Little skeletons are often discovered in houses like that. It wasn't so difficult to conceal births in days gone by. And of course the shame of having an illegitimate child was something terrible. And insufferable for respectable people. That's why John Lewis's daughter went away. John Lewis said she'd gone to work in a large town overseas. But no one ever saw her coming back in the holidays and she was never heard from again. Then Mrs Lewis died and John fell ill soon afterwards, he didn't know how to cook and he wasn't eating properly. He fainted at a meeting of the Society for the Promotion of the Idea that God Exists. He had to be taken to hospital. Well, while he was there, still unconscious, his house started to go to rack and ruin. And someone spotted rats in the back garden. So some of the Society's Elders went into the house to see what they could do about it. And Llywelyn James heard a noise in one of the bedrooms. And the Elders went up together expecting to see hordes of rats. But who was there but Mai Lewis, John Lewis's daughter. Her hair was all white and she had no teeth, her nails were like old claws and she was completely out of her mind, and she was blind, too. Her father had locked her up in a room without a window and light for more than twenty years after she'd admitted to him that she was expecting a child by a lad who worked in the bakery — he'd fled when Mai told him she was carrying his child.

-Was she still alive when the door of the room was opened?

-Yes. But she didn't live much longer — the shock was too much for her after being in a dark cell and living on crumbs and cold water for so long.

-What about the child?

-No one knows anything about it.

-What about John Lewis?

-He died without regaining consciousness.

The Queen looked dreamy for a while as if she could see the past all about her in close-up.

-There were many skeletons in cupboards and under floors in the Twentieth Century, by all accounts, said the Queen.

I too looked around me, at the remains of the old houses. It was still possible to make out where the rooms and doors had been. As I listened to the Queen, who had lived in one of these houses, I had the chilling feeling that I could hear the old stones in the floor and the walls speaking and telling stories about what had happened when they had stood there.

-Why do you call your home Ianto, Queen?

-Ianto was the name of my first sweetheart when I was a lad at the end of the Twentieth Century.

A puff of cold breeze came in from over the sea.

-Let's go into Ianto again, said the Queen, I've got something to show you.

Back in the shed the Queen went over to a small chest in the corner. Bending down beside it, she opened it. It was full of papers.

-Seeing all these papers reminds me of the sad end of the Howells brothers.

-What happened to them?

-They were two bachelors, living in this street, she said, as if the street were still standing.

-Harri Howells and Wiliam Howells. Harri, the older of the two, was a librarian and Wiliam a clerk or something in town. But they had both retired. Harri took to his bed when his legs grew weak. Old Wiliam used to come into town every morning to buy tins of baked beans and the newspapers. And sometimes he'd buy a book. I remember seeing him often. A small thin man walking slowly because his arms were full of tins of baked beans and a load of newspapers. Wiliam was so regular — he came into town every day and to the same shops and bought the same things at the same time every day. Then in the winter he stopped coming. Three days went by without anyone having sight or sound of him. Then some of his neighbours went into the house. No one had been in the place for years. After knocking and knocking at the door, they decided to break in. None of the men expected to see what was awaiting them. The place was chock-full of papers standing in tidy piles, and columns of empty tins, too. Every so often, as the neighbours went through the house, these heaps came tumbling down. It was obvious that someone had set traps in them. The place was a labyrinth, a maze of these snares, and the men had to go through them carefully — if there hadn't been quite a few of them it would have been impossible — and they had to try and locate the traps before proceeding further. Anyway, at last, they came across old Wiliam dead under a pile of papers and books. Caught in one of his own snares. He'd set them to catch burglars. But old Harri was sitting up in bed expecting his meal of beans as usual — there was such an importunate look about him — but he'd gone blind and hard of hearing. He died still waiting. With no idea of what had happened to his brother. The bed was full of maggots — Wiliam never washed clothes and by the time the neighbours arrived the maggots had started on Harri's body.

The Queen was rummaging through the papers in the chest, looking for something. At last she found it and said:

-Here it is, the letter I wanted to show you.

The Queen handed me a bundle of old sheets of paper which had once been white but which had now gone grey like the clothes of the Queen herself.

-Read that, she said.

-What is it?

-Read it.

It was an old letter in scribbled writing, not the Queen's hand, but that of someone who was not used to writing often. And there was no beginning to it, for the first page or pages were missing. The letter began in the middle, as it were. This is what it contained:

... three. I don't know. I don't know where they are. They've grown up, gone off and stayed away. That's what being a mother is all about. I've been married twice. The first one was the father of my sons. And you know what he did? He'd had a row with our youngest son because he wanted to go away like his brothers, but he was only sixteen. His father wasn't willing but the lad went all the same. My husband was so upset, he felt as if he'd failed as a father, he went down to the river in the early hours of the morning and hanged humself from the bridge. So I married again. I was a middle-aged woman and my new husband was ten years older than me. And as it happened, I'd been in town shopping and when I got home the house was cold and quiet. I knew at once that something was wrong. My husband wasn't downstairs. I went upstairs to look for him. And in the box-room I keep locked now he had slit his throat with a kitchen-knife. His blood was all over the place. He was depressed, see, because he'd lost his job and there was no hope of finding another one at his age ...

After I'd read the letter, or rather the extract of a letter, since its beginning and end were missing, the Queen said —

-A sad and unfortunate coincidence, isn't it? A woman losing two husbands by suicide. But there it is, it's a strange thing, life, and we live in perplexity.

-Who was she?

-A woman who lived in these houses. We were at school together.

-How did you come by the letter?

-She wrote the letter to me, of course, after her second husband did himself in. She'd gone away and I hadn't heard from her for years. But after that disaster she didn't know where to turn. Her three sons left her as she says at the beginning, so she wrote to me in order to share her troubles.

-What happened to her afterwards?

-She was taken to a mental hospital and there she died, as far as I know.

-Have you any children, Queen?

-I used to have a child. A girl. A most unusual child. Yes, she was exceptional. She wasn't very pretty, unfortunately — her nose was rather long, like her father's, and her eyes too close to each other like my own father's. But she was very unusual and everyone recognized it. I used to go and meet her from school — she always refused to go to school, or come home, on her own, even after she was thirteen. She'd just stand and wait for me in the schoolyard. On her own usually, but sometimes with a swarm of

185

other children around her. But even in a crowd there was always something about her that set her apart.

Silence fell like a curtain in the hut.

-What happened to her? I ventured.

-She went down to the village, on her own for once, on an errand for me and to post some letters — she had begun to go out alone at last — she went to the shops and to post letters, one to my sister and the other to my cousin. The letters were delivered but no one has seen my daughter since ... That was thirty-five years ago.

The Queen offered me a cup. It was impossible to refuse.

-I worried and grieved for her for years. What had happened to her, was she safe, was she still alive? The police were unable to find any trace of her. I became suspicious of all men. I believed she'd been abducted. Then I changed my mind — this was years after she'd gone missing — I realized that she'd vanished. No one could have abducted her in broad daylight around here, everyone knew her too well, and the place is too open. No, she'd vanished. I don't understand but I do know that's what happened to her.

She was quiet for a minute with a faraway look in her eyes.

-But I still expect her back. That's why I refuse to move from here even though they've demolished the houses.

Presently the visit came to an end. I'm looking forward to the next one, when the stories will once again be different.

The Pizza Man

Owain Meredith

He looked at his watch for the umpteenth time, and still it was 6:50 am. Perhaps the battery had gone; but he'd put a new one in only that morning in case the one he'd put in last week was dodgy.

Last week his boss had left a memo on his desk informing him that they were going to have to spend a working weekend in Milford Haven. He'd read it while drinking his coffee, speaking to a dissatisfied client on his mobile, and eating a low-fat prawn-sandwich. He'd been so excited that he'd begun talking about New York Pizzas to the prawns, chewing the LCD of his mobile, and spilling coffee down his best white Marks & Sparks shirt.

And now he was sitting in the reception area of Pizzas R Us on the Gelli Industrial Estate just outside Bridgend, waiting for Melfyn Melville, his boss, to pick him up and take him on a three-day sales trip to Milford Haven. They were going to sell frozen pizzas.

He'd bought a new suit at Next for £199 and navy socks from Marxies, and spent an hour trying to decide whether to wear a laddish, flowery, trendy tie or a sober, professional one. He'd chosen a quiet maroon one, but when he got home his partner, Clare, had done her nut, explaining that what he needed to demonstrate to Melville that he was cool was a really zany tie.

For some reason Clare kept a very peculiar tie at the bottom of her wardrobe; it had bright red pepperoni on a green background. He had no idea why she kept such a thing; he would have to ask her about it. Anyway, this morning — after going to the loo for the fifth time — he decided against the flashy tie, put it in the bin, and chose a grey one instead.

Where the hell was Melville? He was already beginning to feel knackered. He'd had very little sleep, tossing and turning in the pine bed, going over in his mind what he was going to say. This trip with Melville was his big chance. He'd heard from Karl in Accounts that the West Swansea job was coming up because Siôn Dalzell had gone to work for Pizzas U Like, the firm's main competitors. He had to make a good impression on Melville. In fact, Karl had been an endless source of info about how to make an impression. So why was he still a clerk? Well, that didn't matter now.

According to Karl, you had to demonstrate a thorough knowledge of the product and, at the same time, be a bit of a lad. The occasional dirty joke wouldn't be out of place, he'd said. He'd have to show that he understood the strategy of the latest toppings and that he knew the whole thing was a rip-off. He was grateful to Karl for this advice, and gave a nervous little smile to Marjorie, the receptionist.

He'd just let off a sly fart when the automatic doors of the main entrance opened and Melvyn Melville came straight up to him. He leapt to his feet like a scalded cat, trying to shake off the unfortunate smell.

As the silver Jaguar slipped noiselessly down the fast lane of the M4, Alun ap Rhidyll took a deep breath. Okay, okay, so things weren't going too well so far. He'd got off to a bad start, running towards Melvyn Melville and slipping on the shiny floor of the reception area : unknown to him, Clare had polished the soles of his shoes. Falling, he'd clutched at the waistband of his boss's trousers, tugging them down so that Marjorie and everyone else in reception became aware that Melville — an admirer of Eric Gill — wasn't in the habit of wearing underpants. No, the day hadn't got off to a good start at all. Perhaps that was why his boss was so taciturn.

As they whizzed past the Port Talbot steelworks, Alun tried to bring Karl's words to mind. With a slight cough, he said,'I was reading Pizza News the other day ... ' The driver went on staring through the windscreen, his face expressionless. 'And, um, I read an article by John Friedland-Evans ...' Alun paused. Mentioning Friedland-Evans, the expert on Deep Pan pizzas who was based in Abergavenny, was something of a trump card. Melville said neither boo nor bah, and Alun's throat began to feel very dry. 'He was on about the ratio of garlic to tomato-sauce and how it differs from France to Germany ... Um, I was just wondering what you think ... um, about it.'

Clearly, Melville didn't want to express an opinion, perhaps because he disagreed with Friedland-Evans, thought Alun. He tried desperately to dredge up some other clever snippet from somewhere in the depths of his memory, something from a report he'd read on the most promising pizza salesmen of the year ... then he remembered the anchovies.

Although he had the feeling that his seed was falling on barren ground, he said, 'Good to see the price of anchovies coming down ... how will Pizzas R Us react, I wonder?'

He was aware that he'd lowered his voice, but Melvyn Melville stirred from his reverie, and the large sweaty man turned to him and said, 'Alun, I talk pizzas eight hours a day, six days a week, every week of the year ... Can we talk about something other than bloody pizzas until we get to Milford Haven?'

The white-haired bear of a driver went back to staring through the windscreen and Alun noticed that his foot was pressing hard on the accelerator. He started biting his nails. He'd really cocked things up now. He could hear voices tormenting him and in the wing-mirror he saw a blurred image of Clare and himself, tipsy in a pub.

'I told you, didn't I? This is the annus mirabilis for me ... I can feel it in my bones, Clare. This is my big chance to make a better life for both of us, love.'

Clare had wrapped her arms around him and whispered loud enough for everyone in the bar to hear, 'You're my hero,

Pizza Man!'

The apparition vanished as a gang of bikers overtook the car. Alun tried to recall what Karl had said: 'The important thing, Al, is to be a bit of a lad — make the old fart feel young, one or two jokes in the bar ... you know the score.'

Alun wasn't very good at telling dirty jokes, but sometimes a man had to ...

'Hey, I heard a good one the other night ...' When his boss didn't respond, Alun suddenly remembered that he was supposed to tell this joke in a bar and after eight pints. But it was too late. 'Um, d'you know the difference between one of the Pizzas R Us girls and a ten-pin bowl?'

The silence in the car intensified. It was pressing down on him from all sides. He felt breathless and very hot. In the night-club the other night the joke had sounded hilarious, now it was only sad and dirty and pathetic. Could he avoid the punch-line? Pretend to have sunstroke? Announce he was gay and start making advances to Melville? What if ... ? It was as if he was listening to someone else as he said, 'You can only get three fingers into a ten-pin bowl.'

Another option was suicide. Open the door and fall under the wheels of that Irish beef-lorry. But perhaps honesty was the best policy ... or what if he cried like a big baby? As these ideas flashed through Alun ap Rhidyll's mind, the car sped through the village of Steynton, down the hill, along Hamilton Terrace and down Milford High Street.

It was a fine day: a blue sky, a slight breeze making the masts of the boats rattle. While Melville fetched some reports from the boot of the car, Alun turned to look out to sea, inhaling deeply. Things weren't so bad, after all.

After applying the handbrake, Melville said, 'Rhidyll, this is an important contract for us. I expect total professionalism.'

Evidently Melville had confidence in him.

Paul Creedy, the prospective buyer, was a small man, thickset, with a mop of black hair. He wore a cheap tee-shirt and had a heavy gold chain at his wrist. He managed all the burger vans of southern Ireland; he could have turned anyone into a beefburger if he'd felt like it.

They were sitting in a garish room — the window-frames needed painting — and Alun noticed Melville fidgeting. The nightmare of the journey to Milford Haven had dispersed like morning mist because, in introducing him to Creedy, Melville had referred to Alun as 'my most trusted, up-and-coming pizza salesman'. Alun sat upright and self-important in his chair. Although he couldn't make out a word of what the Irishman was saying, he could see that Melville was in some difficulty. He wore a pained expression. Time to break the ice. A dash of bonhomie was called for.

'Your furkin' cheese is Welsh best, so you charge an extra furkin' fivepence a pound, you furk' ... I don't care if it's furkin' up-your-arse best, you bastard ...'

What on earth was this Mick on about? Alun cleared his throat and then, with a little knowing smile, said, 'Of course, Mr Creedy, we all know that we're selling pure shite, don't we? If only the punters knew that our tomato sauce is eighty-five per cent tap-water, eh?'

Alun laughed loudly but not for very long.

Two hours later, Alun ap Rhidyll and Melvyn Melville were sitting in the bar of the Trafalgar. Melville sat motionless, gazing dully at Alun and clutching the arm of his chair. He'd been like this for an hour and a half. There was only one other person in the place, the proprietor, who stood behind the bar staring miserably over the pool-table at the horizon.

Outside, darkness was falling and, for some reason, the barman hadn't put the lights on. Alun knew now what the future had in store for him — the sack from Pizzas R Us, with a recommendation from Melville that he be publicly executed. The end of his relationship with Clare, which had been based on his promise that they would move into a three-bedroomed house by the time she was twenty-five, and on the fact that the terminology of pizzas never failed to turn her on.

He rose from his chair and announced, confidently and calmly, 'I am just going outside, and may be some while ... .'

The streets of Milford Haven were deserted at six in the evening. He walked for about an hour: down the quiet, shabby High Street, finding that even the Chinese take-away was shut; to the marina, where the ropes of the masts were quiet now, and the small waves slap-slapping against the holds of the pleasure-boats, with one or two faint lights gleaming through the portholes.

On the other side of the harbour, he could make out a village, its streets climbing up the side of a steep hill. He could see a pub, its lights warmly yellow against the dark-blue of the dusk. He crossed a pontoon and went through the huge gates of the harbour, then climbed the unlit back-streets until he reached the entrance to the pub. It was called The Hakin Arms.

There was quite a crowd in one of the bars. He could see their shadows against the murky windows of the lounge and hear the murmur of voices. But when he went into the bar, only two people were there — a middle-aged woman wearing too much make-up and a thin, bony man in his thirties sitting on a high stool and knocking back a pint of stout.

He sat down at the far end of the bar and asked for a pint of lager. The bony man placed his glass carefully on the counter in front of him.

'A 'ard day, mate?' Something in the man's voice invited conversation, but Alun didn't feel like chatting.

'Mmm.' He raised his pint and made for the lounge.

'Can't go in there, sorry,' screeched the woman behind the bar. 'Private party.'

Alun sat back down, two stools away from the bony man, and swallowed his marvellously cold pint of lager in one gulp.

'Only a hard-working man has that kind of thirst, mate. Let me buy you another.'

Another pint of frothy lager was set before him. Alun began to unwind, especially as the barmaid offered him one on the house.

God! they were nice people. The man had been a fisherman

for years, he informed Alun. He'd sailed round the world, but always came back to Hakin in the end, where Myfanwy was waiting for him. Yes, explained the barmaid, she had a Welsh name, though she didn't speak the language. Her father, who'd also been a sailor, had met a girl in Greenland by the name of Myfanwy. Such sociable, warm, nice people.

Suddenly, without any warning, the man put his face in his hands. Looking up again, he asked, 'So, mate, what d'you do?'

The floodgates of Alun's feelings burst open. He told them about his work as a pizza salesman, of his hopes for the industry, about the development of the pizza as one of the most popular take-away foods in the western world. He went on to speak about which fillings would be popular in future and which ones were popular now. He also told them about his disastrous day and what a bastard that Melfyn Melville was.

These two nice people listened to him attentively, their eyes gleaming. Alun could hardly believe they were so interested in him, in the story of his life — in pizzas. In his inebriated state he thought he could see them licking their lips with excitement.

'Tell you what, mate,' said the man. 'Old Jimmy would love to have a chat with you about all this. He's next door. He speaks Welsh. Go on, he'll bore you to death, mate.' The fisherman laughed crazily.

God, yes! Alun felt well-disposed towards the whole world. He picked up his tenth pint, took leave of his new friends and went through into the lounge.

It was a comparatively small room with red walls and old-fashioned wooden chairs placed here and there, a slate floor and pictures of local celebrities. To Alun's great surprise, there was only one old boy sitting there. He wore a dark jumper and a cloth cap.

Alun went over to greet him, lifting his glass and spilling beer down his sleeve as he did so.

'D'you speak Welsh? ... It's Jimmy, isn't it?'

'Aye, I do, lad ... come and sit by 'ere in the corner with me. Where are you from? From Cardiff! 'Ell, you're only a youngster. 'Ow old are you? Christ, not like me, ninety-eight, y'know, yes, yesterday. Been in ill-'ealth for years, like. I was in an iron-lung at the age of twelve, you know. 'Ad TB, you youngsters don't know you're born. I 'ad it from the cradle, see ... '

Hell, the old boy could talk, but anything was better than Melville's reproachful silence. Alun looked at the old man's face, creased like that of a pink elephant, with large watery eyes like an old dog's.

'Aye, want to see the bugger? Want to see the scar one of the Kaiser's bullets left on an innocent young lad? I'll just roll up this sleeve. Look at that. Wouldn't fancy one of these, kid, would you? But that's nothing to the scar I got when I fell under the 'ay-cutter years ago. 'Ere, I'll open my shirt so you can see.'

Alun was feeling ill. The old boy never stopped jabbering about one disease after another, and he didn't want to see the bloody war-wounds in his pale flesh. The fisherman had told him that the old boy was interested in pizzas.

'Awful, Jimmy ... anyway, I'm a pizza salesman ... '

'Pissas? What the 'ell's the matter with you, what interest do I 'ave in pissas? I caught food-poisoning during the war with that bloody Italian grub. Came out in pimples all over, I did. Still 'ave 'em, take a shufti at this ...'

Oh my God, he was going to throw up. Alun turned away to avoid having to inspect a large white pimple under the old gasbag's cap. That was when he noticed a young couple sitting at the far end of the room. He hadn't seen them coming in. The young man waved.

'Right then, nice meeting you, Jimmy ... very nice.'

He got to his feet and went over to the couple. The young blonde smiled.

'Okay, mate?'

Alun was so relieved to hear a rational voice.

'God, can I come and sit by you? That Jimmy's been giving me his medical history since the turn of the century and ...'

The good-looking, athletic young man gave a sly laugh.

'Don't worry, mate. No one's ever been able to shut old Jimmy up.' His voice was starting to harden, his smile not quite so wide now. 'Whenever Cerys and me want to talk to him about *Deep Space Nine* he doesn't pay no attention, does he, Cer? Last week we were in our voyager suits and all the old fool did was laugh and show his scars.'

'Aye,' said the girl, 'I'm not saying we mind talking about other things, see ... what's your name? Right, Alun, but we're very fond of *Star Trek*, see — not the new series, mind you. Well, anyway I don't like it, I preferred the old Scottie and his crew ... '

Alun began to feel a bit uncomfortable. These two were nutters as well. The idiot young man was explaining why *Space Precinct* was better than the original *Star Trek* and the new series of *Deep Space Nine*. God almighty! Alun was starting to feel giddy.

'Right,' he said, interrupting the young man, and saying the first thing to cross his mind. 'From around here, are you?'

They fell silent and looked shiftily at each other. Then the girl leant towards him.

'Don't tell anyone, Alun, but Siôn and me are captains on the imperial Crumble fleet, the nearest milky way to the lesser Mihangel sun. We come from the planet Elbachni in the thirtieth dimension and ... '

What the hell was wrong with that pint of lager? The glass seemed to swell every time he looked at it and he just couldn't finish it. He tried to gulp down the half that was left but again to no effect. The girl was looking at him earnestly and had started going on about the bloody X Files.

'You see, we're the real Mulder and Scully, 'cos when General Eigionaeth was planning the first trans-stellar mission ... '

Why didn't she stop this bull-shit? Alun had a headache and he was beginning to sweat.

Suddenly he noticed from the corner of his eye that a middle-aged man was sitting alone on the other side of the room. He had a rollie in one hand and a copy of the *Mirror* in the other. Alun pulled himself together.

'Hey, that's Wil over there ... Well, thanks for the interesting chat ... See you.'

He leapt to his feet and went over to the man. He sat down

close enough, he hoped, to make everyone else think they were friends, but far enough away from the stranger so that he didn't have to speak to him. He concentrated on finishing his pint and got ready to leave. He began gulping down the lager, spilling it all over his shirt and suit. He was downing it like a horse, but was still unable to make any impression on the drink.

As he put his glass down on the table, the rollie-smoker came to sit at the table opposite. He was smirking at Alun.

'Don't worry, I'm from around here. I come here every night. You've met some of the village weirdos tonight.'

Alun smiled wanly. There was a very tight feeling in his chest. What did this fella want?

'Mind you,' the man said, in a calm and fatherly voice, 'there are some who say that I tend to go on a bit. But every man should love his work, shouldn't he? I'm a tyre-salesman, just outside town, on the way to Haverfordwest.' He lit a fag and drew on it vigorously. 'All kinds of tyres, you know — big ones, little ones, medium ones, motorbike-tyres, car-tyres, tyres for lorries, buses, I've even got tyres for bicycles, you know. Let me have a butcher's at you now. You look to me like a man who drives a Peugeot or something similar. So you'll be needing a Michelin 1.8 pressure, and you can always get remoulds, of course ...'

Alun was drunk, he felt ill, his chest was hurting as if someone was tightening a cord around his ribs, he had a splitting headache, and this blasted man was going on as if tyres were the most interesting things on God's earth.

Oh shit! Jimmy was shuffling over and shouting something about a wound that had re-opened on his backside. Alun was about to get to his feet, but the two paranoid trekkies were standing over him and whispering something about a time-warp and crossing the boundary between this universe and another. The bony fisherman and his wife were sitting on either side of him. Where the hell had they all come from?

'Of course, haddock is nicest cooked in white wine but I don't like fish myself,' the fisherman's wife was saying.

'Please, please, I've got to go,' pleaded Alun.

But Jimmy's hand was on his left shoulder.

'Aye, see, it was bloomin' gangarene. I was in the hospital for two years. I hate hospitals, see, you go in healthy and come out dead ... '

Alun tried to get up but the trekkie's hand was on his right shoulder.

'Have you seen the ninth episode where they meet the Klingons and ask, "Where have you hidden the protector?" '

Alun threw a wild glance at the rollies man. He was grinning broadly at him.

'Of course, I'm not saying that Veltrum makes better retreads for tractors than for cars ... '

Alun's head exploded under the weight of the platitudes — and then everything went black.

It was a young girl with pigtails, dressed in an Adidas top.

'Hey, sorry to bother you. I'm a bit lost. I'm looking for Hakin Hall. The Gorkies are playing there tonight and the man in the bar said you'd know where it is.'

Alun smiled. 'Yes, 'course I do ...'course I do. I expect a teenager like you is very fond of pizzas ... Sixty per cent of Welsh teenagers like ham and mushroom, you know ... they make all kinds of pizzas there — big ones, round ones, some with cheese ...'

The Woman Next Door

Angharad Price

The woman next door told me. She above all others persuaded me
to renounce three things: my job in a large bank in London; my
lover and colleague, George; and all other follies. I was summoned
home by the death of my grandfather, and the need to put his
things in order, and whether to keep or sell the house, Gorffwysfa.
Ours was an ordinary and friendly village somewhere between
Snowdonia and the sea. The people, in the main, were kind and
considerate, and sometimes shy. There was a shop, two garages
with petrol pumps — the village lay between two larger towns —
three chapels and a primary school from the nineteenth century.
Occasionally the chip-shop would re-open until we grew tired of
potatoes and fat.

It had a Hebrew name: Bethlehem. I'd been brought up
under the frown of Grandfather and neighbours on both sides.
Bethlehem had been built by the quarry-owners in the heyday of
the slate-industry. Few quarrymen were still alive; some had died of
old age and the remainder of dust. Most of the children's fathers
weren't quarrymen; nor was my grandfather. But, like Prince
Charles himself, we'd observed in the museum the craft of
extracting, splitting and loading slate. We walked along the track
of the old quarry-line as far as the Menai Straits; we learned 'The
Old Quarryman' by heart for the village eisteddfod; we went to
Sunday School to give thanks and pray for those less fortunate, and

on a trip to Rhyl in July.

The terrace was somewhat apologetic, puny — though not by choice — and aware of it. It snuggled back-to-back with a longer terrace. There was a Methodist chapel at the far end, also aware of its obscurity. We stooped on entering and squatted as we peered through the window in search of daylight.

The house on the corner was a shop. The owner — a stout, slow woman — kept a pigeon-loft opposite. She raced the birds on Saturday afternoons and their cooing was louder than hers. Sometimes children would pause on their way round the village and tease the birds — out of boredom. Another meeting place was the telephone box on the main road where we'd ring each other's houses without inserting coins. All this in a village which was otherwise quiet.

Gorffwysfa had two bedrooms — one for me, one for Grandfather. The beds in both were now empty, but in one bedroom lay Grandfather's coffin, waiting to be taken to Llanddeiniolen cemetery. Old man's smells pervaded. I wouldn't be keeping Gorffwysfa. Strange to think: bricks and mortar were my only connection with home now. What were the people to me?

'Your grandfather left here in order to fill his soul with hope and despair.'

The woman next door rushed this sentence. She seemed disconcerted and was observing me. Gorffwysfa was no longer the axis and she'd become a woman with no address. Having left next door, she'd become strange and real. Grey-eyed, her glance caressed all objects, and her skin was pale. There was a peace about her, not unlike the peace of the grave. She was a handsome woman but had never married, and now sought acknowledgement of those words.

'Grandfather was a hymn-writer,' I assured her.

'A hymn-writer and a psalmist, but with poetic aspirations. As a youth he'd wandered the mountains of Snowdonia. Never really saw them, only heard rhymes in every echo.'

I nodded and confirmed: 'The Snowdon echo.'

'Yes. He left Snowdon's people to seek colours other than

blue. It was a difficult thing to leave like that. People didn't in those days — they stayed put.'

'Just like today then.'

'No, it was different then!' the woman next door retorted, ceasing to look at me, bowing her head and seeming to stare at the sky beyond the quarry. 'You know nothing about the time before you're born.'

She'd always been quick-tempered and yet ready to forgive. Not surprising that many around here were jealous of her. I brought her back to her story by saying: 'Heaven is blue, isn't it? But living here between Snowdonia and the sea, Grandfather had nothing to compare it with. A spectrum of blue.'

'You're right, my girl.'

She caressed the space between us with a stroke of her hand, as if brandishing a paintbrush, dirtying an image in the air. Perhaps she did possess the artist's imprudent nature. Bold and splendid, she daubed truisms between the two of us, then used words to prevent the colours from fusing. 'Your grandfather possessed a triple conscience: that of the puritan, the poet and the Welshman. He left Bethlehem in order to lose himself, and took neither his religion nor his Welshness with him. No, he retained only one vocation, that of the poet, which bridged the gap between here and there.'

'Where did he go then?'

'He came to Tuscany ... '

I'm sure the woman next door said 'came', but when she repeated herself, 'came' had changed to 'went'.

'Your grandfather went to Tuscany and discovered the lapis-lazuli ceilings of the cathedrals with their golden stars, calm and symmetrical. He fondled the breast of the Madonna, touching the body of her suckling child, felt the child's hand clutching his hand and heart. He discovered the black and white marble pillars in the churches of Siena and Lucca, marvelled at the colours of Giotto and Masaccio, sensed the pain and pleasure of going beyond, and desired it for himself. He delighted in Francis of Assisi's love of creatures. He cowered beneath Donatello's prophets as they challenged him to respond. He viewed Brunelleschi's red dome, felt the mystery of its brickwork and ribs. In the octagonal baptistry the devil was punishing sinners.

'Boys and girls in the street in sunglasses spoke in tongues. There was colour on their faces as they acted in the street's pageant.'

The woman next door paused. She removed the saliva from the corner of her mouth with finger and thumb, then swallowed.

'Your grandfather let go. He tasted of the plums and olive-trees in the orchards, and of the juices in the fields. It left a sweet green taste in his mouth, familiar to Tuscans. He drank deep of the red wine of Montalcino.'

But Grandfather had never been a drinker. He'd frowned on the villagers. On hearing them singing hymns past our house on Saturday nights and early on Sunday morning he would gulp down his tea, clenching the cup in his fist.

'I'm sorry, but I'll have to interrupt. Grandfather didn't drink. Stop lying at once, before I lose my temper.'

She'd made me very angry with her gossip. But to avoid a quarrel with the woman next door, who was strangely calm, I added:

'What I mean is that I can't recall Grandfather taking strong drink. Can you blame me for defending him in his absence?'

'May I proceed?'

'By all means.'

And the woman next door proceeded. I relaxed and leant back against the chair, listening for any sound from the bedroom where the coffin lay.

'Drinking deep of Montalcino's finest wines, his thirst was such that no one could quench it. Your grandfather's lips were stained with Brunello wine, his teeth and tongue the colour of blue slate, redness mixed with the sun's freckles on his nose. It was the redness of flowing blood; he never touched the colourless Grappa.

'Your grandfather was a handsome man, as I said, intent on becoming a poet and experimenting with colour and sound.

Helpless and charming, he knew when to laugh and when to sulk, and when subtly to mention his own innocence. He handled the women well, yes, he learned how to love when he left here for Italy.'

When the woman next door finally paused her colours still hung in the air, filling our house, Gorffwysfa, spreading over the plain walls, dripping onto Grandfather's bookcase, over the books, forming puddles on the carpet which finally absorbed them.

I was angry with her again on account of the mess she'd made. In truth, her story was familiar. It was my story.

'Shame on you, ridiculing Grandfather like that! What do you know about him that I don't?'

'What does anyone know about anyone?' she muttered.

'Everyone knows everything about everyone around here.'

'So they say.'

'And knows nothing at the same time,' I concurred despite myself, for the woman next door and I were, in the end, rather similar. 'If Grandfather was far away, the Snowdon echo couldn't have known anything, let alone report it. And he never told me about any of that, which is strange as we were so close.'

This was a jibe.

'It was a hot day,' she interrupted. It was difficult not to admire her for her perseverance.

There she was again with her coarse paintbrush, showing up the space between us by filling it with colour: a thick pink stripe here under the lamp; a yellowish-red circle like the yolk of an egg, like the setting sun; a dab of black hovering over Grandfather's clock; a square ruby hanging under her right ear like an earring. She drew an egg shape in gold, pushing it away with the handle of the brush until it came to stand in front of Grandfather's favourite painting — that of the old woman of Salem with the devil in her shawl. The woman next door was having fun painting and laughing at the same time. Her face creased as she enjoyed herself.

The colours were familiar. Nicer to have them in Gorffwysfa than not to have them at all. They were alive, and made a mess of the house and furniture. They filled everywhere. She was welcome to her fun. I refrained from getting upset.

'Is this a new story?'

'A new slant on the old. Hold your tongue and listen, young lady,' she scolded. 'It was a hot day at the convent of San Antimo near Montalcino. Your grandfather was dying of hunger and thirst. Food and drink were provided by the convent for anybody in need. He was unwilling and proud, but faint when he reached the door, suffering from too much wine; his lips were dry and cracked. He was put to bed and looked after for two or three days, I can't be sure. The white nuns of San Antimo all loved him secretly. Who could blame them? And he too loved being there.

'He claimed that he would immortalize them in his poetry. Of course, only God can bestow immortality, but there were those on earth who worked on God's behalf: poets and other artists, for instance. This too pleased your grandfather. He recovered unwillingly.

'He ate in a cool room beneath the refectory. Through the window was the yellow and dark-green Tuscan landscape. He'd been set aside on account of his sex, that's to say, because he was a man. He felt a bit sorry for himself, no doubt.

'A girl from the village, not the nuns, served his food. She was pretty and very young. They knew almost at once that they were aiming for the same place.

'Only gradually did they draw closer. She was wary of the foreigner with his strange lilt — it was said that he wasn't an Englishman — he was altogether more impetuous. But he held back, anxious not to rush things, and feared the gloom after she'd left when he tried to sleep and recover. Slowly, in that cool room, they became acquainted. They would have twenty minutes at a time and weren't supposed to speak. Nor did they, at first.

'For him she was a saint, an angel at least. She shone in the darkness of the room, especially at evening, as if illumintaed by the setting sun. He saw in her face the features of Mary. After she'd gone he remembered the curve of her thigh. The stranger's skin was pale, his shoulders broad, and he had long sturdy legs; he was more like a statue than the local boys.

'They smiled and then spoke, holding each other's gaze and blushing a bit. Talking was a relief, the words conducting the heat from their bodies and into the landscape. They would talk about everyday things. Fearing she would ask about here, he did most of the talking. She gleaned things from the silences without his knowing, and from the movements of his body as he ate. She came closer, sometimes accepting some food. Leftovers were sent back to the kitchen and this caused raised eyebrows. Anna had black eyebrows and black hair, tied back.

'There was no going back. Still cautious, they hadn't touched each other. He was oddly reserved. She was too beautiful. Your grandfather feared losing control. Wasn't poetry his first love? But one day Anna bent over him and her body was smooth as a sickle. Touching was a shock. Her breast was softer than the marble breasts of the effigies. As they kissed the world turned around ... '

The woman next door suddenly fell silent. I looked up and froze as she groaned loudly. And then I saw myself in her.

It was a long time before she went on with her story. I wasn't listening any more.

'Your father finally came back and you with him ... '

'What did you say?'

'Your grandfather came back and you with him as a baby. Soon afterwards I moved in next door. He brought you up here. It was in Gorffwysfa and in Bethlehem that his soul was filled with hope and despair, with you. The words never came again to conduct the heat from his body, nor did they bring it in. What did this blue landscape have to offer except something hard and cold? He forgot everything as he brought you up, attempting to salve two-thirds of his triple conscience. Such poetry as he wrote was lullabies for you. The story was known to all, except you.'

'Stop it!'

And the woman next door stopped. Her voice was hoarse anyway, and the words had failed to prevent the colours from congealing into one another, forming a rust-red smudge. But before she withdrew again to next door, I had one more question.

It didn't embarrass her: 'Why did you never marry?'

'I've been through love and come out the other side. Why marry, except ...?'

'Except what?'

'Except to have children.'

She threw back her head, looked at me and parted the colours which were a mess between us.

'I'll see you tomorrow at Grandfather's funeral.'

'We'll stand closest to him, as it was when he was alive. You in London and me next door.'

I could have run after the woman next door and stabbed her with the handle of the paintbrush, but decided not to. Strange that nobody had said anything. Perhaps the pigeons had cooed loud enough. And as if she were reading my mind, the woman next door turned and called: 'I was closest to him, not you!'

Our house was not sold after all. I came back to Bethlehem to correct my memories. Gorffwysfa was still apologetic. Sometimes I have chips. Occasionally I send letters to my friends from the post-box near the shop on the corner, mostly to George in London. It gives me something to do.

I live by painting pictures on pieces of old slate. Quotations from psalms or verse by local poets, with coloured patterns. They're sold as souvenirs in the museum at Llanberis. Sometimes I daub paint all over the house.

I shan't move away until the woman next door dies. Haven't I some responsibility towards her? Even then, I might not leave. Because then I'll be the woman next door for others. But it was she who showed me how easy it is to lose yourself here. The woman next door taught me to paint camouflage over the house and over myself. It was here, in fact, that I turned blue. Inside me flows the red of Montalcino wine.

The Cuckoo's Time is April and May

Robin Llywelyn

I sat down at the base of a large tree to watch the sunlight play among the leaves and listen to the world. Quietude is difficult to come by, difficult to find. I wonder whether the cuckoo found it somewhere? Or is it still searching the old peaceful lanes of Eifionydd or Meirionnydd? Or is it tasting the warm grapes which ooze towards it through the cloud on the horizon? Anyway, quietude is even rarer. A pity to waste it, I thought, with no one to be seen in the vicinity and none wandering the beach below me. Not a soul today throwing sticks for their dogs. Yes, I was staring up through the leaves of the tree. And the sun was trying to wink at me from under the cloud and my gaze was through the branches towards the acres of sand. The sand of a tidal beach is tidy, isn't it? No weeds growing on it, nor the remains of castles sinking into it.

I never saw her coming through the wood on tip-toe. If it comes to that, I didn't see her going, either. What state are you in? she asked. I don't know, I'm sure, I replied. I put up my hand to stop the sun blinding me through the branches. The walls are the same, I said, and the same old moss is on their tops. That's what you think, she said, with the yellow of primroses in her hair and the blue of wild hyacinths in her eyes, but we didn't hear the cuckoo this year, did we? Perhaps it will come again soon, I said. Or perhaps it sings a different song now. The lands it has to fly over are too much for it, I suppose. I don't know anything about heat, she said, I prefer the rain. Rain is inevitable somehow, although it is also pleasant having the sun to play on your cheeks. But what's weather to me? Storm, a fair spell, winter, summer, I don't know anything about them. Do you sometimes hear another voice whispering in your ear?

She was looking at me as if expecting a reply. What good does it do to ask? I said. Sometimes, she said, it does. Only when the voices resound in the branches and slip between the leaves. Did you see how I searched for you while you were staring far out over the empty estuary? I saw nothing, I said, except the world over there and then I closed my eyes for an instant and saw you here with me waiting for the tide as night comes down. Yes, she said, but it's only leaves that can open without being able to close. I opened my heart once, she said then, and although the wound healed ...

She came towards me and her face was close to mine. I held his hand, she said, and wasn't expecting clay in the river-bed nor the twinkling stars. His hand was cold, she said, but his forehead was running with sweat. I wiped it with my sleeve but he got to his feet until his shadow filled the place and his breath dulled the light coming in through the the panes of the window. How long have I been awake?, he said then. I didn't know you were asleep, I replied, from the doorway, because I knew now that I had to go. I don't know where he is now or what he's doing. I suppose he thinks of me, if only occasionally. I sometimes think of him. I remember once, on the bare hillside, he came over the rise and sat beside me like before except that he was shy as he put his arm around my shoulder and tenderly kissed me under my ear. We won't go up onto the hill today, he said, it's threatening to rain and the hill is higher than I remember it, too. Small things like that make me think he remembers.

It's not all milk and honey for anyone, is it? I said, seeing her grow pale. She too was now staring out across the bay and shadows were moving across her eyes like clouds. Perhaps it wasn't with me she was talking. Only staring out and her lips moving. I never offered him anything, she said, only my heart. I still try to remember what my part in the bargain was supposed to be. And in the end I did get my heart back, though the worse for wear. The wound's healed now and the scar is very small. It's small and white here under my breast.

And when she lifted up her shirt there was the small white scar under her left breast. Love hurts dreadfully, I said, and yet we still crave it. Yes, I know, she said, rearranging her shirt. You're dreadful, too, for saying things that are obvious to everyone. They are easier to say than saying vague things, I said. It's easier to love than not to love, she said. Yes, I said, trying to think of something similar. It is easier to break than to uproot, I said then. It is easy to dirty fine white silk, she said. Faults are large where there is no love, she added. Great the hatred, and the love, she said again. Please, can we not talk in allegories all the time? I said. It is easy for the healthy who have no pain to urge the infirm to take solace, she said. Yes, I know that, I said, trying to recall my proverbs. Sufficient unto the day is the pudding thereof, I said. Enough of crowder and harp, I added. Enough is enough of singing the same song, enough is enough of honey on the fire. Enough is a little more than what you have, and enough pudding will choke six dogs. And then I shut up.

She was sitting at the base of the green tree and watching me intently. Every bird enjoys its own song, she said, starting to undo her shirt again. I didn't know any proverbs for things like that. It's pleasant to wear two shirts, she said sternly as she slipped the fine white silk from her shoulders. And here is skin without any shirt! And then she whirled the garment about her and flung it away over the gorse and I saw her angrily bare-breasted before me and her eyes were flashing lightning and her hands on her hips. She threw back her head, lifting her hair to the breeze. Wear it, then, she said, wear it over your shirt. Let me see you, in your two shirts. And she pointed at the gorse-bush with its thorns pricking the light silk, and the moon was rising over the rim of the mountain.

I held the shirt between finger and thumb and its perfume was of May flowers and I drew it through my fingers and wrapped it round me like a white flag, like the sail of a sunlit boat on Aber Henfelyn and the breeze in the flowers of the gorse was yellow and the silk fell around me like foaming waves. For such a petite one she likes her shirts large, I thought. This isn't a blouse of a shirt, I said to myself, but a Bendigeidfran's cloak of a shirt, the rough apron of the Anglesey giantess, a parachute of a shirt, by jiminy. You must be a sort of goddess, I said, having managed to get my head out between two buttons, only goddesses could wear a shirt as noble as this.

The moonlight was bathing her skin and the sound of the tide filling the beach. The next thing I knew she was pulling off her skirt. I was still struggling with the silk shirt. Take it off, she said. What? I said. Why? Because it's high tide and a full moon, she replied. Come on, we'll go for a bathe. I don't like bathing in the sea, I said, and the gorse needles are thick underfoot and it would be best if we started thinking of going home. And who said I'd come with you? she said, kicking her skirt away and starting to step gingerly over the gorse needles towards the sea-rocks. Come on, she said, the water isn't cold ... well, not very. By the time I had climbed down to the rocks she had swum half-way to the island; I could see her bobbing like a white cork in the middle of the bay as I dipped my toes into the water. I'm coming, I said, trying to shout but the breeze was against me. And the water was cold.

I didn't catch up with her, no, I had no hope of overtaking her with her swimming like a white eel. Perhaps she's a mermaid, I thought, but then they don't have any legs. She was waiting for me on the rocks of the island. Come on, she said, hurry up. Where are we going? You'll see. The sea-water ran like pearls down her back and her hair hung in coils over one shoulder. I saw her white hand being raised and her fingers beckoning. We joined hands and they were cold. Some Englishman's bought the island, she said, and he has a smashing holiday home over there. And that was where we went — she knew how to get in — and wrapped ourselves in blankets and lit a fire. This Holiday Home Englishman has some fine whisky, I said as we lay on a sheepskin in front of the fire, with crystal glasses tinkling like stars in our hands. It's only in this kingdom that we live like this, she said. What kingdom's that? I asked. No-man's kingdom, she replied. The old faraway look was back in her eyes. Yes, she said. Where we recognize without touching and get without seeking but seek nothing that's not already got. She glanced at me, adding, Do you recognize me? Yes, I said. You didn't, she said. Will I again? I asked. There's no next time in no-man's kingdom, she said. Why? I asked. Because there's no yesterday and no tomorrow, no watch and no grandfather clock. How do they know what time it is, then? I asked. Be quiet, she said. Only in no-man's kingdom are we allowed to live like that. But you won't gain it by searching, remember. And don't let your hand fail you when your turn comes to try and catch it, or you won't ever see it again. I see, I said, not fully understanding. So are you happy? Yes, she said. But why, I asked, if nothing lasts? Everything lasts for ever in no-man's kingdom, she said. But it was you who said it doesn't last, I said. The fire was dying in the grate and the dawn was grey at the window. I got to my feet and my shadow filled the floor and I wiped my breath from the window-pane to see the blue light of morning.

We could walk back along the beach, she said. The tide must be out by now. Yes, I said, looking across the dark sands.

I wonder whether that Holiday Home Englishman missed the two blankets; he probably did the whisky. Our feet were squelching in the sand and there were whisps of wild cloud in the distant east. Strips of pools lay like oil where the sea had been. Sea-birds calling. And part of the night lingered in the woods of the estuary and the dawn-chorus of small birds drowned the scream of the lonely seagulls out on the beach. My feet were tender after the sands, making me hop on one leg when the gorse-needles pricked my feet. She walked over the gorse needles without stumbling and grabbed her shirt from the bush. The morning light slunk towards us from every direction. She put on her shirt and it fitted her. I pulled on my trousers and did up my fly. I wiped my lips with the palm of my hand to taste the salt. She went over to her skirt which lay like a wreath on the ground and picked it up and shook it free of creepy things and leaves. The dew had soaked our clothes. She shivered as she drew the skirt over her ankles and up her legs. I was struggling to shove my feet into shoes that had just become two sizes too small for me. The din of the birds was filling the wood and ringing in my head. And she combed her hair with her fingers and brushed it back. And with the palm of her hand she caught a chink of the morning sunshine percolating through the branches onto her and held it as if it were a mirror in her hand. She turned to me and smiled. I caught the scent of bluebells and the smell of the beach. The light in the mirror of her hand was bright, and shining from her primrose hair and blue eyes. Slowly she turned her palm towards me and the light sparkled over me and filled me with its blessed warmth. I put my hand to my face and saw the hand light up as if a flashlamp were shining on it. I put my hand out to steady myself against the trunk of an oak-tree at my side. I could see the light burrowing into the recesses of the bark and disturbing insects and sending them scuttling to new hiding-places in their fright. No more than they could I look into the eye of the sun. And she was laughing through a cloud at the beginning of summer. I didn't see her go. I thought she was still there and that I should turn to her and laugh with her and talk about what we had seen. Then I thought I should see her when the cloud lifted from the face of the sun. But instead, raindrops began to fall on the leaves. Somewhere in the wood pigeons could be heard imitating the voice of the cuckoo. The cuckooo didn't call again this year. It wanted quietude, probably. I wonder whether it found it?

Mr and Mrs Tiresias

Siân Prydderch Huws

They say (how 'they' stick their noses into everything!) that the way you and your partner sleep speaks volumes about your relationship. So poor old Maj and Wil: their relationship hardly exists, judging from their sleeping arrangements now. Mind you, we're not about to witness the break-up of a marriage in this story. No, this is the tale of a quite ordinary couple: Mr and Mrs Jones, the middle-class, middle-aged version — her with her dog and Women's Institute, him with his secretaries. They're both still lying there, back to back but not touching. I can hardly see the top of Maj's head because she's slipped down under the eiderdown. She feels safe in her nest, the coverlet drawn up tight around her and her nightdress even tighter. Not that she has much to fear: she was released years ago of any obligation to satisfy Wiliam's requirements — others have that job now, poor dabs, though he still holds interviews from time to time. He looks like a whale compared with Maj's slim body. The coverlet slips off his chest as he breathes slowly and regularly, revealing a lot of hair.

Maj stirs like a langourous cat in the sunshine, as if her body senses that the alarm clock's about to ring. She puts her hand over the clock in anticipation: it's half-past seven, the clock rings. It's not much of a clock, though, one of these modern contraptions that aren't loud enough to wake a rottweiler let alone a big old codger like Wiliam. Maj stabs at the clock's mechanism; a pity it isn't possible to shut everyone up so easily, she thinks. She sits up and looks at Wiliam: he's still sleeping soundly. She waits for him to sense her waking presence as dogs do, but Wiliam isn't even up to dog standard! He continues to breathe quietly; she can see the crown of his head, white and large like the skin of a cold custard.

'Wiliam, wake up, it's half-past seven.'

He doesn't move. Maj gets up and shakes the eiderdown roughly as you do when beating a rug, making a whirlwind around Wiliam's body.

'What the hell are you doing, woman? Can't a man wake up in his own time?'

Now that the first chore of the day is over, Maj breezes down into the kitchen to make breakfast.

'Bloody women!' says Wiliam under his breath. Then he remembers it's only Tuesday and there are days to go before the weekend, and his heart lifts. Days of lunches, golf, chatting with the boys, poking fun at the girls — long, pleasant days at the office before he'll have to spend any more time with Maj and the dog. He starts on the daily scratching ritual. He scratches for at least a quarter of an hour every morning; he feels this does a lot for his circulation. In fact, without being particularly aware of it, he spends the better part of the day scratching some part of his sweaty anatomy. He begins with his head, scratching until the skin falls like snowflakes onto the pillow. Then he scratches his chin; there's a practical reason for this — to find out whether he needs to shave. Then he proceeds to scratch under his armpits and his breasts, boobs any woman would have been proud of. He then scratches in a straight line from his navel to his balls.

'Bloody hell!'

He feels for them again, running his hand between his legs and up his stomach. He sits up with a jolt, bends down, stands up, gropes, stumbles — there's nothing there! He tears off the eiderdown; perhaps they've fallen down between the bed and the wall, he tells himself. But they're not to be seen anywhere. Perhaps he's still asleep, having a nightmare.

'Wiliam, what's all that noise?' bawls Maj from the foot of

the stairs. No, he's wide awake, he's certain of that. He starts trembling and feels pressure in the pit of his stomach. It's disappeared! Is God punishing him for all the sins he's committed? It's bad enough taking his prick away, but putting this woman's thingamyjig in its place is unforgivable! It's intolerable, a sort of sexual slit, a useless aperture, a crack in the body. He rubs it furiously.

'A bloody twat!'

He sniffs his fingers and wrinkles his nose. He can't go to work stinking like this. He runs into the bathroom and starts scrubbing the scarlet sleeve vigorously. He imagines he can wash it away, but there's no shifting it. He pours half a cannister of talc over it, hoping that will help disguise the smell.

He goes back into the bedroom and quickly dresses, in case Maj begins to suspect something's wrong. Perhaps it was she who's arranged all this by giving him some pill or other; though perhaps she doesn't have the imagination. He comes to the conclusion that it's all Jesse's fault; she's just been on holiday and maybe he's caught some new-fangled disease off her.

'Wiliam, your breakfast's been on the table for ten minutes,' shouts Maj from the kitchen, and she thumps the ceiling with a stick she keeps for the purpose, in case he hasn't heard her the first time. There's nothing for it but to carry on as if nothing's happened, thinks Wiliam; it's possible that he's been overworking.

'Don't shout, woman, I'm coming!'

Wiliam walked into the office as self-confident as ever, his Maxwellian swagger very much in evidence. He felt a twinge of lust on seeing three shapely girls trying to get the duplicator to work. They were like the three Gorgons. He fumbled in the pocket of his trousers to see whether they'd managed to turn his vital member to stone. The grin faded as he remembered that he wasn't all man today. As he went past Price's office the door was open.

'Good-morning, Wil, fancy a game of golf and a couple of drinks and stuff after work?'

'Some other time, Price.'

Wiliam hurried by. He wasn't up to 'stuff' today. Jesse was at her desk, typing busily. He went past her in a hurry too, closing the door of his own office behind him. But Jesse had followed him in.

'And how's little Wili today?'

'Not very well, as it happens,' Wiliam complained.

Jesse rolled her eyes and pursed her lips in a mock-kiss; then she reached to fondle his prick.

'But you haven't got any appointments till this afternoon.'

'I don't feel well and I'd like to be left alone.'

'Who's got out of bed on the wrong side this morning, then?' she said, and still pouting, went back to work.

Maj had been in a hurry to clean the house that morning because she wanted to catch the ten o'clock bus to the library. She called there every other Tuesday, and she was willing to admit that she thought more of the library than the chapel. Her favourite reading was local history, but old Islwyn Ffowc Elis was quite high in her estimation too. If she hadn't had to look after the dog and Wiliam she would have liked to work at the library, but for the time being she had to make do with being a customer.

After another glance at the kitchen to make sure everything was in its place, she put on her coat ready for the bus. As she reached for her bag she felt a sudden craving for a bar of chocolate and went back to the cupboard where they kept sweets. It was Wiliam's cupboard; well, Maj bought the sweets, of course, but only Wiliam ate them because Maj had to watch her weight. But today she'd scoffed the whole bar almost before she'd torn off the paper. She didn't feel at all guilty; she ignored the blandishments of the women's magazines. She went back to the cupboard, grabbed a packet of crisps, then went to catch the bus.

Having bought a ticket, Maj decided she'd like to sit upstairs for a change. Usually, she sat on the lower deck because there were always youths on top making a din. But today it was as if something had taken possession of her: she was changing all her habits. She struggled up the stairs; these old bus-drivers ought to be prevented from restarting the bus until everyone's in their seats, she thought. She reached the top of the stairs and looked around for a vacant seat. She held her head high; the usual self-conscious feeling had vanished. Several seats were empty, but Maj found herself sitting next to a young man. He was a bit alarmed to see this middle-aged woman shoving herself in beside him, particularly as she gripped his leg for support as she sat down. Maj could feel his muscular body at her side; she imagined him swimming naked like in that aftershave advert. She was alarmed that she'd thought such a thing and tried to banish the image from her mind, but the lad went on swimming, his thighs shapely and his prick flaccid. An odd sensation went through her body; she could smell the sweat of the boy's discomfort, feel the churning in the pit of her stomach, and something moving in her bloomers. Her skirt began to lift as something started to swell. She and the boy looked at each other in astonishment; was this what was meant by The Change? She broke out in a cold sweat. She didn't know what was happening. She sat perfectly still until the bus reached her destination.

On arriving at the library, she went straight to the toilet. She nearly had a heart-attack when she saw what was causing the swelling — she had a prick! This wasn't what was supposed to happen at The Change, was it? To make the situation worse, it was hard as a fist; she had never played with herself before, but she had to do something — and for the first half-hour of her visit to the library she remained in the toilet. The librarian was surprised to see Maj behaving so oddly, because she was usually so ready for a chat. She was even more surprised at Maj's choice of books!

Wiliam sat at his desk reading *The Sun* and shaving for the fourth time that day. He shaved dozens of times a day; he had nothing better to do, apart from pinching the bottoms of his female colleagues, signing one or two letters, and looking in on meetings from time to time. He was fond of his shaver, it was so handy, running over his chin like a swan on the surface of a lake. Shaving thus behind his desk, he looked the spit and image of Victor Kiam, he of the plastic smile. Indeed, that was what Jesse sometimes called him. After about five minutes, he switched off the shaver and began arranging his papers for one of the rare meetings he had to attend that week. Having done up the buttons of his jacket and straightened his tie, he made for the committee room with his file under his arm.

It was easy to tell the committee room because you sank into the expensive carpet up to your knees. The council had spent all its budget for the last financial year on furnishing this room. The table was long enough to hold the Last Supper and the Bryn-coch Football Club's Christmas party at the same time. Whenever he was in this room Wiliam felt like Alice after she'd drunk the magic potion; everything was so big that he seemed lost in his chair.

Wiliam was to open today's meeting. He started off well enough and everyone seemed to be supporting him. (There's no need to describe everyone present, that is to say the others attending the meeting; suffice to say that all ten were exact copies of Wiliam.) Reaching the climax of his speech, he felt for his prick; he always did that when he wanted to impress, for that was where the truth lay. (The word 'testament', by the way, derives from 'testes'.) The ten men were staring at one another uneasily; Wiliam was still standing before them, his mouth wide open and no sound coming out. He was wishing the floor would open up and swallow him; all self-composure deserted him when it dawned on him once again that his balls and prick were no longer there. He managed to hobble through the rest of his speech before going back to his office with his tail between his legs. Jesse was waiting for him eagerly, keen to give him another feel.

'Wili ...'

'Oh damnation!' he shouted, turning on his heel.

Maj pulled the chain of the thunder-box and went to wash her hands. She'd never seen such a thing; her arms would be aching tonight; it was no wonder Wiliam had rheumatism, she thought. She'd cleaned the house again after coming back from the library in an effort to put it out of mind, but nothing seemed to work. She put the telly on and sat in an armchair. She was trying to relax but her hand kept playing pocket billiards. The doorbell rang and Maj went nervously to answer it.

'Hiya, love, I've come to clean the windows, look. Four for two quid.'

'Four what, my darling?' Maj replied provocatively.

'Hell, been at the sherry, Mrs Jones? Four windows I mean, but I can do you some more if that's what you want,' grinned Twm Windows, his tongue hanging out like a dog's.

'Come in then, sugar.'

Maj didn't know why she was behaving like this but she was enjoying the game. The strange thrill went through her again and she couldn't think about anything except Twm's naked body up on the ladder doing her windows with his rag and bucket. For his part, he'd sensed Maj's animal desire, and although he'd never thought of her sexually before, she'd do for this afternoon. He felt like a bull, he was going to give old Mrs Jones one till she sparkled. But Maj had a quite different idea. She'd had a bellyful of men like Twm, these blasted macho men. It was always the men who prided themselves in having their own way all the time, using women — 'giving them one'. Today she had the wherewithal to get her own back; well, on Twm, at least. But that was enough for the moment.

'Turn round, sugar, I want to see your backside ...'

'Bloody hell, woman ... or man, is it? ... what are you doing?'

'Now you know how King Edward the Second felt, don't you?'

Wiliam had never been so glad to step over the threshold of his home. He went into the kitchen expecting Maj to be there preparing his supper. But she was sprawled on the sofa watching football on the telly.

'Since when have you watched soccer? And stop staring at me, it's not ladylike.'

Maj didn't answer, just let off an enormous fart.

'What's for supper?'

'I had chips from the shop, thank you very much, Wiliam.'

'Chips? Since when did you eat chips?'

She got up suddenly and stood quite close to Wiliam. She breathed deeply down his throat like a rampant old mare.

'I want you, Wiliam — now!'

'Hell, what's come over you, woman?'

'Don't tell me you've got a headache, Wiliam.'

She chased him round the sofa for a few minutes before grabbing him by the collar after cornering him between the coffee-table and telly. She leapt on his back as if mounting a horse. Wiliam winced; he felt like a turkey being stuffed.

'Lie back, darling, you don't have to enjoy it, just take it, see.'

Wiliam's whole life flashed before him; he was galloping through hell and Maj was the harpy on his back, red-hot sparks falling from her lips. All he could think of were Mercutio's words — 'O flesh, flesh, how art thou fishified!'

A Fantasy in Memory of the Anglesey Bone Doctors

Sioned Puw Rowlands

This is the sixth time Sigrid Williams of Caerpwsan knocks on the doors of the Anglesey Bone Doctors.

How does she look, knocking?

Incandescent, lashing her tail, her belly long and bellicose, sweeping her feet; her glasses off her nose, being rubbed frut-frut in her petticoat.

What on earth has brought her all the way from Clynnog Fawr on a hot June day? For the sixth time?

It's her spectacles, all dulled and dim. They are lying higgledy-piggledy in the sideboard drawers, piled high inside the settle, taking up room for blue plates, family knives and forks, clothes and beautiful little flowers which could be opening their delicate colours in holes and corners. All useless!

Remembering this, the glasses everywhere, good for nothing, and all the money she's spent on them, Sigrid clenched every sinew in her body as if prepared to pluck each hair with a pair of tweezers. Yet her tonsils were a swollen, raw cushion across her throat, pulling rather painfully as she swallowed her spit between each mouthful of air.

The door was opened by a man, his hair coming out from under his hat like steam. He was tall, with the smallest of heads and the largest of eyes.

Sigrid could have said neatly enough, a revelation!but she wouldn't have dreamt up anything that simple, so she stares right into the steam and says,

I'm afraid that the glass-cleaning stuff you gave me doesn't seem to be doing anything at all. I'm still going through one pair after another, rubbing them all with my blue might, yet I can't see much through them, you know.

What on earth do you expect, my dear? More crumbs underfoot, or what?

You know well enough that all I ask is to know precisely what's before my nose. No more, no less.

But a pair of glasses won't give you much knowledge. I suffer knowledge, I don't rub my nose in it with the hairs around my mouth relishing its way like a gormless rake into honey ice-cream.

Sigrid laughed all over, as if bewitched. She laughed again until her breasts were rubbing against her pale little cheeks. And she laughed yet again until her petticoat tickled her ears.

Are you then telling me that there's no curiosity about you? Tell me how you manage to move bones into places as if they were nothing more than jigsaw pieces, being without curiosity? Eh? Some kind of birth-right, I suppose? Knitted into the tips of your fingers long before you slipped down your mother's red sleeve.

Come on. We'll go in, rather than standing here like two flies tinkling electricity.

Richard Evans notices Sigrid's lips fondling themselves into a sea anemone. He looks at her a while before stepping over the threshold, trying to get rid of the terrible sight sticking to his eyes — Sigrid clutching his arm by the mouth, like a limpet. He who loves Anglesey oysters. Yeuk. Really now. He thought — I could say that she dried up in the sun, just like that, in the time it took me merely to chew my toenails — too far from sea-water.

Sigrid's hair had widened and stretched its way out like the wind, like oil; her two legs quietly bent at the knees as she straightened and gave her bottom and belly a lift in and up, and for a split-second it was as if some lazy dangling piece of ivy had plucked some life into itself.

Richard Evans thought — seaweed is hair moving in the wind.

He decided to look out through the drawing-room window, down over the bent back of the garden, to the stone beach and the sea — a lazy sea which rippled without passion even in the throes of a storm. He wouldn't want to wash his grey soles in such idleness.

Apart from rubbing your glasses, what do you do with your quality time, Sigrid? Are you one of these people who believe time can move?

Sigrid imagined time tickling her skin, making its serendipitous way up her back or lying stubbornly in the troughs of her wrinkles, wilfully greedy, heavily weighing its nail-booted feet, to the delicate smoothness of her bones.

Then Richard Evans said,

People do all kinds of things with their time, don't they? They carry umbrellas over their heads along streets; sleep on beds like curdling custard; eat one saucepan after another of porridge with black treacle; or play with their feet. I mumble, you know. I garble a mutter, until the hairs around my mouth start quavering and my bones start knocking away quietly: dym-dy dym, dy dym-dy deym, and so, de-dâ, da de-dym da-dé-om, dy deyêom.

(If you're not happy with the soft sounds landing inside your ears like small balls, one after the other, like Safeway peaches, you can give up this story forthwith, and go and change your shopping-list.)

Come! Come, let us nurture a bit of filth in our little bashful heads; let us be greedy in our understanding of these two — and swallow them whole, feeling their shapes pressing their way down and up our intestines.

Her skirt is tight around her thighs. How did she manage to walk here?

And her petticoat shows.

Her head is like a puppy's, leaning forwards until she's in danger of losing her balance.

But it's a devil of a big head, isn't it?

What about her legs then? What are they like?

Solid. Duff like that.

But she has malleable ankles, and toes which are enough of a wonder.

It's a haystack on her head.

Yes, seaweed is hair moving in the wind.

But there's no whiff of a cockle about her.

Give her a good splashing of vinegar. It'll do wonderfully.

He's a doctor.

Yes, a bone doctor.

He has a wife.

So where is she then?

He was on his way with his wife to Llannerch-y-medd market. In a cart, and a donkey to pull them. And they came to bold lads leaning over the back of a wall, pulling faces, as if they had broken arms. Richard Evans gave one arm among many a good plucking, and broke it for real — imagine — until one started yelping like a dog after an escaping cat. But fair play, he gave it another tug until the arm was back in place.

So he has a wife.

He has a beetroot of a face. What he has for a face is red — on fire. And two cow eyes, blue-grey on either side of his nose. Two flat lakes. So that one expects to see them overflowing their banks and dripping their way down the ridges of his cheeks, towards the hole between his lips.

Is there any danger they might dry out then?

Of course not. He lives with his feet in the sea.

Heavy bones weighing twice her size. (Sigrid now.) And an ostrich of a man who dribbles over oysters, his eyes overflowing his head. What is this then? A story about doing sums, about division and multiplication and apportioning; the ribbons of May merrymaking or the long face of a limp tragedy?

Sigrid's magnifying glass was lightly tapping her bosom as she went into the back room in the shadow of Richard Evans. She always keeps her magnifying glass on a piece of string round her neck, in case it goes astray among Caerpwsan's trifles.

I'm a fantastically practical woman.

Richard Evans gave his head a sudden nod to show that he was listening intently and that he understood perfectly.

You're quite certain now, Sigrid, that you're doing the right thing? Tell me. There's reason in everything, you know. And remember that bones are made of 'lastic; that thumping and pulling is finite. If you change your structural shape too often, you're in danger of one day not being able to open your eyes. What would you do then? Who would do the baking? You know, everyone needs a profession.

I'm absolutely certain, Richard Evans. I'm quite witched, it has to be said, with these glasses. I can't be done with it any longer. And you're a dab hand with these bones.

Then,

Shall I sit here on the bed?

Richard Evans thought — is she on for a netting of fish to swim through her, helter-skelter? He watched her forming a right-angle with the naked face of the bed, the pockets of air forming between the line of her thighs and arms, against the rest of her body, against the line of the bed.

He thought again — one does not come to a decision like a swimmer coming up for air. It's the style I accept as a medium for events which makes me decide about things. Hum-ho.

He watched her making her face more comfortable with a pout, coaxing her mouth into a mealy kiss.

As for her, she thought — he will send me beyond his eyes, in and beyond his blue-grey cow eyes, into the soft belly of the sea.

She was immediately ashamed of having woven such a wasteful fantasy. She had wanted to be able to see properly, to see properly, once and for all, and that was all; to be rid of the wire frames and the pairs of glasses everywhere underfoot, which were driving her lover out of the house, through the front door, to spend his time leaning and muttering over the shoulder of Pont y Cim. What of treading water, with her mouth pulled into a bustle-free smile in the centre of the sea of thought, and thinking? She started to yearn for home, for a proper spring-clean.

Said Richard Evans,

You're a mighty literal one, you know.

Sigrid's eyes lit up like two lumps of red-hot coal.

Richard Evans started on his job in his white coat, his mumbling of a song filling Sigrid's ears. She was spread out underneath the palms of his hands. She was kneaded; her bones were pulled until her head was between her legs.

It's a nasty thing, curiosity, isn't it, Sigrid? said Richard Evans as he fondled her frame in jerks — It sinks into us, doesn't it?

But there aren't many who refuse its mouthy bezels.

It's enough to make me float lightly away, to see it from a distance, its feet pulled straight, covered in seaworthings, worth nothing.

In a tock of a tick, Sigrid will be on her way home, her movements a quarter of a way to being inside out. Her bones will be sore, but will be stout enough in their new harmony of fresh angles, leading her to stare at other things, driving her head to poke its tongue into new corners.

In an hour or two, Richard Evans will be on his belly in his bed, his feet over the side, thinking of hair spreading and two legs bending.

Foreign Investments

Wiliam Owen Roberts

I know you'll laugh. Before I even open my mouth, before I tell you anything ... I know you'll laugh. And I've had a bellyful, just so you'll understand, because even someone like me comes to the end of his tether and goes stark raving bonkers sometimes ... I'm talking to some young lecturer at a party, she's just finished her first term ... 'And what exactly do you do, then?' ... I pretend not to hear her ... And the conversation drags on ... And soon she'll ask, 'I'm sorry, but I didn't catch what you said ... 'I mumble ... But sooner or later, they're all sure to ask again, and insist on knowing what sort of work exactly, and with a sigh, I have to admit ...

Bursts of laughter then and hands over mouth to hide the smirking ... And not light-hearted, giggly laughter either, but laughter out of disbelief, the kind of incredulous laughter that insists on asking, 'What?' Because my confidence is shaken I hear myself saying, ' ... Do you know, for example, what our annual expenditure is?' And they purse their lips and shake their heads for a moment, their wine-glass held to their cheek. 'Did you know that £1,892,000,000 is spent annually on Health?' And they open their eyes wide and say, 'No!' 'Oh yes, it is, and £635,000,000 on Housing ... Not to mention £166,000,000 on Industry and Employment ...' Even I know as I speak that all hope is lost. I'd better not admit it, but I have a sort of weakness for facts.

And just so that you'll understand, I'm going to Japan tomorrow with the Secretary of State. Yes, putting it like that I don't doubt it sounds quite grand. Lucky man, I hear you say ... or I hear older people say, because in their eyes I've landed myself 'a cushy job'. But if you had spent six weeks rushing around the cities of North America with this Secretary of State, and the one before him, I can assure you with hand on heart that's it not all fun by a long chalk. This constant coming and going all over Wales is very laborious work. I'd like to see what your backside would be like after walking out into the foyer on the forty-fourth floor after nine hours of trying to get the Bosch Management Board to see sense, and all that time you've been on your knees persuading them to open a factory at Miskin. And them hesitating and ranting and us feeding them with all possible positive information, e.g. the local grants available, the willingness of the work-force to work long hours, flexible hours, shifts of all kinds, their hostility towards unions, and how grateful they are for any kind of work on whatever terms you, Herr Bosch, see fit to arrange ... And I can't begin to tell you about the trouble we had with the Managing Directors of Panasonic in Hiroshima, but that's another story ... I'm sorry, but I have to tell you; did you know that there are more than forty Japanese firms in Wales? The largest cluster in any part of Europe? Employing 12,000 people, mainly women? But I'm sure you're familiar with that fact already, aren't you ... ?

The air-ticket to Japan is in my breast-pocket. I can feel it rubbing against my right nipple as I hurry out of the Welsh Office past the Law Courts ... Can you guess why, I wonder? Well, so you'll get the picture, I've been corresponding with a young lady. I'd become a bit depressed by all those women making fun of me and all that travelling to the four corners of the world, so one evening I hit on the idea of putting a small ad. in *Y Dinesydd*. Nothing happened for about four months, then one morning I received a letter in Welsh, north Welsh, and in very neat handwriting, too. To tell you the truth, looking at it closely, it wasn't unlike the handwriting of Sir Wyn Roberts, and for a moment I thought perhaps he'd caught wind of my intention and was pulling my leg. It wouldn't have been the first time, because I remember being in this bar in Bangkok (when we stopped overnight on the way to Taiwan), but that's another story and I'm starting to get off the point now ...

We've been corresponding for six months (36 letters from me, 35 from her). Her name's Olwen. She's refused to say what her surname is. Just Olwen. And no picture, just thirty-five letters and all smelling of some lightly scented soap. Mmmmm. I'm hurrying past the Oriel Bookshop now because, at my request, we've arranged to meet for the first time today, a meeting in the flesh, as it were. (I've walked from the Welsh Office to Cardiff Central Station every lunch-time this week, without any sweat, and I can tell you, hand on heart, if ever you're in a hurry to catch a train, it's exactly fourteen minutes and twenty-six seconds by the shortest route. So if you allow yourself twenty minutes, you'll be there in plenty of time to buy a ticket and a book or whatever it is that takes your fancy ...)

I'm striding through the indoor market now. The reason why I insisted on meeting her was the simple fact — damn it all! another fact! I'll have to stop talking about facts all the time — stop, stop, stop it — (I'm slapping both my cheeks) — was that I'm beside myself thinking about going to Japan tomorrow and leaving her here without even having met her. Five weeks away and being with the Secretary of State? But even worse, the Secretary of State and the Overseas Economics Unit of the Welsh Office talking in the way Economics Unit people always talk, and even worse than that, the way the Secretary of State talks? Can you imagine a worse torture? I'm a fairly neutral sort of person, naturally ... but having said that, some things get on one's toot from time to time, don't they? Not to have seen Olwen would have done for me and I just had to arrange to meet her. At least, we would have broken the ice then and, hopefully, that would have eased the pain of the trip to some extent and given me something to look forward to on my return, instead of that empty flat I have in Fairwater. And yet ... yes, yes, I know what you're thinking ... You think I'm taking quite a step today, don't you? By taking the plunge like this, by

228

arranging to meet her? because what if she and I don't ... ? Yes, I know, I know ... But there, as Sir Wyn said to me in his great wisdom once in Detroit, 'What's love but a gamble ... ?'

Fourteen minutes and twenty-one — two — three — four — five — twenty-six seconds and I'm there. But there's no sign of anyone else. Right. Patience. Steady now. Steady. Steady. A quarter to one. It was a quarter to one we agreed in the letter. Doesn't love, doesn't pursuing the hope of love, do strange things to one ... ? Even to neutral men ... I'm waiting. And I'm still waiting. It's now ten minutes to one and there's no sign of anyone with a red rose ... No, half a tick ... someone's coming. Yes. I swear it. Someone's approaching me ... A young blonde with a white rose in her hand ... And she's standing at the far end from me ... She's sort of peeping at me out of the corner of her eye and naturally I'm doing the same to her ... But, unfortunately, Olwen has dark hair and we agreed in the last letter it was to be a red rose...

What shall I do? It's five past one now and I only get an hour for lunch ... I'd better get it over with and start chatting to her ... I'm a bit shy ... (Well, come on, with a red rose in your fist how would you feel?) ... I say hello and she brushes her hair from her eyes ... And we start talking ... But you're not going to believe this: by a strange coincidence, she's arranged to meet someone called Gary at this very spot ... And I tell her about Olwen ... Twisting the roses in our fingers, we sympathize with each other, what a pity, very awkward, bad luck, and so on ... To keep you in the picture, her name's Melanie and she says, 'Nice to meet you' and I reply, 'Nice to meet you, too' ... It's now twenty minutes past one and time's flying by with neither of us noticing ... And do you know what? ... (Yes, you've guessed already, haven't you?) I might as well be honest and admit nothing, but I'm sorely tempted ... The neutral heart is warming to the girl with the white rose despite the fact that I've been preoccupied with the red-rose girl for months ...

I'm being squeezed into a dilemma. I'm so confused I'm trembling. I'm in something of a tiz. I'm in pain ...

All the same: I remember all the love that's about to come true in those letters, all thirty-five of them ... And yet, the girl with the white rose and I are getting on like a house on fire, like birds of a feather. Oh, if you could see us laughing and talking here — I can't begin to describe how I feel, we're perfect partners, as perfect together as ... well, what? I'm so taken with her that I can't even think of a comparison ... as perfect as the Welsh Office and the Language Board ... seeing eye to eye on everything, sharing the same pleasures, the same interests, the same aspirations, the same kind of ideals, complementing each other splendidly ... Oh, heck! I'm tempted to chuck the red rose away ... but, unfortunately, the girl with the white rose looks at her watch and has to go ...

An instant of hurriedly trying to make up my mind: now or never! Now or never! Stop her! Say something to her! Say it! Say it!

But the civil servant in me whispers, 'Don't'.

The girl with the white rose gives me a wistful look ... If you could see the way she's looking at me it would be enough to break your heart for ever. She's taking her sad leave of me ... Moving away and half-turning to glance back over her shoulder for the last time before disappearing into the crowd ... And now she's gone. And I feel so flat ... I can't begin to tell you how I feel ... Down in the dumps ... I don't think I've ever felt as sad as this ... As if some quarry chamber has opened up in the pit of my stomach ... And I'm looking at my watch and it's nearly half-past one ... Two taxi-drivers, with arms folded, gob onto the pavement ... Suddenly it's the pits here ... take a good look at the tramps and winos with their bottles of cider in brown paper bags ... A young girl over there, eyes spinning with drugs ... The whores of Newport doing some lunch-hour trade ... The living dead ... The mess and the waste ... And that old woman, well over fifty, walking slowly towards me through the filthy pigeons, with a red rose ...

'Eurwyn?' she says.

'Olwen?' I say, and you can imagine how I feel.

'Fair play to you, you waited for me ...'

'Yes,' I said, feeling really low.

'Look,' she says, 'that young woman over there has asked me to give you this.'

I take the red rose and stride over to the Burger King where Melanie's sitting on a high stool with a Florida of a smile on her face.

'Olwen?' I say.

She puts her arms around my neck. And I wrap my arms round her and look deep into her eyes. And we kiss. Kiss and kiss until we're screeching and laughing and squealing crazily ... And the air-ticket to Japan was never used, by the way, and you should have been at Gatwick next day, apparently, to hear what the Secretary of State had to say ...

The Writers

Martin Davis was born in Llanrwst in 1957 and educated at the University College of Wales, Aberystwyth, where he took a degree in Irish and Welsh History. Since 1988 he has worked as a freelance editor and translator; he also writes for radio and television. He has published a volume of verse, *Chwain y Mwngrel* (1986), two collections of short stories, *Llosgi'r Bont* (1991) and *Rhithiau* (1993), and a novel, *Brân ar y Crud* (1995).

His story '*Rhith Rheolaeth*' appeared in *Rhithiau* (Y Lolfa, 1993*)*.

Sonia Edwards was born at Cemaes in Anglesey in 1961. She was educated at the University College of North Wales, Bangor, and is a Welsh teacher at Llangefni Comprehensive School. She won the Prose Medal at the Anglesey Eisteddfod in 1992 and since then has published two collections of short stories, *Glas ydi'r Nefoedd* (1993) and *Gloynnod* (1995), and two novels, *Cysgu ar Eithin* (1994) and *Llen Dros yr Haul* (1997).

Her story '*Prynhawn Gwyn*' appeared in *Gloynnod* (Gwasg Gwynedd, 1995*)*.

Dyfed Edwards was born in Bangor in 1966. Educated at the Normal College, Bangor, he is now employed by the *Daily Post* in Liverpool. He has published two novels, *Dant at Waed* (1996) and *Y Syrcas* (1998), and a collection of short stories, *Cnawd* (1997).

His story '*Y Llyfrgellydd*' appeared in *Cnawd* (Y Lolfa, 1997).

Meg Elis was born in Aberystwyth in 1950. Educated at the University College of North Wales, Bangor, she was Secretary of Cymdeithas yr Iaith Gymraeg and a leading activist on behalf of the Welsh language. She became deputy editor of *Y Faner* in 1982 and since 1987 has been employed as a translator by Gwynedd County Council. She is the author of a volume of poetry, *Cysylltiadau* (1972), two novels, *I'r Gâd !* (1975) and *Cyn Daw'r*

Gaeaf (1985), a collection of short stories, *Carchar* (1978), and a visitor's guide, *Eglwysi Cymru* (1985). With her second novel she won the Prose Medal at the National Eisteddfod in 1985.
Her story '*Mynd i Mewn*' appeared in *Carchar* (Y Lolfa, 1978).

John Emyr was born in Llanwnda, Caernarfonshire, in 1950. Educated at the University College of Wales, Aberystwyth, he was a Welsh teacher before becoming an editor at the Language Studies Centre in Bangor in 1988, and is now a freelance writer and tutor. He has published two novels, *Terfysg Haf* (1979) and *Prifio* (1986), and a collection of short stories, *Mynydd Gwaith* (1984). He has also written studies of the work of Kate Roberts, Lewis Valentine, Saunders Lewis, W.J.Gruffydd and Bobi Jones.
His story '*Wrth Afonydd Babilon*' appeared in *Mynydd Gwaith* (Gwasg Gee, 1984).

Aled Lewis Evans was born in Machynlleth in 1961. Educated at the University College of North Wales, Bangor, he teaches Drama and Media Studies at Ysgol Morgan Llwyd in Wrexham. He has published three volumes of verse, *Tonnau* (1989), *Sglefrfyrddio* (1994) and *Mendio Gondola* (1997); a collection of short stories, *Ga'i Ddarn o Awyr Las Heddiw?* (1991); and a novel, *Rhwng Dau Lanw Medi* (1994).
His story '*Dean a Debs*' appeared in *Barn* (1995*)*.

Bethan Evans was born at Dolgellau in 1962. She graduated in French at the University College of Wales, Aberystwyth, and is now a freelance writer based in Bethesda. She has published a novel, *Amdani!* (1997) and a journal, *Dyddiadur Gbara* (1997).
Her story '*Un Letusen Ni Wna Salad*' appeared in *Straeon Siesta: Tocyn Tramor* (gol. Delyth George, Y Lolfa, 1997).

Lowri Angharad Evans was born in Cardiff in 1966. She took a degree in Welsh at the University College of North Wales, Bangor, and lives near Llanllechid, Gwynedd. She joined BBC Radio Cymru as a researcher in 1991 and is now a Director in Training with Ffilmiau'r Nant. She has contributed to *Golwg* and the series of radio talks *Sglein* (Gwasg Gee), and since 1995 has written scripts for the television soap *Pobol y Cwm*.

Her story '*Y Gôt*' is previously unpublished.

Siân Prydderch Huws was born at Bodedern in Anglesey in 1970. She graduated in Welsh and Drama at the University College of Wales, Aberystwyth, and now lives in Ireland, where she is a freeelance writer. She won the Literature Medal at the Urdd National Eisteddfod in 1993 with *Cenhedlaeth Wag* and has contributed stories to the series *Straeon Siesta*. She also writes scripts for television and edits *Lingo!*, the Welsh-learners' magazine.

Her story '*Mr a Mrs Tiresias*' appeared in *Straeon Siesta: Rhosod a Chwyn* (gol. Delyth George, Y Lolfa, 1997).

Aled Islwyn was born in Port Talbot in 1953. He took a degree in Welsh at St. David's College, Lampeter, and worked as an editor with Gwasg y Dref Wen in Cardiff before joining the Press and Public Relations Office of S4C. He has published six novels: *Lleuwen* (1977), *Ceri* (1979), *Sarah Arall* (1982), *Cadw'r Chwedlau'n Fyw* (1984), *Pedolau dros y Crud* (1987), *Os Marw Hon* (1990) and *Llosgi Gwern* (1996), and a collection of short stories, *Unigolion, Unigeddau* (1994). His third novel won the Daniel Owen Prize at the National Eisteddfod in 1980 and his stories won the Book of the Year Prize in 1995.

His story '*Stori Linda*' appeared in *Unigolion, Unigeddau* (Gomer, 1994).

Meleri Wyn James was born in Llandeilo in 1970 and lives in Carmarthen. Educated at the University College of Wales, Aberystwyth, where she read Welsh, she has worked as the Arts Editor of *Golwg* and as a researcher with BBC Radio Cymru. She is now a freelance journalist and is following an M.A. course in Creative Writing at Trinity College, Carmarthen. After winning the Literature Medal at the Urdd Eisteddfod, she published some of her stories under the title *Mwydyn yn yr Afal* (1991) and her first full collection, *Stripio,* in 1994; she has also contributed to the anthology *Mwys a Macabr* (1996).

Her story *'Stripio'* appeared in *Stripio* (Y Lolfa, 1994).

Alun Ffred Jones was born in Llanelli in 1949. Educated at the University College of North Wales, Bangor, where he took a degree in Welsh, he is a film and television producer with Ffilmiau'r Nant. Among the serials for which he has written scripts is *Pengelli.* A selection of stories about the Bryn-coch football team, written in collaboration with Mei Jones, was published as *C'mon, Midffild!* (1990).

His story *'Y Reff'* appeared in *Rhagor o Hanesion C'mon Midffild!* (Hughes, 1990).

Goronwy Jones is the pseudonym of Dafydd Huws, who was born in Bangor in 1949. He took a degree in Welsh at the University College of Wales, Aberystwyth, and was a schoolteacher in Cardiff before becoming a freelance writer. He has published three volumes of prose: *Dyddiadur Dyn Dwad* (1978), *Un Peth 'Di Priodi* (1989) and *Ser y Dociau Newydd* (1996). He has also written scripts for television, including *Pobol y Cwm, Iechyd Da, Mwy na Phapur Newydd* and *Un Dyn Bach a Rôl.*

He is represented here by an extract from *Dyddiadur Dyn Dwad* (Cyhoeddiadau Mei, 1978).

Dafydd Arthur Jones was born in Bangor in 1957. Educated at the University College of Wales, Aberystwyth, he is now a senior lecturer in the History Department at Trinity College, Carmarthen. He has published stories and reviews in the Welsh periodical press and won the Drama Medal at the National Eisteddfod in 1983. He has also written a monograph on Thomas Levi in the *Llên y Llenor* series.

His story *'Myfyrdod ar Fin y Pwll'* appeared in *Taliesin* (83,Gaeaf 1993).

Angharad Jones was born at Dolgellau in 1962. She graduated in Welsh at the University College of North Wales, Bangor. She has been a lecturer at the Normal College, Bangor, and is now Drama Commissioner at S4C. She has published a collection of stories and poems, *Datod Gwlwm* (1990), and a novel, *Y Dylluan Wen* (1995). She has also written scripts for television.

Her story *'Annwyl Mr Atlas'* appeared in *Datod Gwlwm* (Gomer, 1990).

Mared Lewis was born in Bangor in 1964. She took a degree in English at the University College of Wales, Aberystwyth, and spent a year in Los Angeles in 1991-92. After working for CELTEC for four years, she became a full-time writer in 1997. She is a regular contributor to Welsh magazines and some of her stories have appeared in the series *Straeon Siesta;* she also writes scripts for *Pobol y Cwm*.

Her story '*Los Angeles Drws Nesa i Afallon'* appeared in *Straeon Siesta: Tocyn Tramor* (gol. Delyth George, Y Lolfa, 1997).

Robin Llywelyn was born in Bangor in 1958 and educated at the University College of Wales, Aberystwyth, where he graduated in Welsh and Irish. Since 1984 he has been Managing Director of Portmeirion, the Italianate village near Penrhyndeudraeth which was created by his grandfather, Clough Williams-Ellis. He has published two novels, *Seren Wen ar Gefndir Gwyn* (1992) and *O'r Harbwr Gwag i'r Cefnfor Gwyn* (1994; Trans. *From Empty Harbour to White Ocean,* 1996), and a collection of short stories, *Y Dwr Mawr Llwyd (*1995). An essay about his childhood at Llanfrothen was published by Gwasg Gregynog in 1996.

His story *'Amser y Gwcw yw Ebrill a Mai'* appeared in *Y Dwr Mawr Llwyd* (Gomer, 1995).

Owain Meredith was born in Cardiff in 1969 and lives in Trefforest, near Pontypridd. He took a degree in Welsh History and Art History at the University College of Wales, Aberystwyth, in 1991. He has been editor of the pop magazine *Sothach* and has

published a journal, *Diwrnod Hollol Mindblowing Heddiw* (1997). He works as a film archivist with HTV.
His story '*Y Dyn Pizza*' is previously unpublished.

Twm Miall is the pseudonym of Llion Williams who was born in Trawsfynydd in 1956 and lives in Cardiff. Educated at Coleg Harlech, he has worked as a bricklayer and in forestry, and is now a full-time writer, working mainly in television. He has published two novels, *Cyw Haul* (1988) and *Cyw Dôl* (1990).
His story '*Gerald*' appeared in *Golwg* (101, 1992).

Mihangel Morgan was born in Aberdare in 1955. He trained as a calligrapher and then took degrees in Welsh at the University College of Wales, Aberystwyth, where he is now a lecturer in the Welsh Department. He has published two volumes of verse, *Diflaniad fy Fi* (1988) and *Beth yw Rhif Ffôn Duw?*(1991); three collections of stories, *Hen Lwybr a Storiau Eraill* (1992), *Saith Pechod Marwol* (1993) and *Te Gyda'r Frenhines* (1994); three novels, *Dirgel Ddyn* (1993), *Tair Ochr y Geiniog*(1996) and *Melog* (1997); and a study of the work of Jane Edwards in the *Llên y Llenor* series (1996). His first novel won the Prose Medal at the National Eisteddfod in 1993.
His story '*Te Gyda'r Frenhines*' appeared in *Te Gyda'r Frenhines* (Gomer, 1994).

Elin Llwyd Morgan was born in 1966 at Cefnbryn-brain in Carmarthenshire. After graduating in French and English at the University College of Wales, Aberystwyth, she worked as a journalist and as an editor with Y Lolfa, but is now a freelance translator and writer. She has published a guide to the pubs of Wales, *Tafarnau Cymru* (1992), and a volume of poems, *Duwieslebog* (1993), and has contributed poems and stories to magazines such as *Golwg, Barn, Tu Chwith* and *Poetry Wales*.
Her story '*Farewell, Frank*' appeared in *Mwys a Macabr* (gol.Delyth George, Y Lolfa, 1997).

Eleri Llewelyn Morris was born in Bangor in 1950 and lives near Pwllheli. She read Psychology at the University College, Cardiff. She has worked as a journalist and was co-editor of the women's magazine *Pais* from 1978 to 1983. Among the books she has published, more than a dozen in all, are two collections of short stories, *Straeon Bob Lliw* (1978) and *Genod Neis (*1993). She also writes scripts for radio and television.

Her story *'Mae'n ddrwg gen i, Joe Rees'* appeared in *Straeon Bob Lliw* (Christopher Davies, 1978).

Angharad Price was born in Bangor in 1972 and read Modern Languages at Jesus College, Oxford, where she recently completed a doctorate on contemporary Welsh literature with special reference to the work of Robin Llywelyn. She is one of the editors of the literary magazine *Tu Chwith* and, with Frank Meyer, translated into German the stories by Welsh writers in the anthology *Tee mit der Königen (*Cambria Verlag, 1996).

Her story '*O Fan Hyn'* appeared in *Straeon Siesta: Rhosod a Chwyn* (gol. Delyth George, Y Lolfa, 1997).

Manon Rhys was born at Trealaw in the Rhondda in 1948. Educated at the University College of Wales, Aberystwyth, where she graduated in Welsh, she is a freelance script-writer for television and lives in Cardiff. She has published a collection of short stories, *Cwtsho* (1988), a play, *Pwy Biau'r Gân?* (in collaboration with T.James Jones, 1991), and two novels, *Cysgodion* (1993) and *Tridiau ac Angladd Cocrotshen* (1996). She has also contributed to *Pobol y Cwm* and wrote the script of the television drama, *Y Palmant Aur* (1997), which was published in 1998.

Her story *'Cwtsho'* appeared in *Cwtsho* (Gomer, 1998).

Wiliam Owen Roberts was born in Bangor in 1960 and now lives in Cardiff, where he is a freelance writer. He was educated at the University College of Wales, Aberystwyth, where he graduated in Welsh and Drama. He writes for television and the stage and has

published two novels, *Bingo!* (1985) and *Y Pla* (1987; translated by Elisabeth Roberts as *Pestilence*, 1991), as well as a collection of stories, *Hunangofiant* (1990).
His story *'Rhosyn Coch'* appeared in *Straeon Siesta: Rhosod a Chwyn* (gol. Delyth George, Y Lolfa, 1997).

Meleri Roberts was born in Bangor in 1967. Educated at the University College of Wales, Aberystwyth, she is head of the Welsh Department at Ysgol Syr David Hughes, Menai Bridge, Anglesey. Her story *'Gwyn y Gwêl'* appeared in *Straeon Siesta: Rhosod a Chwyn* (gol. Delyth George, Y Lolfa, 1997).

Esyllt Nest Roberts was born in Pwllheli in 1972. She graduated in Welsh at the University College of Wales, Aberystwyth, and holds an M.A. in Folk Studies from the University of Cardiff. She won the Crown at the Urdd National Eisteddfod in 1995 and is now an editor with Gwasg Carreg Gwalch in Llanrwst.
Her story *'Calon Dafydd Bach'* appeared in *Cyfansoddiadau Llenyddol Buddugol Eisteddfod Genedlaethol Urdd Gobaith Cymru,* (UGC ,1995*).*

Gwenan M. Roberts was born in Bangor in 1974 and lives in Llanfairpwll in Anglesey. She graduated in Welsh at Cardiff University in 1995 and is now completing a doctorate for research into the plays of Gwenlyn Parry. She has contributed articles and reviews to the magazines *Barn* and Golwg.
Her story *'Llithro'* appeared in *Taliesin* (95, Hydref, 1996).

Sioned Puw Rowlands was born in London in 1972. She was educated at New College, Oxford, where she read Philosophy and Modern Languages, and spent a year teaching English at Mendel University in the Czech Republic. She is at present writing a doctoral thesis in comparative literature at St. Anthony's College, Oxford. She is employed by the Arts Council to promote the translation of literature in Wales and also works for the Mercator Project in Aberystwyth. With *Diogi a Chynhyrfu* (1996) she won the Literature Medal at the Urdd National Eisteddfod. She is co-editor of the magazine *Tu Chwith* and a frequent contributor to the Welsh periodical press.

Her story '*Ffantasi Deyrnged i Feddyg Esgyrn Mon*' appeared in *Barn* (402/403, 1996).

Eirug Wyn was born at Machynlleth in 1950. He studied Welsh and Drama at Trinity College, Carmarthen. Formerly a bookseller, he is now director of a television company and lives at Groeslon near Caernarfon. Among the books he has published are *Y Drych Tywyll* (1992), *Smôc Gron Bach* (1994), *Elvis* (1996), and *Blodyn Tatws*, the last of which was awarded the Prose Medal at the National Eisteddfod in 1998.

His story '*Y Trwsiwr Ffenestri*' appeared in *Golwg* (1995).

The Artist

Elfyn Lewis was born in Porthmadog in 1969. His distinctive large-scale, abstract canvasses appear in a number of public and private collections. He is a founder member of the artist group *Quincunx*, who are at the forefront of Welsh contemporary art. His work has appeared on record covers for numerous Welsh bands including *Big Leaves* and *Catatonia*. He was educated at the Universities of Lancashire and Cardiff. His work has been widely exhibited throughout the U.K. and overseas.

The Translator

Meic Stephens is an editor, translator, journalist, literary agent, and part-time lecturer at the University of Glamorgan and the Centre for Journalism, Media and Cultural Studies at the University of Cardiff. Born at Trefforest, near Pontypridd, in 1938, he learnt Welsh as an adult. Among the books he has translated are *The White Stone* (1987), a selection of essays by T.H.Parry-Williams; the memoirs of Gwynfor Evans, *For the Sake of Wales* (1996); Saunders Lewis's novel *Monica* (1997); from the French of Luis Nunez Astrain, *The Basques: their Struggle for Independence* (1997); an anthology of short prose by Welsh writers, *Illuminations* (1998); and two novels by Islwyn Ffowc Elis, *Shadow of the Sickle* (1998) and *Return to Lleifior* (1999). He also compiled and edited *Cydymaith i Lenyddiaeth Cymru* (1997) and *The New Companion to the Literature of Wales* (1998).

Translator's Note

The short story in Welsh has a long and illustrious tradition. From Kate Roberts in the 1920s down to the present, the form has been practised with flair and distinction, and at present it is enjoying a new vogue.

The stories in this anthology, the first of its kind ever published, continue and extend that tradition into our own day. They were written by authors born since 1948, so that no writer represented here was more than fifty years old at the time of publication; over half were in their twenties and thirties in 1998. I shall leave it to readers and reviewers to ponder why so many are women.

My selection, necessarily a personal one, is intended to reflect something of the range and quality of the short story as it is being written in the Welsh language today. Some of the authors have established reputations, whether as short-story writers, novelists, or script-writers for radio and television, while others have only just begun publishing their work. All have a commitment to the form and are aware of its requirements.

I am grateful to the contributors for agreeing to cast an eye over my attempts to render their work in English and, in some instances, for drawing my attention to how the translation might be improved. In this process I also had the help of my friend Don Dale-Jones, who made a number of valuable suggestions. For any infelicities which may remain I alone should be held responsible.

Meic Stephens
Whitchurch
Cardiff
December, 1998